For her he'

Eyes burning with   nd
her scent of almo   n't
go back, Gray. I can't just sit there and wait for the
next shot through the window."

He crouched beside her and reached for her hand,
trying to ignore the kick-in-the-gut need touching
her brought. He thought the distance of years had
made him immune to her power to dazzle him.
But there it was, fizzing through his veins like a
shook-up can of soda. "If you testify, you destroy his
make-believe world. Without that power, he loses
everything."

"You don't get it."

"He's just a man, Abble, not some sort of a superhero."

"He owns me."

Gray pounded a fist against the tabletop. "Nobody
owns anybody."

She turned her face away from him. "As long as Rafe
is alive, he can get to me."

"Not if we destroy him."

Dear Harlequin Intrigue Reader,

Summer's winding down, but Harlequin Intrigue is as hot as ever with six spine-tingling reads for you this month!

* Our new BIG SKY BOUNTY HUNTERS promotion debuts with Amanda Stevens's *Going to Extremes*. In the coming months, look for more titles from Jessica Andersen, Cassie Miles and Julie Miller.

* We have some great miniseries for you. Rita Herron is back with *Mysterious Circumstances*, the latest in her NIGHTHAWK ISLAND series. Mallory Kane's *Seeking Asylum* is the third book in her ULTIMATE AGENTS series. And Sylvie Kurtz has another tale in THE SEEKERS series—*Eye of a Hunter*.

* No month would be complete without a chilling gothic romance. This month's ECLIPSE title is Debra Webb's *Urban Sensation*.

* Jan Hambright, a fabulous new author, makes her debut with *Relentless*. Sparks fly when a feisty repo agent repossesses a BMW with an ex-homicide detective in the trunk!

Don't miss a single book this month and every month!

Sincerely,

Denise O'Sullivan
Senior Editor
Harlequin Intrigue

EYE OF A HUNTER
SYLVIE KURTZ

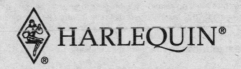

HARLEQUIN®

TORONTO • NEW YORK • LONDON
AMSTERDAM • PARIS • SYDNEY • HAMBURG
STOCKHOLM • ATHENS • TOKYO • MILAN • MADRID
PRAGUE • WARSAW • BUDAPEST • AUCKLAND

ISBN 0-373-22866-X

EYE OF A HUNTER

Copyright © 2005 by Sylvie Kurtz

This edition published by arrangement with Harlequin Books S.A.

® and TM are trademarks of the publisher. Trademarks indicated with
® are registered in the United States Patent and Trademark Office, the
Canadian Trade Marks Office and in other countries.

www.eHarlequin.com

Printed in U.S.A.

ABOUT THE AUTHOR

Flying an eight-hour solo cross-country in a Piper Arrow with only the airplane's crackling radio and a large bag of M&M's for company, Sylvie Kurtz realized a pilot's life wasn't for her. The stories zooming in and out of her mind proved more entertaining than the flight itself. Not a quitter, she finished her pilot's course and earned her commercial license and instrument rating.

Since then, she has traded in her wings for a keyboard where she lets her imagination soar to create fictional adventures that explore the power of love and the thrill of suspense. When not writing, she enjoys the outdoors with her husband and two children, quilt-making, photography and reading whatever catches her interest.

You can write to Sylvie at P.O. Box 702, Milford, NH 03055. And visit her Web site at www.sylviekurtz.com.

Books by Sylvie Kurtz

HARLEQUIN INTRIGUE
527—ONE TEXAS NIGHT
575—BLACKMAILED BRIDE
600—ALYSSA AGAIN
653—REMEMBERING RED THUNDER*
657—RED THUNDER RECKONING*
712—UNDER LOCK AND KEY
767—HEART OF A HUNTER†
773—MASK OF A HUNTER†
822—A ROSE AT MIDNIGHT
866—EYE OF A HUNTER†

*Flesh and Blood
†The Seekers

CAST OF CHARACTERS

Abrielle Holbrook—Abbie witnessed her father's murder and has been running for her life since. The WITSEC program that was supposed to protect her has become a minefield of death.

Grayson Reed—Abbie was once the golden girl of his dreams, now he has to take all he knows about her, Echo Falls and tracking prey to protect the woman he loves, but can't have.

Deputy Marshal Phil Auclair—How had the old marshal survived three deadly attacks on his subject when younger deputies had died? Was it simply devotion to his job or did he have inside help?

Raphael Vanderveer—Abbie's camera caught him murdering her father. Now he wants her and his freedom back and nothing can stop him from getting what he wants—not even the inconvenience of being on trial for murder and treason.

Elliot Holbrook—He gave his life to protect his daughter, the family business and the town he loved.

Hale Harper—The new Seeker has a chip on his shoulder the size of California. Is he willing to trade Abbie's life to ease his own pain?

Brynna Reed—Gray's sister is not the girl he remembers. She's embroiled in troubles of her own. Does she need money badly enough to betray her best friend?

Pamela Hatcher—Rafe's assistant longs for action and adventure.

Sister Bertrice Storey—How could Abbie's mother's best friend betray the girl she'd treated as a daughter?

Chapter One

Abrielle Holbrook was watching cable television in yet another cheap motel when Deputy Marshal Ed Kushner's chair was thrown backwards. His body toppled against the television screen, blotting out Gene Kelly, who was singing in the rain.

In the next instant the lamp on the table at her elbow shattered, throwing the room into the flickering gray haze of the television's moving pictures. WITSEC Inspector Phil Auclair tackled her to the stained burnt-orange carpet and shoved her toward the connecting door between their rooms. "Stay low."

She knew the drill by now. Pulse frantic and hyperventilating, she crawled to the bathroom, still steamy from Phil's shower, and hugged the floor. So much for witness security. Three weeks. Three relocations. Three dead deputies. She didn't even know where she was. What day it was. Couldn't remember her current alias. It was all too much. Her chest cracked under the spasm of her tears. When would this nightmare end?

Phil shouted into his cell phone while Gene Kelly tap-danced in the next room. At this moment Abbie would give anything to slip into Debbie Reynolds's role and join Gene on the wet movie set. Even rain sounded good. Maybe it could wash away the image of blood constantly tainting her vision. Closing her eyes, she let the *click-clack* of taps and the beat of familiar music form the colorized pictures of the oft-seen movie. And against the screen of her mind she shadowed Gene's every move.

The next thing she knew, someone was tugging on her elbow. She blinked up at him and for a second mistook the gray hair and worried blue eyes for her father's.

Phil all but yanked her to her feet. "Time to go."

Even though there were half a dozen armed men patrolling the parking lot, Phil scanned every shadow as he hurried her to the waiting armored car with the tinted windows. He'd barely slammed the door shut before the car sped off.

Abbie sank into the seat that smelled of cigarette smoke and canned deodorizer and let her heavy head plop against the window. "I can't do this anymore."

Phil patted her elbow. "Ten more days, princess. Once the trial's over, you'll be safe."

She tried to draw reassurance from the man who'd become her lifeline in the past year since her camera lens had captured her father's murder at the hands of his partner. But the soul-deep cold wouldn't leave. Safe? She didn't think she'd ever feel safe again. "I can't."

"Don't you want to clear your father's name? Don't you want to see Vanderveer pay for his crimes?"

What good was she doing her father like this? "I just want my life back."

"If Vanderveer is set free, you never will."

You won't ever be free from me, Abrielle. I won't

ever let you go. I'll be in your dreams and in your night-mares. I'll follow you wherever you go.

Somehow even behind bars Rafe Vanderveer had managed to do just that. Even from behind bars he would kill her. When was the last time she'd slept without having a nightmare about him? When was the last time she'd slept through the night? "Ten days is a long time to stay alive when my protectors keep dying."

In the dim light from the dashboard Phil's jaw seemed to sag with the weight of his responsibility. "I'll keep you safe. I promise."

But doubt tailed her the three long hours until the car stopped again. It followed her in the shower, where even blistering heat couldn't loosen the icy horror glued to her skin. It cozied up to her on another too-soft mattress of another motel bed with sheets that were too stiff and a pillow that was too flat.

Phil checked the doors and window, made a call, then slid into the second bed fully dressed. "Try to get some sleep."

Code phrase for *We'll be moving again in the morning.*

She aimed the remote at the television, turned the volume down low and flicked through channels until she landed on *West Side Story.* As Richard Beymer sang his heart out to Natalie Wood, Abbie relaxed. Then later, as the Sharks and the Jets duked it out, the doubt mutated into a fear so sharp, it cut her breath.

Someone knew. Not just anyone. Someone on the inside. How else could they have found her? The first time was her fault. She'd needed to hear a familiar voice and had called a friend from back home. But not the other two times. She'd trusted Phil. She'd believed he had her best interest at heart.

She craned her head toward the man who'd become a friend since she'd entered the program. Deep lines bracketed his mouth and wrinkled his forehead. Purple moons bruised the skin beneath his eyes. Eyes that were kind and understanding like her father's. Was experience enough to account for his being alive while three younger men were dead? What reason did he have to betray her?

Even if he hadn't, someone else had.

He couldn't keep her safe. No one could. Raphael Vanderveer had too much to lose by letting her live.

WITSEC had taken everything from her, erased her past as if she'd never existed. But it wasn't enough. Rafe remembered her. He wouldn't let go. Not when she was the only thing between him and his freedom.

Somehow he'd done this to her and would keep doing it until she was dead. Then the town, the mill, the house, everything that was still part of her fondest memories would be his to abuse and destroy.

If she was to stay alive to avenge her father and make sure his murderer never left prison or touched her beloved town, if she was to have a chance to once again live an ordinary life, she could trust no one.

When Phil's gentle snores told her he was asleep, she slunk out of bed. No point trying the front door. He'd be up with the first clink of the lock. She stumbled to the bathroom as if she'd just woken up. He'd heard her do that often enough in the past three weeks to think nothing was out of the ordinary.

In the bathroom she checked out the small window. Doable. Like Phil, she'd crawled into bed fully dressed. She'd given up on pajamas after the second attack. She glanced at her feet and wriggled her toes. No shoes. But she couldn't risk going back for them. Hiding the slide of the window with a flush from the toilet, she took a deep breath. Then, balancing on the seat, she pushed herself onto the sill.

Outside, cold asphalt met her bare soles. Panic snaked up her spine until her teeth chattered. *If Phil can't hide you, what makes you think you have any chance to stay alive on your own?* Glancing at the window, she thought of crawling back to her only safety net. A safety net full of holes. No, her best chance to stay alive was on her own.

A thick gray fog wrapped around her like a shield, giving her a skin of courage. *Become smoke.*

From not far away came the sound of trucks rumbling by on a highway. Like the swish of a lighthouse, the beams of the trucks' headlights cut starry circles into the dark murk. She couldn't go home, but she could disappear. All she had to do was hide for ten more days.

With one last look over her shoulder she faded into the mist.

"HEY, HOLLYWOOD, CONGRATULATIONS on your successful hunt."

Grayson Reed paused at the door of what served as a briefing room in the basement bunker of Seekers, Inc.—also known as the Aerie—surveyed the four men around the conference table through the mirrored lenses of his glasses and copped a superhero pose. "No sweat."

As Noah Kingsley strode past him toward the octopus of wires attached to the computer system, he jabbed Gray in the ribs with an elbow. "Never any sweat with you."

Not that his target had made the game of hide-and-seek easy, but once he was cornered, he'd seen that walking out willingly was the wisest of options—especially with the LAPD SWAT team surrounding him. Gray had dealt with bullies often enough to have learned a few tricks. Even scum wanted to believe it deserved respect. Gray let them think he gave them what they wanted; then they gave him what he wanted. He was always one for win-win.

Dominic Skyralov studied the plate of muffins in front of him, chose a lemon-poppy seed and grinned his good-old-boy smile as he peeled the paper. "How was the mother state?"

They all thought Gray was a California boy born and bred. They'd choke on their coffees if he told them he'd lived less than an hour from Wintergreen until he'd graduated from high school—then he'd gone as far away as he could from the butt-end-of-nowhere town that was Echo Falls. Moving away to someplace where no one knew him, where no one had any expectations, had allowed him to reinvent himself. He flashed Skyralov a toothpaste-commercial smile because the blond cowboy expected it. "All sunshine and surf."

As Kingsley set up the computer for whatever presentation Falconer had planned, he eyed Gray up and down. "What happened to you? The dry cleaner run out of perchloroethylene?"

Gray smoothed the wrinkles on his silk-blend dove-gray blazer. What was the point of buying cheap when suits took such abuse in this line of work? Cheaper to buy top-of-the-line in the long run—not that any of them gave him a break for his good sense. "Red-eye. Couldn't wait to see you guys, so I didn't even stop home."

Skyralov and Kingsley smirked.

Gray dropped into a leather chair around the cherry-wood conference table. Farthest from the door—his usual post. Lounging against the wall, Sabriel Mercer, with his dark and dangerous looks, nodded acknowledgment but didn't speak. Never did unless he had something important to say. Hale Harper, the new guy, was still feeling his way into the group. He was almost as dark and brooding as Mercer. For the life of him Gray couldn't figure out why Falconer had hired someone with such a big chip on his shoulder. That could only lead to trouble.

Sebastian Falconer, head honcho of Seekers, Inc., strode in and took his place at the head of the table.

As Gray reached for an orange-date muffin in a basket with a lacy doily, he chuckled. "You really ought to tell Liv that lace clashes with the macho image we're trying to build here."

"Eat up those blueberries." Falconer's features remained stiff and formal while he shuffled papers in readiness for their meeting, but amusement leaked into his voice. "Liv wanted me to mention they're good for the prostate."

Laughter exploded. Skyralov scooped blueberries onto the plate next to his muffin. "Next she'll issue Kevlar vests every time we leave the bunker."

"Back-ordered. Won't be here till next week." The corner of Falconer's mouth twitched in what, for him, passed as a smile. His wife, Liv, had sustained a brain injury a year and a half ago. She couldn't remember a thing of her life before the accident, but since then, the organizational skills she'd had to learn to cope with her condition had made her an invaluable part of Seekers, Inc. She fussed over them all as if they were family. None of them minded.

Falconer tented his hands on the table in front of him. "Okay, bring me up to date."

Grasping his red suspenders, Kingsley gave the daily security update. Mercer clipped through his usual terse report on the activities of his current tracking cases. Between bites, Skyralov announced he was leaving for Louisiana in an hour to follow up on a tip on the serial marrier who squeezed his brides dry, then left them hanging. An Austin society dame had hired Seekers, Inc. to find the man who'd defrauded her daughter out of her fortune. The mother didn't care how long it took or how much it cost as long as the "dirty, rotten scoundrel" never enjoyed a penny of her family's money.

The screen at the front end of the room went blue, and Kingsley said, "Ready when you are."

Falconer reached for the remote that controlled the PowerPoint presentation. "Yesterday afternoon we were hired by our old outfit."

Skyralov paused, a spoonful of blueberries hovering just outside his mouth. "The U.S. Marshals Service?"

Falconer nodded. "One of their WITSEC subjects bolted and they need her back."

Gray leaned back in his chair as if that would help him take in the whole situation. "Why are they involving us?"

"They seem to think one of their own is responsible for compromising her security."

Gray gave a low whistle. Admitting that one of theirs was dirty was never easy for the Service. Having worked the WITSEC program in the past, he knew its usefulness even as he saw the possibilities for betrayal. Every good had its ugly side.

Falconer aimed the remote at the screen and a face

popped onto it. "We've been tasked with finding Abrielle Holbrook, daughter of Elliot Holbrook of Holbrook Mills in Echo Falls, Mass."

Everything in Gray stilled. Though the mirrored lenses of his glasses shielded his eyes from everyone, the gray tint was light enough for him to see every detail clearly. Abbie's picture filled the screen, and the past he'd worked so hard to leave behind slapped him between the eyes. There in front of him was the image of everything he'd ever wanted. Everything he'd been told he could never have.

Abrielle Helena Holbrook. A.H.H. Not just her initials but also the sound people usually made when they saw her.

Abbie was golden—from her honey hair to her honey eyes to her achingly sweet personality. You wanted to hate her for all she had, but you simply couldn't. He had never met a single person who didn't like her. Seeing her face on the screen knocked him off center. She was the absolute last person he'd have thought would ever need WITSEC. How could the girl every guy had been in love with and every girl wanted as a friend now be running for her life—not only from the scum who'd forced her into WITSEC but from the program itself? The girl was allergic to conflict.

"Isn't Holbrook Mills involved with the Steeltex project?" Skyralov asked.

"They are," Falconer said.

Harper frowned so deeply, his eyebrows met in the center of his forehead. "What's Steeltex?"

Falconer clicked the remote, and a picture of a soldier dressed in camouflage came onto the screen. In the next slide, only a miragelike shimmer distinguished the soldier from the brick wall behind him. "It's a new fabric the U.S. Army is working on. It transmits visual information about color, light and patterns through the fiber to make whoever wears it nearly invisible against any background. Microdots are woven in to locate a downed soldier. The latest model contains conductive fibers in the chest area that can monitor vital functions of an injured soldier. This information can be relayed by wireless signal to a remote location such as a field hospital."

The V between Falconer's eyes deepened. "That project and the safety of our troops out in the field are compromised if Abrielle Holbrook isn't found in time to testify at her father's murder trial. Because of the Steeltex project, the trial's high threat."

"Her father was murdered?" Gray's nerves were running a marathon, but he spoke as casually as if he were relaxing beachside.

Falconer clicked the next slide forward, flashing a picture of Elliot Holbrook on the screen. Gray-haired, blue-eyed, fair and generous. The man had kept the small mill town of Echo Falls alive when everyone else had given it up for dead. No one was good enough for his daughter. But, then, when you had a daughter like Abbie, how could they be?

The next photo was of a younger man who'd tried his best to present a Pierce Brosnan 007 image but couldn't quite cut the right attitude. He wore the better-than-you sneer of the typical bully. "Elliot Holbrook was murdered by his business partner, Raphael Vanderveer."

The next slide turned Gray's stomach. In color that was so vivid it almost looked fake, the James Bond wannabe held a pistol at Holbrook's head. Smoke puffed out of the muzzle. Red mist sprayed out from Holbrook's head. Gray recognized the place—Holbrook's office in the back of the mansion on the hill.

Mercer's voice floated from the shadows of the wall. "Where'd that photo come from?"

"The subject took it."

Abbie had photographed her own father's murder? The fast-food egg-bagel sandwich he'd wolfed down on his way here turned to brick. He hoped to heaven someone was there for her. She adored her father. Her whole world revolved around pleasing him. Losing him, witnessing his murder, would've torn her apart.

"Over the last month," Falconer said, "information on her whereabouts was compromised three times. Three deputies are dead. After the last attack she disappeared and hasn't been seen since. The Service is worried about her safety."

Six slides clipped by, showing a photo of each of the three men as it appeared on their badges and a crime-scene photo of each of their corpses. Gray's skin grew cold. His mind couldn't wrap itself around Abbie having to witness such violence. That was his world, not hers. Hers was all softness and light. She could capture magic with her camera, render a child's face into a work of art, a family portrait into an intimate revelation of cohesion. The photograph she'd taken of him and his sister at Brynna's sixteenth birthday party was the only thing he'd taken with him when he'd left Echo Falls. Had she shut down as she had when her mother died? Without her tight-knit group of friends who would have shaken her out of her mental fog? Where had she run?

"Here's our subject's profile." Dry statistics that

couldn't even begin to describe the life that buzzed around Abbie glared at him from the screen.

Skyralov sipped green tea. "What was her last location?"

Kingsley popped a suspender. "Ed Kushner was killed in Providence, Rhode Island. After that, Inspector Auclair took her to a small motel outside of Hartford, Connecticut. She escaped through a bathroom window." Pictures of the motel, the window and the surroundings clicked across the screen. A lone imprint of a bare foot on the shoulder of a road. That more than anything made it real. Abbie's foot in the sand. How often had he seen that image?

Gray shook his head. *Don't go there.* "Where's the trial?"

"Boston," Falconer said. "Eight days from today. We have to find her. Without her, Vanderveer has no reason to reveal the extent of his treason. We have cause to believe he's behind the attempted murder of Abrielle Holbrook."

Falconer's chair whispered as he turned to face Mercer. "Mercer, I want you to track the witness and bring her back. Reed, since you've worked WITSEC, you'll go in posing as a deputy to find the inside—"

"I'll track." Gray sat as still as an art-class model. He could not let Falconer know how much he wanted to lead the retrieval team.

Falconer frowned at him. "This isn't multiple choice."

"I'll track." *Be firm. Keep it cool.* "I know how to find her."

Falconer contemplated him with his hard eyes and sharp face. Without breaking eye contact, he said, "Harper, you'll go undercover. Mercer, you'll help Reed track."

"I can track alone. No sweat."

"That's all, gentlemen," Falconer announced. "Check your PDAs for updates. Reed, stay behind."

Four sets of curious eyes appraised him as they filed out.

After Kingsley closed the door, Falconer sat on the corner of the conference table. "How much sleep have you had?"

Gray flashed him a smile. "You know me. I can sleep anywhere. I got some shut-eye on the plane."

"It cuts close to home."

"I know."

"Can you handle going back?"

The strange thing about Falconer was that he asked for everything and somehow you felt compelled to give it to him. He knew the deep, dark secrets of each of his team's men. But the courtesy didn't extend both ways. He was still a mystery to them. But there was trust. And that said a lot. Falconer knew about Echo Falls, knew about the strained relationship between him and his sister, Brynna, knew the hard time he'd had surviving the unforgiving label of coward branded onto him by small-town narrow-mindedness.

But he didn't know about Abbie. Gray had never told a soul about Abbie.

Gray leaned back in his chair, hands behind his head, arms splayed wide—the image of relaxation. "Yeah, I can handle going back. That's why I took your job offer in the first place." Sort of.

Falconer turned the remote in his hand. "You've been here over a year and you haven't set foot in Massachusetts."

Gray popped a careless shrug. "Guess I just needed

a push." If he had, he'd have known about Abbie's father and could have helped her.

"I'm not sure this is such a good idea."

"I know her. I know Echo Falls. I can find her faster than anyone here."

Someone within the program wanted to harm his golden girl. He might have had nothing to offer her thirteen years ago, but now he could keep her safe from the bullies who wanted to hurt her. "I understand her. I understand where she's coming from. I understand the program that betrayed her." He was her only chance.

"It's not just Abrielle, Reed. There's WITSEC's reputation and the lives of soldiers at stake."

"I get that."

A long silence loaded the room with tension, highstrung and expectant. *Never let them see you sweat.*

Falconer reached forward and with a finger flicked Gray's glasses so they rested on top of his head. "Tell me about Abrielle."

Gray willed his naked gaze to meet Falconer's straight on. *Never let them see your pain.* He grinned and made a joke out of the feelings that had nearly eaten him alive. "She was the princess in the mansion and I was the guy from the wrong side of the tracks."

"I see."

Gray feared maybe Falconer *was* seeing too much. "I never stood a chance."

"A schoolboy's first crush can make him blind to boundaries."

"But he still understands their restrictions." Especially when they were pounded into him.

"Make sure you do." Falconer rose and gathered

his files. "You find her and you bring her in. Is that understood?"

"Crystal clear."

"Mercer's my best tracker. He's going with you. This is too important."

Just what Gray needed—a shadow to witness his weakness.

ALL PRISON TELEPHONE conversations were taped, so Raphael Vanderveer had to learn to talk about what to the censors would sound like treason as if it were apple pie. But what did the little minds know about how the world really worked? They didn't understand he was selling defective merchandise to the enemy while working on the real thing for the U.S. government. Why shouldn't he profit from the enemy's greed? "I'll need a new suit for court."

"Check."

That's what he liked about Pamela Hatcher—her efficiency. With just those few words she'd know what to do. It wasn't that they were intimate. He'd hired her because he *wasn't* attracted to her. She was a steel stork of a woman, with a face like a scarecrow and delusional fantasies of being the next Lara Croft. But her mind was sharp enough to cut paper and she understood him. So few people did. A vengeful woman was a force more fearsome than an atomic bomb, and he never wanted pleasure to interfere with business. No sex. No jealousy. No need to worry about female revenge. Pamela got that. What she wanted from him wasn't passion; it was adventure.

"Have my tailor cut a dress for you while he's at it." Raphael pulled on the cigar he'd paid a small fortune for.

"Really?" Pamela's squeal of delight was real. In his generous understanding of her fantasy, he'd offered her the kind of assignment that would send someone like Pamela in throes more satisfying than any orgasm. How often had she asked for a more hands-on part in this game he was playing with his captors? Now she'd get to tackle the role of private investigator.

"Any word on the Belgian chocolates yet?" Abbie was a sweet more delicious than any candy, as Pamela already knew. But Abbie had escaped the box he'd put her in, and he needed her back.

"You don't pay me enough for all this runaround." Pamela pretended to whine.

Another little ruse. The censors heard an overworked, underpaid assistant. But Pamela knew the worth she brought him, and he paid her accordingly. Nothing Uncle Sam could get his hands on, mind you. All part of the fun for Pamela. "I just gave you a designer dress." Out of fabric so secret, being caught wearing it would have her tried for treason.

"Um, so you did." She giggled like a schoolgirl, already anticipating the thrill of the hunt. He beamed at his foresight to hire her.

"Check the order confirmation and track down that chocolate. And make sure the contents aren't damaged." He blew out rings of smoke. As soon as he got what he needed from Abbie and erased her from the picture, he could get back to business. She'd already cost him almost a year of his life. He'd make her pay for all of her sins. "I want to celebrate my release in style."

Chapter Two

Gray had sent Mercer to sniff Abbie's trail at its last known point, but the shortcut to information lay in this armpit Gray had sworn he'd never come back to.

The skeleton of houses forming the backbone of Echo Falls appeared through the rain-drenched windshield of his Corvette. How could so little have changed in thirteen years?

Echo Falls squatted in northwestern Massachusetts, east of Highway 91, north of Route 2. A town lost in time, tucked in its own little world. Settlers had followed the law of least effort, taking advantage of the natural fall of water from Holbrook Pond to Bitter Lake, which then emptied into the Prosper River and into the Connecticut River. To make up for the falls' lack of grandeur, the founding family had somewhere along the road built a spectacular granite arch bridge over the fast-moving river.

Originally water powered the wool mills; now it was electricity. The surviving mill buildings still stood on their original site, reflecting on the pond on sunny days. Built in 1774, Holbrook House still faced south, overlooking the river. As the family grew, more estates were built on Holbrook land. Five grand brick homes once lorded over the lower village where the peons lived in boardinghouses on Peanut Row. In the late 1800s, that constituted enough political power to divert a railway to this nothing town.

The train had long ago stopped coming and the tracks turned into nature trails. Modern gabled capes, contemporaries and colonials mixed in with the old brick homes, Victorians and farmhouses. Posh homes still cropped up in the small upper village. Working stiffs still lived paycheck to paycheck in the larger lower village. Of course, Holbrooks didn't own all the fancy homes now, only the original house on Mill Road.

As Gray crested over the last hill, he let out a breath he wasn't aware he'd held. Orange construction barricades closed off the old bridge and redirected traffic through the lower village. Great. He'd hoped to avoid meandering through the center of town.

At least the rain watered down the hard edges. He didn't really want to see the old hometown and all the bitter memories that stagnated there. The plan was to talk to his sister, get a lead on Abbie and get out of this hellhole as fast as possible. *Take it in like a reporter, Gray. Or a travel writer. Notice, don't feel.*

He gritted his teeth as he passed the middle school. Even through the slosh of rain and the tint of his sunglasses every ugly detail glared at him. His grip tightened on the steering wheel and he pretended not to see the redbrick building. Voices from the past crowded in, making his skin shrink too tightly around him. *Crybaby. Loser. Wimp. You can't do anything right. Run, you coward, run.*

Coward.

He rolled his shoulders, trying to dislodge the old taunts that had been the steady staple of his school years.

To his left, the high school's mustard-brick facade smeared between swipes of his wipers. There he was voted most likely to fail and end up in jail. This in spite of being ranked ninth in a class of one hundred and three, lettering in three sports and working twenty-five hours a week. Ironic really that his job was putting scumbags back behind bars where they belonged. Including, once, a former classmate. The all-grown-up Mr. Soccer Star still liked to pick on boys who were smaller than he was.

Who's laughing now?

It was all in the past. He was no longer the runt who had to play class clown or run to save his hide. He no longer had to fight his sister for the last scrap of food on the table. He could stand up straight and be proud of who he was and what he'd become. He was good enough for anyone—including Abbie.

Yeah, right. Her old man would still have found fault with him.

At Peanut Row he slowed. The old weight of doom he'd dragged around like a ball and chain fitted itself around his neck. He loosened his tie. *You're not that kid anymore.*

Spinners' Tavern still stood on the corner. Still had a steady clientele even at eleven in the morning. His mother had probably spent more time on the second bar stool from the right than she had at home. Like a stick of peppermint gum was going to mask the booze and fool them into thinking she'd actually gone to work for a change.

The last house on this dead-end street looked better

than the last time he'd seen it. The door and shutters wore a fresh coat of lipstick-red paint. But not even the bright color could erase the tired slouch of the roofline or the defeat of the sagging siding. The wipers taunted him, *coward, coward, coward.*

Now that he was here, he wasn't quite sure what to do. The last time he'd talked to Brynna, she'd screamed at him to never call her again and had slammed down the phone. All of his calls after that were screened through a voice box, and she hadn't returned any. But then Bryn had never played by anyone's rules; she'd made up her own. That's what got her kicked out of the police academy. Last he'd heard she'd gotten a P.I. license. He couldn't imagine that business was booming for her here.

Maybe she was right. Maybe he was a coward for not pushing the issue. Maybe he had run from his responsibility to her. But only an idiot went where he wasn't wanted.

Rain drummed impatiently on the ragtop of his Corvette, reminding him of his mother's red nails clicking against the cracked kitchen table. *Are you just going to sit there?* Her shrill voice taunted. *For heaven's sake, Grayson, grow a spine. Do you want to end up like your father?*

Don't know. That might be a good thing.

The imagined smack of his mother's slap stung his cheek.

He twisted off the ignition and, rounding his shoulders against the pelt of rain, trotted across the street to the red door. For a second his hand hovered above the glossy red paint, then he knocked.

A volley of small yips answered him. "Quiet, Queenie!"

Bryn. Yet not Bryn. Something was off in her voice. "Bryn, it's Gray. Open up."

The silence on the other side of the door was so deep, it seemed to suck the breath right out of his lungs "Bryn. Please."

"Go away."

"I need to talk to you."

"Yeah, well, you're a decade too late."

"Open the door, Bryn."

"I can't." The broken tone of her voice tore him apart. What on earth had happened to her? Why was her hatred of him so deep? He was the one who had been all but driven out of town. What could she possibly hold against him?

Something slid down the other side of the door, rattling the wood on its hinges. "You left me, Gray. You left me with her." Her voice, low on the other side of the door, hardened. "You left me with *them*."

Gray swore silently and slid down the front side of the door. They sat back to back with the door between them. "I couldn't take you to basic training. You know that."

"You left me, Gray."

Rain blitzed his face, soaked his suit and sank into the Italian leather of his shoes. "You liked it here. Mom always took your side. Mama's baby never had to do anything. You and Abbie, you were the toast of the town. Queen of this. Princess of that. Brynna Reed and Abrielle Holbrook. Everybody's friends. Why would you want to leave that?"

"Things change."

Hands draped over his knees, he closed his eyes and leaned his head against the hard wood. "Talk to me."

"It doesn't matter. You should leave now."

He thought he heard tears in her voice. What the hell was he supposed to do with that when she wouldn't talk? "This isn't about me, Bryn. It's about Abbie."

"Abbie's safe wherever she is."

"No she isn't. Someone within WITSEC is selling her out. If I don't find her, she could die."

Silence, except for the sting of rain spiking against the concrete stoop and rattling against the siding.

"She's already lost so much," Gray said. Noncriminals paid a higher price than criminals in WITSEC. Loss of identity, self, dignity. Abbie was a woman of her world. She belonged here in the same way he never had. Losing her father, her life, her world, he couldn't imagine how she'd survived it all. "She doesn't deserve to die for a mistake her father made."

"Elliot died to protect her."

"What makes you say that?" That tidbit wasn't in the briefing notes.

"I'm not going to betray her."

"It's not betrayal when you're helping her."

"She's safe."

Stubborn. Hardheaded. Foolish little witch. It wasn't her life she was playing with; it was Abbie's. But he swallowed the barbwire of anger and talked to his sister as if logic would make a difference. "People on the run tend to go back to the familiar. I need to know if she came to you for help."

"She's safe."

"Did you know that her safety was compromised three times in the past three weeks? That three deputies died trying to protect her? That right now Raphael Vanderveer is negotiating with teams of lawyers and that, if Abbie chooses not to testify at the trial, he could end up out on the streets again."

"Like you said, she's lost so much. Maybe she feels she has nothing more to lose."

"There's her life."

"What's the point if she always has to live in fear? Maybe she's tired of running, Gray. Did you think of that?"

A skewed barb? "I couldn't take you with me, Bryn. And even if I could have, you wouldn't have come. You fit too well here."

"Yeah, maybe you're right."

Nothing he could say would change her mind. "I care about Abbie. You know that. I have to find her before Vanderveer's snitch does. In your heart you know that, too. Where is she?"

But Bryn didn't answer. The push of her body against the door yielded a loud creak.

He sprang up and pounded on the door. He wrenched the doorknob, but the lock wouldn't give, and he'd long ago lost the key. "Bryn, you have to help me. Please. I don't care if you hate me till the day you die. But you have to care that Abbie's life is in danger."

Bryn's footsteps padded away. The dog's toenails clicked on the linoleum as it followed its mistress.

A moment later "Stayin' Alive" blasted from a stereo.

He wasn't stupid. He got the hint. As always in this town, he was on his own. He turned and strode toward his car. His being here was causing Bryn grief, and whatever he represented to her was a threat. Too bad she couldn't think of her friend. He needed to find Abbie to help *her* stay alive. Couldn't Bryn see that? He yanked the car door open and fumbled in his soaked-through pocket for his keys. With one last look at the sad house that looked like a tired, made-up whore, he cranked on the ignition.

As the engine growled to life, a smile cracked his lips. He reached into the glove compartment for the holey gym sock he kept there to wipe fog off the windshield and dried his sunglasses.

"Stayin' Alive." From the soundtrack of *Saturday Night Fever.* Maybe Bryn hated him, but she did care about Abbie after all.

DON'T THINK OF IT, Abrielle. Nobody knows where you are. Nobody can find you. Still, the edge of her peace started to curl at the sound of the ferry's horn. Once a day it brought supplies, mail and possibly people. And a troop of fear. That was the one chink in this otherwise perfect armor.

Out here in her refuge of growing fog, she listened for Bert's footsteps on the rocky path that were the pre-arranged all-clear signal. Only the gentle lap of water against rocks reached her. Was there a problem this afternoon? Had someone suspicious gotten off the ferry? She fiddled with the aperture ring on the camera Bert had loaned her. *Let it go, Abbie.*

Bert wouldn't spill her secret.

Strains of "High Noon" crept into her mind as Abbie imagined five-foot-two Bert in a showdown with one of Rafe's thugs. She laughed out loud and the fog swallowed her voice, replacing it with the quiet push and pull of water on rock.

After the chaos of the past year, this quiet was a blessing. She lifted the camera and forced herself to relax into the calming rhythm of nature around her.

Back to basics, Abbie. The first essential of a good photograph was awareness. What personal statement did she want to make today?

"Part of finding your God," Bert had said when Abbie first showed up on the convent doorstep begging for sanctuary, "is finding yourself."

And here in the cool afternoon air, with a pale white haze on the horizon, Abbie could almost believe she'd have a chance at connecting with her lost self—and surviving for another eight days.

Though the Sisters of Sacred Heart were in the midst of their summer tourist season, Bert—Sister Bertrice Storey to everyone else—had found a room for her in the old granite convent. People came to Retreat Island at times of transition—divorce, death, milestone birthdays—that made one want to look deep into oneself or beg some higher source for answers to questions that really had none. But the quiet did heal and it had a way of leading one to some sort of peace.

There were no televisions here, no mad schedules, no hectic running from one appointment to the next. There was room for a dozen overnight visitors to find their own voices in the silence. They could join the sisters in their daily prayers. They could work in the gardens. They could walk in the woods. If someone needed to talk, a sister was there with a willing ear. Chapel bells woke the residents at six every morning, and small signs on the walls discreetly reminded guests that their silence was their gift to their companions.

Though Bert had insisted they had a full house, the island was big enough that Abbie hadn't run into any of the other guests. They, like her, were seeking solitude. And two days into her ten-day retreat, that sense of peace was starting to envelop her as thickly as the fog bank tucking in around the island.

Fear retreated and she lost herself in the beauty of nature around her. Viewpoint and composition. Light, form and tone. Texture. Pattern. Through the lens of the camera she searched. The scent of spruce and sea air and damp earth connected her to the here and now and grounded her to her surroundings. Crouched among the rocks and boulders that lined the western shore, she aimed the camera at the departing ferry that was moving into the fog like some sort of spaceship and snapped the shutter.

Fog folded in around the ferry's departing bulk, swallowing it whole. Bert's footsteps crunched on the path. All was safe for another day.

Her sigh filled the night air. With a smile she straightened, threw her head back and spread her arms like Julie Andrews at the beginning of *The Sound of Music,* then twirled on her rocky perch to meet Bert. Before she could start singing, the sight of a wind-carved spruce bending over a ledge of rocks caught her eye. She lifted the camera and focused on the image that gave the impression of a pointy-hatted gnome stroking its long, bristled beard.

Bert's footsteps stopped on the trail.

"What took you so long?" Abbie asked, moving one foot to a neighboring boulder in order to accentuate the spruce gnome's nose. "I was starting to think something happened."

"Your Sister Bertrice is one tough cookie. It took me a half hour to convince her I was one of the good guys."

At the sound of the male voice Abbie jerked around, lost her footing on the wet rock and landed hard on her backside. Fear serpentined through all of her limbs, setting them shaking. How could Bert have trusted anyone after what Abbie had told her? Men—all men—were a threat to her. No matter how charming—especially if they were charming—they belonged to Rafe, and the only thing Rafe wanted from her was permanent silence. Scrambling, she managed to get up and over the rock, away from this threat.

"Abbie! Hey, wait, no!" The dark shape scurried after her, swearing as he slipped on the slick rocks. "It's me. Gray."

"Gray?" Heart hammering, she froze, holding the camera against her heart like a pitiful shield. Gray had once had a way of making her feel as if her mere presence in this world made it a better place. What teenage girl didn't want to see herself as a goddess in a handsome boy's eyes? Then she'd ruined it all with just a few words. "What are you doing here?"

"Can we climb down from here?"

"No." She needed distance. This was too unexpected, too startling. Gray, here, now. Wrong time. Wrong place. She shivered and wished she'd worn a sweater over her sleeveless blouse. He detached himself from the fog, and she sucked in a breath.

Familiar features formed as he drew closer, and the sizzle she'd thought of as teenage infatuation stirred her blood. His sandy hair now sported a salon do instead of the home-butchered bowl cut. His high cheekbones still begged for a camera's attention. His lips were still tempting. He still wore the mirrored shades he'd taken up in high school. Cool then, scary now because she couldn't read his intent in his eyes.

Her hands tightened around the camera and she

struggled with her desire to inch it up to her eye to capture this ghost from her past. That sleepy smile. That careless pose. That air of endless time on hand. They were all a skin he wore to protect himself and hid a steely determination. She'd admired that survival instinct in him, that fire to succeed that no one could douse no matter how much water they threw at him. That relentless ability to pursue suited his job, but it would also return her to a captivity that doomed her to die. "Stay where you are."

"I'm here to help you, Abbie."

"I was safe until you showed up." She stepped up to the next boulder and away from the frustrating tug of outgrown teenage hormones that had once made her do crazy things like swan dive into the quarry to get his attention.

Balancing himself on the slippery soles of his leather shoes, he followed her. "I don't work for Vanderveer. I don't work for the Marshals Service. I work for a private firm. I'm here to help you. You know me, Abbie. Trust me."

"I can't. Leave me alone." She continued putting distance between him and her on the path of rocks she'd traveled time and again over the past few days. She couldn't trust him. She couldn't trust anyone. She was learning that lesson blow by painful blow. Look where trusting Bert had gotten her. Where would she go now? "How did you know where to find me?"

"A lucky guess."

"Brynna." Tears blurring the path, Abbie reached out to steady herself on a neighboring boulder, then continued her upward climb to the stand of spruce. How could Brynna have sold her out? Even to Gray? Especially to Gray?

"She didn't say a word." Gray puffed too close behind her. "Why won't she open the door for me?"

"You left her."

"I had no choice."

"You asked me to go with you."

He slid and mumbled a curse. "That was different."

"Not to her." Not when Bryn knew her only protection from her mother's hard life was Gray. But he couldn't know, and it wasn't Abbie's place to tell him. "How did you find me?"

"It wasn't that hard. People tend to go back to what's familiar. Your parents are dead. Brynna's too obvious and too close to home. Who else could you trust? Then I remembered your mother's college friend who used to take you to see all those musicals in Boston when you were a kid. Had a hell of a time tracking her down. Who would've thought a theater major would end up in a convent?"

She'd hoped no one. Her mother had died so long ago and Bert hadn't been an active part of Abbie's life since then. Abbie had assumed Bert wouldn't show up on anyone's radar. Except Gray's. Because he knew her so well. What if Rafe's hired goons had followed him? "Please, Gray, if you ever cared for me, go away."

"You know, between you and Brynna, my ego is taking quite a beating."

"Then you shouldn't have come back to the people who can hurt you."

"You have to testify. I can keep you safe until then."

Rain started, pecking at the fog. She reached the stand of spruce and looked down at Gray's dark shape struggling for footing on the rocks below. She'd missed him. But after the way she'd hurt him, she had no right to expect him to put his life on the line for her. She wasn't the old Abbie, and he wasn't the old Gray. Too much had happened to both of them. "Go, Gray. Please leave me alone."

"I can't, Abbie. Not this time."

She didn't wait to see if he made it safely over the last muddy stretch of cliff. She ran through the woods, following not path but memory. Something moved to her right? A deer? She turned her head but saw nothing in the soupy murk. Gray had her imagining Rafe's minions all around her.

"Abbie!" The alarm in Gray's voice froze her. A moment later he tackled her to the ground. The hard knock jammed the camera into her chest, stealing her breath. A second later something bit into the tree at her side, drooling chunks of bark onto her arm.

"Stay down," Gray said, then took off after whoever had shot at them. He disappeared into the fog she'd counted as a blessing only moments ago.

Desperately trying to rasp breath into her lungs, she clawed at the earth at her side. This could not be happening. Not here. This was a safe place. Drops of rain splattered around her. She'd been wrong. Rain didn't wash away the fear. It was still there. Big and immovable. *Raindrops keep fallin' on my head.* She shook her head. *Don't go there. Not now.* She had to get away. Tonight. She had to disappear again.

"Can you stand?" Gray's hand reached down to help her up.

She nodded and sat up, finally getting air into her lungs. "I'm fine. Did you get him?"

"No. He got away."

She hadn't realized until then that she'd counted on

Gray to catch him and give her a chance for a safe get-away. The bitter hiccup of tears joined her lung-filling breaths. "I have to get back. Bert'll worry."

Gray's hand didn't let go of her arm. "Abbie." He opened his left hand. There on his palm rested the proof that her safety was nothing more than illusion.

Chapter Three

"How did he get hold of this?" Abbie's fingers shook as she picked up the ripped square of fabric from Gray's palm. Like a chameleon, the square rippled from light to dark, then settled, taking on her skin's color, and all but disappeared. Steeltex. The experimental fabric her father had developed for the U.S. Army. "How could Rafe's goon get into the mill? It's fenced now. Gated. Guarded night and day by military police."

"I don't know, but we have to get out of here." The tautness of Gray's voice, the protective stance of his body and the predatory way he scanned the area around them ratcheted the tightening squeeze of anxiety in her chest.

"Is he still out there?" She craned her neck and probed the shifting shadows that pooled the woods into shades of black. Her body was strangely numb, as if it didn't quite belong to her, and it automatically shrank closer to Gray.

Gray poked at the scrap of material peeking out of the top of her fist. "He's got the advantage. He can see us, but we can't see him."

He shook off his jacket and wrapped it around her shoulders. "We need to get moving."

The jacket had trapped his heat and his clean scent, and both swaddled her like a security blanket. A muscle in his jaw twitched as he adjusted the lapels around her neck, then his face settled into a sharp set of unreadable lines.

"I don't need this—"

He stopped her efforts to remove his jacket. "The white of your blouse drinks in what little light there is and turns you into a beacon."

Her gaze dropped to his chest. The pearl-gray of his shirt shimmered in the fading light. "But now you—"

"Shh. Let's go. We have to get to the convent."

A look in his eyes yielded only a reflection of her dazed-deer look in the lenses of his glasses. This running, this constant fear, wasn't going to end. Not until either she or Rafe was dead. "We won't make it,,," *Alive* stuck in her throat. Their hunter was too close. Behind that tree? Behind that rock? The noises of the island became skulking footsteps on the undergrowth, sour breath in the fog, evil glee on the water. "It's too far."

"We will." He tugged on her hand, breaking her paralysis. "One step at a time. Like old times."

Like the time when she couldn't run one more step at track practice and he'd fallen back to her pace and joked until she'd forgotten the cramp in her side. His no-worries tone, the warmth of his hand holding hers, the solidness of his body pressed against hers almost had her believing this could be just another training session.

How easily she'd fallen back into the old roles. Him watching out for her, her letting him. Except this time there was no smile to seal the lie that everything was okay. His vigilant scanning and cautious movements erased all delusions this was anything but a hunt and they were the prey.

Trailing behind him, camouflaged in his jacket, she was once again his kid sister's best friend, one of the girls he continually had to get out of trouble. Then she'd wanted his attention. Now his taking charge was making her feel small and helpless.

Just like her father's well-meaning control.

Just like Rafe's manipulations.

Just like WITSEC.

With Gray it was supposed to be different.

Comfortable. Easy. Safe.

At the edge of the woods Gray paused. His breath puffed close to her ear as he took in the obstacle before them. In the creep of fog and darkness the ground continued to slope gently toward the darker mass that was the convent. Like an invitation an irregular patchwork of fog-blurred lights burned at some of the windows. Between her and Gray and the granite walls of the building was a wide expanse with nothing but open space. The manicured lawn with its meandering stone path, park benches, birdhouses and fragrant rose border was magnificent in sunlight, inspiring a slow pace and self-contemplation. Now it seemed peppered with armed mines and much too exposed.

Three deputies had already died trying to keep her safe. The thought that Gray might be next terrified her.

"He'll see us. We won't make it." The imagined infrared dot of the assassin's scope burned her back.

"Walk in the park, hon." He flashed her teeth, but the false smile didn't fool her. He removed his shirt and dropped it behind a rock. His tanned skin blended in better with the darkness of the approaching storm, even with the rain giving it sheen. "Like the quarry parties. Think of it as racing the park ranger to the gate."

"Not exactly the same." The park ranger hadn't pointed a gun at them, and even if he had, he would have shot to miss.

"We'll give him the smallest target possible and take a path he can't anticipate."

"Right." Everything in her screamed to stay in the relative security of the shadows. *Don't move. Stay.* Just a bit longer. Just until she could dig a little deeper for her last scrap of courage. "Why you? Your firm could've sent someone else."

"I figured that by now you'd need a familiar face."

She did. Desperately. She gazed at the face that had given her countless sleepless nights, at the face she'd been looking for in crowds for more years than she cared to admit, at the face that could still jolt her heart like a double shot of espresso. He'd come to her when it would surely have been easier to let someone else take the job. Had he forgiven her?

He squeezed her upper arm. His chin jerked toward the convent that seemed a hundred miles away. "Come on, Abbie. Let's make a run for it."

Right. "If you remember correctly, I was never much of a sprinter."

"That's all right. I've got you covered."

And even as they crouched at the edge of the woods waiting, he did. The firm planes of his body curved over hers. The breadth of his shoulders stretched across hers. The hard weight of his arm was armored plate around her. Her awareness of his heat and his scent and his steely determination to protect her hurt with its acuteness. After thirteen years, shouldn't she have moved on? Oh, no, not homebody Abbie. She hung on to things that did her no good. Like a magnum of champagne, just one touch and her mind uncorked with all her unfulfilled childhood fantasies starring Gray. But being around Gray had always been like that—a combination of confusion and longing she'd never quite known how to handle.

"Ready?" he asked.

And just like that the fantasy popped. The man Rafe had hired to silence her was somewhere out there in the fog and storm. He was real and he was after her. Not Gray, not side trips into fantasyland could take away the fact that she was a target. For all she knew, the assassin was standing right there beside her, laughing silently, waiting for her to move. *Deal with it, Abbie.*

Throat too tight to speak, she nodded.

"Stick close." Not that Gray was giving her a choice. Hands hard on her shoulders, he plunged them into open space and steered her into a zigzag path toward the kitchen door of the convent. She pumped her arms and legs hard until her lungs burned and every muscle shrieked from the assault.

To their right a shape rose and darkened against the fog, then disappeared again. Something whizzed by her ear and plunked into the pole holding the multiapartment birdhouse. Martins exploded out and scattered like buckshot.

Rafe's assassin was shooting at them. She was going to die. Rafe was going to win. She wasn't ready to die. She hadn't even figured out the basics—like what she wanted to do with the rest of her life. For sure it wasn't running. Or hiding.

Gray cursed as he pressed the armor of his body closer to hers and shifted directions, practically lifting her off her feet. "Faster!"

She was nothing more than a rag doll at the mercy

of her protector and her hunter. A bank of tears dammed her throat. Her legs were moving, but she could no longer feel them. Rafe had promised to destroy all she cared for. He'd poisoned her existence. He'd raped the mill and Echo Falls. He'd killed her father.

Another bullet screamed past her, blasting rose petals on the path. She stumbled. Gray held her up. She couldn't see a thing. Not the convent lights. Not the ground at her feet. Not even the end of her own nose. The dam of tears broke and spilled.

You won't ever be free from me, Abrielle. Rafe's laughter echoed in her mind. *I won't ever let you go. I'll be in your dreams and in your nightmares. I'll follow you wherever you go.*

"Hang on, Abbie. We're almost there."

Gray's voice and Gray's push shoved her back into the chase.

Life and death. The line was thinner than she'd ever imagined.

If Rafe knew about Gray, he would destroy him. Rafe reveled in exploiting weaknesses to his best advantage.

She couldn't allow Gray deeper into this mess. Not unless she wanted to lose him, too.

GRAY SHOVED ABBIE THROUGH the convent's kitchen door and barred the heavy wood door behind them. His Glock wasn't a match for a sniper's rifle, and he doubted the good sisters packed heat. Would the shooter dare to violate the sanctuary of a convent? Would he kill defenseless nuns to get to Abbie?

When the local marina hadn't had any rentals available, the daily multi-island ferry ride had seemed safe enough. An open target was usually riskier than fading into a crowd. But now it was clear he'd messed up. He had to get Abbie off this bull's-eye target and behind Seekers, Inc.'s thick walls as soon as possible.

At their noisy entrance, Sister Bertrice, who was standing at the counter, gasped and whirled around, brandishing a knife like a sword. A spatter of strawberry juice plopped onto the dark gray of her skirt.

"What happened to you?" she asked, clutching the silver cross dangling at her neck with her free hand. She took in the bits of twigs and dirt that clung to Abbie's shoulder-length honey-brown hair and the mud that streaked her jeans and white blouse.

"Nothing," Abbie said, but the compulsive wringing of her hands gave away her anxiety.

"You look as if the devil was after you." Sister Bertrice dropped the knife on the cutting board and rushed to Abbie's side. "Are you all right?"

She ushered Abbie to a backless bench, polished by years of use, and skewered him with a look of accusation.

"I'm fine," Abbie said, tripping slightly over the toe of her sneaker as she sat down at the table. "Really. I think I'll just go to bed."

She started to rise again, but Gray caged her in. "Someone shot at Abbie."

"Shot at?" Sister Bertrice crossed herself and hugged Abbie. "How can that be?"

"Is there any way to get off this island tonight?" Gray asked. Mercer was somewhere in Connecticut, thanks to Gray's reluctance to have a witness when he first caught up to Abbie. The rest of the team was just as far and time was of the essence.

Eyes pinched with worry, Sister Bertrice said, "The

ferry comes only once a day. You won't be able to leave until tomorrow afternoon."

Unacceptable. Clothed in Steeltex, Vanderveer's hired gun was essentially invisible and able to move as he pleased. He'd be watching and waiting for Abbie to move. For another chance to earn his pay.

The homey aromas of dinner's home-baked bread fresh out of the oven, vegetable ragout bubbling on the stove and strawberry shortcake scented the air, but the cold granite walls reeked of primitive defenses easily breached. "What if you had an emergency?"

"Then we can call a medevac helicopter, but this doesn't qualify."

"Why not? It's a matter of life or death."

Sister Bertrice's white dandelion puff of hair swayed with the shaking of her head. "They answer only medical emergencies."

"Whoever shot at Abbie is still out there." Gray paced the span of the double-wide arched kitchen door leading to the outside, more to keep Abbie in than to keep anyone out. Her body was tensed for flight. Her gaze kept darting to the door. He didn't like the pallor of her skin, the dazed look in her eyes or her stubborn insistence that she was fine when her body betrayed her shock at the near miss.

Seeing her again had been a shock to his system— like jumping into ice-cold water—and had knocked him for a loop. But he could not let his teenage infatuation with her get in the way of doing his job.

"Have any new guests arrived since Abbie got here?" Identifying the shooter would make keeping Abbie safe that much easier.

"Other than Abbie, you're our only arrival this week.

Do you think there's a danger to any of our other guests?"

"No, the shooter is after Abbie."

"What can we do?" Sister Bertrice clutched her cross as if it would provide her inspiration. He'd leave the prayers to her and rely on a solid plan of action.

Vanderveer couldn't have bought every cop in the country. Though Gray couldn't pull jurisdiction, he could get the USMS to, if it came to that. First he'd try the cooperative route. He'd explain the situation to the locals, then hitch a ride back to the mainland. "We'll have to call the local cops."

"Gray, no! I can't go back into protective custody." Arms wrapped around her middle as if she were in pain, Abbie turned to Sister Bertrice. "If you hadn't told him where I was, I'd still be safe."

"If I hadn't told him, dear, you might be dead."

Abbie blinked as if to hold back tears and made a small sound low in her throat that made him want to wrap her into his arms and promise her a happy ending. She'd always been a sucker for happy endings.

"Your young man is right, Abbie. This is too big. You can't handle this alone. You have to trust someone. I wouldn't have sent him after you if I hadn't remembered him from your seventh birthday party, when you got hit with the piñata bat. He's the one who held a napkin to your temple until your father could whisk you off to get stitches. He has your best interests at heart." She patted Abbie's hand with obvious affection. "I'll go place that call now."

Abbie hung on to the lapels of his jacket that was still draped over her shoulders. The gold feather earrings hanging from her lobes shivered. Her eyes beseeched him. "I can't go back, Gray. I can't just sit there and wait for the next shot through the window."

He crouched beside her and reached for a hand. It was cold in his—as cold as the diamond-and-topaz ring on her finger. He rubbed her fingers to bring back warmth and tried to ignore the kick-in-the-gut need touching her brought. "Seekers is as safe a place as there is. It's outfitted with the latest security technology. It's a damned fortress. No one will be able to get to you there."

"Except Rafe. You don't know him. He's a manipulator. He'll use you to get to me, and you won't even know it until it's too late."

"Is that what happened to your father?"

She pressed her lips into a thin line and nodded.

He didn't like the mechanical stiffness of her body or the flat look in her eyes. She tried to pull her hand free. He hung on to it, needing to keep that small connection between them. "A bully has power only as long as people believe in his vision."

"My point exactly."

Eyes burning with fervor, she leaned forward and her scent of almonds and honey teased him. He'd thought the distance of years had made him immune to her power to dazzle him. But there it was, fizzing through his veins like a shook-up can of soda. "If you testify, you destroy his make-believe world. Without that power he loses everything."

"You don't get it."

"He's just a man, Abbie, not some sort of superhero."

"He owns me."

Gray pounded a fist against the tabletop. "Nobody owns anybody." Especially not a bully.

She turned her face away from him. The same living-dead expression she'd worn after her mother had died cloaked her face. He hadn't known how to reach her then, and the same kind of bewilderment rippled through him now. His golden girl should glow with happiness, not have the weight of sadness dull the light in her eyes. "Abbie."

Her restless fingers knitted themselves with the hem of his jacket. "I know I have to testify. My father used to tell me that with privilege came responsibility. He owned the mill, but he was responsible for the well-being of the people who worked for him. He believed that if he took care of his people, they would return his loyalty."

"I read about the fire. About his keeping his employees on the payroll while the mill was rebuilt." Her father's selfless actions had turned him into a hero. And a hero's image was a tough one to uphold.

"To keep his promise he had to take on a partner. When George Vanderveer died, Rafe inherited his father's options in the mill. Without Rafe's money Dad couldn't have bid successfully on the Steeltex project, and the mill desperately needed to win that contract. I owe Dad. I owe the employees who trusted him." She turned to look at him, her eyes an open window to the knock-out-drag-down brawl between her fears and her duty. "But don't you see? As long as Rafe is alive, he can get to me."

"Not if we destroy him." For her he'd conquer the world. She had to know that.

"How exactly do you plan on doing that? He's already in jail, Gray. What will a life sentence do to him? He'll still have his pack of goons to send after me. Even if Massachusetts had a death penalty, what would it do to him? He'd still have years of appeals to torture me. After he's convicted, he'll be even more desperate for revenge. I won't *ever* be safe."

Gray plucked a piece of twig from her hair and tucked a soft dark gold strand behind her ear, catching the tip of his finger on the chain around her neck. "I took care of Trevor Osborn when he was stalking you."

The gold flecks in her eyes whirled as she touched the bump on the bridge of his nose. "He broke your nose."

"And when that dog had you treed when you trespassed at the apple orchard," he said, his voice rustier than he'd expected. "I got him away from you."

Her gaze slid down to his calf, where the zigzag-scar souvenir of that battle resided. "He tore your jeans to shreds."

It was worth every rip of denim and skin to have Abbie fuss over him once the mutt had hightailed it back to the farmhouse. The way she'd clung to his arm all the way back to the mansion had had him preening peacock-proud for days.

Don't go there, Gray. His brain frantically fired warning messages. The past wasn't someplace he wanted to get stuck. He'd worked too hard to free himself from the bonds of Echo Falls to get trapped there. "Good thing I've got a tough hide."

"Not tough enough for Rafe. He has no conscience."

"Bullies rarely do." Gray had to remember all the hard-learned lessons beaten into him in that snake pit of a town.

"It's not the same, Gray. We're not in high school anymore. He'll kill you to get to me."

A frown rucked her forehead, and he had to stop himself from ironing it out. No, they weren't in high

school anymore. They'd moved on. Abbie to her career
and him to his. In spite of her situation, she still belonged in a world of light and color. She'd always be
his golden girl, but he was the wrong kind of man for a
woman like her. He saw that now. She needed someone
who could share Echo Falls and the mill and all the re-
sponsibilities that went with privilege and position. And
he needed to keep showing bullies the error of their
ways. Raphael Vanderveer was next up on the slate.
"Failure is not an option."

Not then. Not now.

There was no need to revisit old patterns of emotions
they'd both outgrown.

"Four people have already died because of me. Three
deputies and my father."

"And you're thinking that because of that you should
go it alone until the trial?"

She gave a small nod and her voice dipped into a
featherlight whisper. "I have to."

His brave, foolish girl. Her willingness to sacrifice
herself for the things she held dear was one of the qual-
ities he'd admired about Abbie. But her sacrifice wasn't
acceptable. Protecting Abbie was his job. Getting her to
Seekers was his job. Seeing her make it in one piece to
testify was his job. "It's out of your hands. There's too
much at stake."

The squish of Sister Bertrice's soft-soled shoes returned. "Because of the weather, the police can't come
until morning."

"Then we'd better lock up tight."

He always got the job done.

"THE CHOCOLATE ORDER SHOULD be in state by tomorrow night," Pamela announced toward the end of their

daily briefing phone call. The faint clanging of a bell buoy pealed in the background and had Rafe cursing Abbie for all she'd stolen from him. "I ran into a bit of trouble, but I have a tracer on it. I know the expected arrival time and destination."

Rafe went giddy with joy at the prospect of having Abbie back in his sights but kept his voice strictly business. "That is good news indeed."

"It's going to be held at customs for a while, though, unless I can get the release numbers I need. It's because of the Limburger cheese that somehow came with it."

Stinky cheese. Cops of some sort. Who had tagged on to Abbie? Phil Auclair again? He thought he'd taken care of the determined marshal. Why did Pamela need information from their inside patsy? Talking to that contact too often could compromise his advantage. "When did this happen?"

"Yesterday. It's from a private reserve."

Private cops? Had Abbie turned to her pathetic childhood pal? He had to nip that in the bud. "Contact our friend and say we need that customs release information. That we can do much to keep this import business thriving if our request is expedited."

"And if there's trouble rerouting the cheese?"

No cop—private, public or paid for—was going to get between him and what was his. He had no qualms about ridding the world of one more badge-wearing bull. "We'll simply make fondue."

Chapter Four

The need to hurry and get back to Abbie pressed at Gray's back like a mugger's knife. He'd left her at the convent guarded by a police officer. MacAllister would keep her busy while taking down her statement. Gray headed toward the patch of woods where the intruder had shot at Abbie. Simms, the chief of police—a scrappy goat of a man as weatherworn as the island—followed at Gray's heels.

A platinum sky met a stirred-up sea of pewter. The scent of rotting kelp, peaty forest floor and rain-heavy spruce boughs filled the morning air. His suit—what was left of it—and shoes weren't exactly the best equipment for this task, but his travel bag was stuck in the trunk of his Corvette on the mainland. The plan had been simple—get Abbie and get off the island.

He should've known. When it came to Abbie, nothing was simple.

"With the storm last night, we aren't too likely to find anything," Simms said when Gray bent closer to the ground for a better look.

"Won't know unless we try."

The ground was saturated from the rain, squishing

moisture into his shoes with every step. He ignored the discomfort and concentrated on his task. The faster he found the trail, the faster he could get back to Abbie.

Spotting indentations in the ground, he stopped. Boots. Army boots. The real thing or purchased off the shelf? One person. That was a relief.

"Watch your step," he told the chief. "I've got something." Careful not to displace the track, Gray placed his foot alongside one particularly good boot mark. The print was narrower, smaller than his. The stride was shorter, too, with the toes pointed slightly inward. A short man? A woman?

Using the camera Sister Bertrice had loaned Abbie, Gray snapped a picture of the track and one with his foot placed next to it for comparison. Maybe Kingsley could come up with an identifier. Simms took his turn at photographing the evidence.

Picking his way along the trail, Gray looked for disturbed vegetation, broken twigs and turned-over rocks. Along the top edge of the bluff, near the spruce Abbie had been photographing when he'd found her, he noted light prints. Suddenly the prints moved backward, dragging heel and toe. A retreat when Abbie had clambered up the rocks?

He touched the imprint of Abbie's shoe running away from him. But he knew the outcome of that trail, so he followed the other. It led to a boulder where the intruder had knelt and used the rock's flat top to prop his weapon. The knee prints were smaller than he'd expect from a man, less deep. Would someone like Vanderveer entrust such an important job to a woman? That didn't fit the bully profile. Bullies needed to elevate themselves by putting others down. And for a man like Rafe, a woman would make a prime target.

Yet what better way for Rafe to fool the people charged with watching his every move?

And there was Abbie in a convent full of sisters. Could one of the nuns be toting a weapon in the folds of her skirt? He itched to get back, but to protect Abbie, the professional in him had to learn as much as he could about his adversary.

Now the prints showed the intruder running. His prints chased hers. But in clear daylight he could see what he'd missed in the fog. He spirited the threads of Steeltex caught in the bark into his pocket before the cop could see them. As far as he knew, the project was still classified.

"Looks like your shooter rested here," the chief said, stroking his close-cropped beard as he studied the scene. His navy windbreaker flapped in the wind.

In her camouflage suit, the shooter had blended well. "I breezed right by her without seeing her."

"Her?"

"That's what the trail says."

The cop shrugged. "Could be a teenager. You said both shots missed."

"Could be." But not wearing Steeltex and not zeroing in on Abbie. Vanderveer wasn't that desperate yet.

Gray climbed down the opposite side of the bluff to the eastern shore of the island. The rocks mostly hid the shooter's tracks until he studied the few inches of mucky beach. There he found a slip mark above the high-tide line. Scuffs of navy paint streaked a rock, and the rainbow slick of gasoline staining shone on another.

"Looks like your shooter came with his own power."

The chief bent down and studied the paint, then photographed the marks. "I'll take a paint sample and see what we can come up with. But I expect he's gone and won't come back."

If she'd actually left the island. The ragged shore was full of little coves. His guess was that she'd stick to Abbie like a shadow.

The chief finished collecting his evidence and taking his notes, then joined Gray at the edge of the water. "Nothing much to do for kids around these parts, so they go out and shoot targets. First time for Retreat, but it happens all the time on the smaller islands."

Probably just as well the chief didn't seem too disturbed about last night's events. He would get their statements and they'd be out of here in less than two hours. Gray planned on hitching a ride back with the cops. They'd be safe enough on the water.

But on the highway, Corrine, his red vintage Corvette, would make them sitting ducks.

IN THE PILOTHOUSE OF THE police patrol boat, Abbie sat stiffly while MacAllister stood at the controls. Her restless fingers clasped and unclasped the buckle of the small leather bag in her lap. Here she was again, in a small enclosed space, surrounded by cops. What if one of them died because of her?

The chop of tarnished-silver water bounced the boat around. Wind whipped her hair. She scraped the flailing locks back into a ponytail and tied them with an elastic band she found in the pocket of her polar-fleece vest. She scanned the horizon for another boat, another threat, another sniper's rifle seeking her out.

Gray leaned against the railing at the prow, looking—even without a shirt under his suit jacket—like a carefree tourist. But his shoulders betrayed tension and his gaze swept the water as if his glasses were X-ray devices able to spot the skeleton of a would-be assassin.

He meant well, of course. He didn't realize that this wasn't just another scrape. That this situation had dire consequences. Mostly for those around her. Maybe he even thought he was keeping her safe just for old times' sake. Because Bryn was her friend and that was the only way he could show his sister he cared.

He'd seen WITSEC from the deputy's viewpoint. He'd gotten to go home most nights and sleep in his own house, in his own bed. He'd gotten to keep his name, his past—himself. He couldn't know what it was like to lose yourself piece by piece, to live in fear that at any moment a bullet would shoot through some window and destroy what was left of you.

She tore her gaze away from Gray's face and tried to focus on the instrument panel as complicated as any jetliner's. It didn't work. The red lines reminded her of blood and dead deputies. She rubbed her hands against the thigh of her slacks but couldn't stop the flow of cold sweat. How long before they got to shore? How long before she was out of this tin-can target? How long before she could get away?

Since high school she'd gained a certain sense of self, of who she was and what her duties and obligations were. She'd embraced both her public goodwill image at Holbrook Mills and her unofficial role as ambassador for Echo Falls. She'd also cultivated a personal passion to capture a person's truth on film. She loved catching kids. Life hadn't tainted them yet and there was such purity in all their expressions.

Until Rafe had taken over his father's role as partner.

He'd chipped at the gleaming facade that was her life and broken it all apart until she'd wondered about her choices, about her values and about the meaning of her life.

Not exactly what Rafe had had in mind. He'd hoped that his remarks would make her as soft and as pliable as the parachute nylon the mill produced. What he forgot was that Holbrook fabric was not as fragile as it looked.

Even though there was nothing left of what she once was, she still wanted that life back. She loved Echo Falls. She loved the mill. She loved the people who made up both.

Rafe had meant to distance her from her environment and had instead brought her closer to her roots.

By now she was supposed to have married him. And what was hers was supposed to be his. She shuddered.

At first he'd charmed her with his polished manners, his dazzling smile and his smooth bass voice. She'd almost fallen under the spell of his persona. Until the press conference, when Holbrook Mills had announced its new contract with the Army. As was her custom, she'd photographed the event. When she'd processed the film, something in Rafe's eyes had shivered dread down her spine. She'd thought it was a trick of the light. But the look of pure evil she'd frozen on film had surfaced again, both at her home and at his office, when he'd thought no one was looking. He'd shown his true colors the day he'd murdered her father.

Because she'd seen his soul, he had to destroy her. He had to destroy everything she cared for.

Against her will, her gaze once again sought Gray. The stubble-shadowed jaw took nothing away from the clean-cut looks he'd sculpted out of the clay of his dirt-poor youth. A leaden weight dragged at her heart.

Her father would approve of the man Gray had become. They shared a deep sense of ethics and the values of honor and loyalty. Bryn probably wouldn't agree, but Bryn tended to forget she was the one who'd slammed shut that particular door. Abbie had seen the letters from Gray that Bryn had discarded unopened. Gray was the one who'd arranged and paid for his mother's stay at the hospice when liver disease had made staying at home impossible. He'd offered to pay for Bryn's college education, too, but pride had made her refuse.

Seeing him again, so strong and solid, so determined to act as her protector, spiked her heart with a quick jump. She wished for one of his smiles that made her feel as if all was right with the world.

She was tired of constantly looking over her shoulder. She was tired of being afraid. She was so marrow-deep tired that she was actually considering letting Gray take her to Seekers, Inc., letting him take care of her. Letting Rafe test just how high-security Seekers' safety bunker was.

The last few weeks of bloody horror were making her weak.

You're as strong as Steeltex.

Sneering, she shook her head and opened the small leather bag that contained the few changes of clothes Bryn had provided her and the camera Bert had loaned her. She took out the Nikon and loaded a fresh roll of film.

She wanted nothing more than to go to sleep, to slide into darkness and stay there until the trial was over. Until someone could assure her that the shackles around

Rafe were so tight and so solid, he could never again rally allies to do the dirty work he was denied.

"We'll find him, you know," MacAllister said, slanting her a look that came too close to pity for comfort. "Something like this, the perp always comes to light."

"Of course." She raised the camera and searched through the magic frame.

"He won't be able to keep the secret. It'll itch at him and itch at him till he bursts and has to tell someone else about the deed. Small town like this, a secret like that won't stay quiet too long."

"Thanks."

His fresh-scrubbed face was still eager and filled with idealism. How long would it take for lines to carve dispassionate grooves around his eyes and mouth like those that etched Simms's face? "Can I take your picture?"

"Me? What for?"

"I like the look in your eye." She wanted to capture the youthful passion shining lighthouse bright on his face. As a reminder that some parts of the world were still worth looking at.

He grinned. She snapped.

MacAllister slowed the boat as he approached the dock. "We're almost there."

One hand on the wheel, the other on the throttle, he twisted around to face her. He opened his mouth as if to add something more. She adjusted the focus ring. Surprise rounded his eyes. Glass shattered. The report of a gun cracked through the sudden rev of the boat's engine. MacAllister crumpled, taking her down with his dead weight.

"CAN WE STOP?" ABBIE ASKED as Gray's Corvette burned up I-95. Red streaked the sky, reminding her yet again of MacAllister's blood all over the patrol boat deck. Another dead cop. Because of her. Her stomach was a tangle of greasy knots, her mind a maddened beehive and her determination would capitulate into a white flag of surrender if she didn't do something soon. "I think I'm going to be sick."

His fingers touched her knee in concern and racked up her guilt another notch. "There's a rest stop up ahead. Can you hang on for another few minutes? I don't want to pull off on the shoulder."

"Just hurry." Would he leave her alone? She searched her memory for the layout of the bathroom but couldn't remember if there was a back exit or not. Gray had changed into khakis, a polo shirt and running shoes. She wished he'd kept on his slippery leather shoes. Then she'd have half a chance at losing him.

"You holding up?" Gray asked as they passed a sign announcing their upcoming exit.

His head remained fixed straight ahead, but the flick of his gaze in her direction snapped like a camera's shutter to judge her mental and physical soundness. "I'm fine."

"You saw someone shot to death. You need to—"

"No, I'm fine."

"You've been through a—"

"No, really, there's nothing to talk about."

Talk wasn't going to solve her problem. As much as he wanted to, Gray couldn't fix this. Another cop had died. And once again the shooter had gotten away. If Gray hadn't called his boss, who had expedited her release, she'd still be trying to answer questions to which she had no answers. Somehow she needed to ditch Gray.

The surprise in Officer McAllister's eyes would haunt her for the rest of her life. It would paint a stain on her conscience—just as Deputy Kushner, Deputy Donaldson and Deputy Tarpley's deaths had. Another bright life extinguished because of her. If MacAllister hadn't moved, if he hadn't wanted to soothe her, the bullet that shattered his heart would have hit her right between the eyes.

She blinked to soothe her burning eyes. She swallowed to loosen the knot in her throat. She shuddered and zipped up the polar-fleece vest she couldn't seem to shed even in the near-eighty-degree heat.

Why couldn't Gray understand that she didn't want to add him—or anyone else—to the ranks of the dead? That Rafe wouldn't stop until he got what he wanted? Her in a grave on which he could spit.

The coming rest stop was the last one before the New Hampshire border. And she simply couldn't let herself get trapped in a place Rafe could find.

Gray slowed and took the Exit 25 ramp. He parked on an outside row of the rest-stop parking lot, leaving plenty of space all around him for a quick getaway.

She rolled her shoulder as if to dislodge a laser sight. "Is someone following us?"

"Just being careful."

He draped an arm casually around her shoulders, but there was nothing relaxed about the action-readiness of his taut muscles. His hand hovered over the gun she'd seen him hide in the holster under the untucked tail of his polo shirt. He studied every car and every person they passed on their way to the building.

To her dismay, he made as if to accompany her into the ladies' room. "You can't go in there."

"I'm not leaving you alone."

"What could possibly happen in there?"

"You're not feeling well."

"Yet another reason not to have an audience." She raked her loose hair back and blew out a breath. "Just give me a couple of minutes."

A bus belched to a stop, unloading a gaggle of older ladies wearing red hats and purple T-shirts. Laughing and talking all at once, they entered the building and swarmed toward the bathroom.

Gray made a small sign of surrender. "Okay, I'll wait for you right here." He leaned against the doorway. His smile had steel around the edges, but to the casual observer it would look like a lover's tease. "If you need anything, call."

Not good. How could she get away with him watching the only exit? The competing scents of cinnamon and fast-food grease wafting in the air turned her stomach. *Think, Abbie.* Out of the corner of her eye she caught sight of the Cinnabon stand near the men's room. "I could use a cup of tea to settle my stomach."

His long and hard stare had her insides squirming like eels. With a barely visible shake of his head he denied her request. "Not a chance I'm going that far from you, honey."

"Do they have ginger ale in the soda machine?"

"We'll look on the way out." There was no give in his voice. He was as determined to keep her trapped in his sights as she was to escape him. "Don't make me wait too long."

"I wouldn't dream of it." With as carefree a step as she could manage, she rounded the curve of the wall, then peered around the corner. Through his damned glasses, his gaze was zeroed in on the entrance to the ladies' room.

Behind her the red-hatted women congregated around the sinks. Their cheery voices pinballed against the tiles. She could slip into the middle of the group as they were leaving. Gray would spot a sea of red and purple, and she'd swim out lost among them. Then she'd have only a few minutes to disappear. Would the ladies notice one more on the tour bus?

The older women headed for the entrance. Just as she was about to join the group, someone bumped into her. Abbie's arms automatically reached out to the tiled wall to catch herself from falling.

"Oh, I'm so sorry," the tall, thin woman said. "I didn't see you there."

"It's all right." Distracted, Abbie glanced at the group. She had only a few seconds more to make her escape. "I'm fine."

Abbie pushed herself off the wall. A heavy, cream-colored envelope toppled from her leather bag. "Miss? You dropped something."

Hands dripping with water, the woman ripped a length of paper towel from the holder and shook her head. "No, it's not mine."

Abbie turned over the envelope and glanced down at the name. "Are you—"

She sucked in a small gasp and ran a finger over the brown calligraphy ink that turned her name into a work of art. Where had this come from? The paper was damp under her fingers, as if it had absorbed moist sea air. Bert must have tucked a note in her bag.

She looked up in time to realize she'd missed her opportunity to escape. The ladies had all left. And Gray still stood there.

Desperately needing a few minutes to think, she slipped into a stall and locked the door. She dragged a nail under the flap and slit the envelope open. Bert's words of encouragement would settle her nerves. Her gaze traveled to the end of the page looking for the curvy angel doodle that always graced Bert's notes. Her heart sank.

Rafe's name contaminated the expensive paper, and his heavy energy crawled under her skin like a poison-ivy rash. She let her back fall against the beige metal wall of the stall for support. The stationery shook in her hands.

In the same calligraphy hand, the message read:

My Dearest Abrielle—
At a time like this, who can you trust?

The WITSEC inspector assigned to keep you safe?

Check his bank account, dearest Abrielle, you'll see how well he's being paid to betray you.

Your childhood friends?

Your Brynna has a crusade to mount now, doesn't she? And crusades are always expensive. Ask her how many cases she's handled this year. Ask her about her expenses. Ask her how she's making ends meet. The answer will surprise you. Did you know that she's used your name to grease her way?

Your Grayson is a man on a mission. On the surface, you're his mission. But ask yourself what is more important to him, you or keeping up the image of the fearless hunter? He can live without you. He's proven that over the past thirteen years. But he cannot live without the weight of his title. A coward always needs a shield. He's run from Echo Falls. He's run from the Navy. He's run from the Marshals Service. When things get tough, Grayson Reed runs. Can you trust that he won't run when you need him most?

Don't be foolish enough to think Seekers, Inc. can protect you. One of them is ready to use you as bar-ter bait. Their deaths will be on your conscience.

You are mine. No one, nothing, can keep us apart. I will find you wherever you go.

I have never shown you anything but the utmost respect. I have loved you and cherished you. I have laid my soul bare to you. I am ready to give you the world. I will stand by you when you need me.

In just a few more days we can put this misunderstanding behind us and live the life that is our fated destiny together as man and wife.

Remember, Abrielle, there is no one you can trust, except me.

All my love,
Raphael.

"Abbie?" Gray's voice echoed against the tiled walls of the bathroom and made her jump. "If you're not out here in ten seconds, I'm coming in after you."

"I'll be right out."

She folded the letter back in its envelope and dropped both in her bag. At the sink she splashed cold water on her face and pasted on a smile, then strode out of the ladies' room.

"Everything all right?" Gray asked. His blasted mirrored glasses covered his eyes, but their burning gaze studied every inch of her for signs of distress. "Still want that soda?"

"Yes, thank you."

Gray maneuvered her to the vending machine, fed coins into the slot and handed her a can of Sprite—the closest thing to her request. Their fingers touched against the cool aluminum. His grip on the can stayed firm and his mirrored gaze seemed to reach all the way down to her soul. "I can keep you safe."

When she didn't respond, he let go. The weight of defeat strained her limbs like deadwood.

The nightmare wasn't going away. Rafe didn't love her. He didn't cherish her. He didn't have her best interest at heart—only his own. She had no illusions that if she gave in to his demands, she would wake up six feet underground.

Still, he was good at using weaknesses to his advantage. He was a master at digging dirt. How much of what he'd written about Phil and Brynna and Gray was true? How much was scare tactic? How much more could Rafe take away from her before there was nothing left?

Chapter Five

Gray stole a glance at Abbie sitting next to him in the car. She held the can of Sprite with both hands and stared at the unopened tab as if it were a missile detonator and the decision to destroy a state rested solely with her. She hadn't said a word in over twenty minutes.

Ordinarily he'd just turn on the radio and let her stew in her own mind, but she'd already gone through so much. More than most men could take without breaking.

Gray had a hunch she'd wanted to bolt back there. The crawl of spiders had knitted a web on the back of his neck. They'd started their frantic construction as soon as he'd shut off the engine and hadn't stopped until they were once again on the road. *Too bad, honey. You're stuck with me until the trial.*

"Talk to me, Abbie."

She continued staring at the top of the can of soda. The lights over the Piscataqua River Bridge turned the purple night into a sour-orange haze. He switched to the middle lane to avoid the odd sensation of falling the rail gave him.

"If I ask you questions, will you answer with the truth?"

"Of course." *What's the catch?*

"No couching to protect me." A certain desperation furrowed her forehead and clouded the bright light that should shine from her eyes.

"I'll always protect you, Abbie, whether you want me to or not." He shot her the smile he'd once reserved just for her, the kind of smile that would provoke an answering grin no matter what her mood. "Talk to me."

"Will you not ask me any questions in return?"

Drawing tiny circles with his back teeth, he stared at the white lines on the road. What was he agreeing to? A debating team took up sides in his head. After a minute neither side had him convinced, so he went with neutral. "I'm not sure I can promise that without more information."

She shook her head, returned her gaze to the top of the soda can and picked idly at the tab with a fingernail. "You're worse than the company lawyers. Listen, answer and don't question. Okay?"

He pulled in a breath. To get, he was going to have to give a little. Getting past Abbie's barrier was more important than satisfying his own curiosity. The pro side won. For now. "Okay."

"Why did you leave the Navy?"

This was relevant to the current situation how? "I put in my five years and moved on."

Her fingernail fiddled with the tab on the can of soda, causing a nerve-irritating *click-click-click.*

"I wanted something more, Abbie, something the Navy couldn't give me."

"What?"

He shrugged, staring at the thickening traffic around Portsmouth. What had he wanted? A sense of accomplishment? Control? Knowing how to put feelings into words wasn't his specialty. "What I found at Seekers."

"Why were you fired from the Marshals Service?"

Continuing an investigation after a cease-and-desist order had not gone down well with his superior. The Service always came first. That was the unwritten rule. But damn if it hadn't felt good to do the right thing, even if it was the wrong choice for career growth. Turned out he'd helped save lives doing it, too. In the end truth had won out and they'd all gained vindication. "I wasn't fired. I was temporarily put on unpaid leave, along with the rest of the Special Operations Group, until an investigation cleared us."

"Why did you quit, then?"

Because following rules and regulations didn't come easy. He'd tried to toe the line in the Navy. He'd tried to go by the book in the Service. But private policing offered much more freedom—and bigger rewards. "For many reasons. The main one being that Sebastian Falconer offered me a job. I respect the man and his vision, so I accepted."

"The people at Seekers—do you trust them?"

By the dim light of the dashboard he studied her with his peripheral vision—the pale skin, the haggard look, the desperation. Was she finally realizing she had no choice but to trust him? "With my life."

"Are you sure?"

"I'm positive."

"How close are you to these people?" She licked her dry lips but didn't crack the tab that could quench her thirst. "I mean, would any of them admit if they'd done something wrong?"

"Like what?"

A sigh escaped her and her shoulders slumped as if she were deflating. "I don't know. Something that might make them betray one of the team?"

"I don't know what you're getting at, but if I was in a tough situation, I'd want a Seeker watching my back."

She nodded but nervously rocked the can of soda between her palms. The rumble of the engine growled between them, a pulse beating out the tension of their silence.

He rolled his tongue in his mouth and did his best to swallow his impatience. "What's going on, Abbie?"

A crinkle of painful lines radiated from her eyes as she winged her shoulders forward. "I can't go with you to Seekers, Inc."

"It's the safest place there is."

"Rafe is going to kill all of you. I can't have that on my conscience. It's too crowded as it is."

"Abbie—"

"No, listen to me." Her head jerked up and her eyes were alight with a gold fire that pulsated with cold fear instead of warmth. "My father is dead. Three deputies are dead. A police officer is dead. Rafe isn't going to stop until he gets me, and he knows where we're going."

Gray's jaw slid back and forth. "He can't know."

"He told me."

Gray's head snapped in her direction. The phantom spiders at the back of his neck went on overdrive. The car next to him honked as Corinne drifted into its lane. "When?"

Abbie set the can of soda aside, dug into the bag at her feet and brought out a cream-colored envelope. "He left this for me."

"Where?" How was it possible for Vanderveer to get

anywhere close to Abbie? How had Gray missed the intrusion? He'd promised to keep her safe. How the hell was he supposed to do that if he couldn't even see his prey? Maybe Falconer was right to question his ability to do this job.

"I'm not sure. I found it while I was in the bathroom."

He kicked himself once more. He should've gone in with her. "Read it to me."

She did. And with each venomous word scratched by Vanderveer's pen Gray's temper rose a degree. By the time she finished reading, he was just shy of boiling over. Hands clawed around the steering wheel, he modulated his voice. *She's afraid. Soothe her.* "He's lying, Abbie."

She folded the note back into its envelope and thrust it into her bag. "About some things, yes. But you have to understand that he's an expert manipulator. Dirt and weaknesses are his tools of choice."

"He's manipulating *you* with his lies."

"Bryn hasn't been herself in a long time," she said. The pleats above her eyes pressed into her forehead much too deeply and made his thumbs itch to smooth them. "How come Phil Auclair wasn't killed when three younger deputies were? For all I know, you did run from the Navy and from the Marshals Service—"

"I didn't run. I chose new career paths—"

"How can you be one hundred percent sure about everyone who works on the Seekers team?"

The picture of Harper flashed into his mind. The guy carried a chip bigger than California on his shoulder. He didn't fit in. And Gray had wondered more than once why Falconer had hired someone like Harper. Was Harper angry enough to trade Abbie's life for whatever mark stained his soul? "Vanderveer is using your fears to get you to do what he wants. If you're running, it's easier to get a bead on you."

"I don't care, Gray. All I have is your word that one of your team isn't dirty. I can't take that chance. I'm not going where I don't feel safe, and I won't feel safe at Seekers. Not knowing Rafe knows where I am. I'm not going there."

"You don't have a choice, honey." *You find her and you bring her in. Is that understood?* Gray had given Falconer his word.

"I'd rather die than give Rafe a reason to kill more people."

Her hand curled around the door handle, and the spiders at his neck went hog wild again. For once he wished he'd gone for a late-model car with all the bells and whistles to lock her in, instead of a classic like Corinne with everything manual.

"You keep going straight through the Hampton tolls or I swear to God I'll open that door and jump out."

She wouldn't. She couldn't. All he had to do was calm her down. "Abbie—"

"Stop the car, Gray, because I'm getting out." The clipped confidence of her tone took him aback. So did the latch that unhooked with a pop.

"Close the door." They were in the middle of traffic. She wouldn't get out. She was trying her hand at some Vanderveerian manipulation.

"Not unless you stop the car."

"I'm in the freakin' middle lane. There's traffic all around us. You'll get yourself killed."

She reached to unclip the safety belt. Swearing, he clasped a hand over the buckle, squeezing her hand to keep her from pressing her finger on the release. She let go of the door. It rattled against the frame. With traffic on both sides, he couldn't maneuver to the shoulder. She hooked the leather bag at her feet into her hand and slammed it into his fist until his knuckles bled. Before she broke bone, he capitulated. "All right. You win."

Her breathing was a jagged rush. Her eyes were wide and wild. She was so wound up, he was afraid she'd spring out from sheer adrenaline overload.

"Stop the car."

"I said you win. I'll drive through the damned tolls." There was more than one way to Wintergreen.

"Stop the car now."

"We're in the middle of traffic."

She reached for the door again. "Stop the damned car!"

"Fine."

He tapped the brakes, warning the car behind him of his intent. He added the hazard lights for good measure. She'd soon see how stupidly she was acting. "We're stopped. Close the door."

"Not until you promise that you won't take me to Seekers."

"It's the safest place for you, but if—"

Before he could finish, she flung the door open and got out. Traffic buzzed around her in a flurry of dizzying headlights, honked horns and raised fists.

Careful of the traffic, he rushed after her. She strode down the middle lane of I-95 as if she were on an empty country road outside of Echo Falls. "Abbie!"

She rounded on him, her face raw with rage, her fists tight at her side. The steady beam of his headlights cut stark shadows across her body, sharpening her cheeks, chiseling her chin and giving her face a hard edge. That hardness scared him more than any special operation he'd taken part in. The headlights of speeding cars flickering like strobes added to the impression of madness.

"I've had it," she said. "I've had it with lies and threats and death. I've had it with people who think they know what's good for me. My father didn't know. Rafe doesn't know. And you certainly don't. Did any of you bother consulting me before you made plans? No! You all just assumed I'd want what you want. Well, guess what? I don't want to be the good little girl anymore. I don't want to pretend I'm somebody else. I don't want to go to Seekers. I just want my life back. Is that too much to ask?"

He reached out to her, desperate to reel her in to safety. She stepped back, clutching her leather bag to her chest. The diamond-and-topaz ring on her hand glared a cautious warning. *She needs reassurance, Gray. Give it to her.*

"No, Abbie, it's perfectly normal. But these aren't normal circumstances. You said you didn't want anyone else's death on your conscience. If you don't testify, then you could have the deaths of thousands of soldiers weighing on you. Seekers can keep you alive so you can get your life back. I can keep you safe until the trial. You have to trust me."

Her throat worked hard and she shook her head. "Rafe knows where I'm going. He knows where to find me. I can't go there."

Even in this humid heat and wearing a fleece vest, shivers wracked her body. The thought that Vanderveer could locate her terrified her to her core. In this state, would she throw herself into traffic rather than walk into a place that would petrify her every second of every day? Seven days of this could leave her unfit to testify. And wasn't that the ultimate aim?

"Okay. I hear you. No Seekers." A faraway siren warbled through the night. "Now get back in the car before the state troopers get here and we have to answer questions."

There was enough doubt rolling around in his head about Harper that he could give her a temporary reprieve until he checked out the situation. He weighed his options and came up with an intermediate plan. "We're going to Boston."

He offered her his hand once more. This time she took it. He used up half a lifetime of restraint to control his urge to wrap her in his arms and blister her ears with how much she'd scared him. But he couldn't let her see how much she'd shaken him. *Never let them see you sweat.*

"What's in Boston?" she asked as she stepped shakily back into the car.

"Relative anonymity."

ABBIE STUDIED GRAY'S EVERY move. She watched for surreptitious advances to his pocket, where he could slyly signal someone from his team. When he noticed her preoccupation with his hands, he tossed her his cell phone and continued driving. She held on to the slim phone with both hands, as if it were a symbol of his trust. Would he do as he said? Would he take her somewhere else? Or was this a long, circuitous road to Seekers? She wasn't sure how far she could trust him, and the uncertainty plagued her with an odd mixture of guilt and regret.

The first thing Gray did when they got to Boston was arrange for a parking stall for his Corvette. He paid for a month in advance to ensure its safety and mooned over his goodbyes to the pile of steel as if he were abandoning a child. What was it with guys and their cars? Next they took the T to the Aquarium stop and hoofed it to the King's Arms Hotel on Rowes Wharf five minutes away. At the marble and brass-trimmed registration desk he asked for Joanna Kingsley.

"Who's Joanna Kingsley?"

"Noah Kingsley's sister. He's a fellow Seeker."

The architects and decorators had worked hard to imbue the lobby with the rich feel of an old castle. The reds and golds and greens of carpets and tapestries and the soft lighting were supposed to lend gilded warmth. But her gaze focused on the facing made of unyielding square stone blocks and the steel bars over decorative crenelles. "I don't think this is a good idea. She'll tell him where we are."

"Not if I ask her not to."

"But—"

"I trust her and I trust Noah."

"I can't afford to trust anyone."

He leaned against the desk, giving the impression he was a patron with time on his hands. She imagined that beneath his mirrored glasses he assessed everyone in the lobby. "It's temporary, Abbie. We have to stay somewhere tonight. We have to make a plan. We can't go running willy-nilly."

"That way we're unpredictable."

"And a moving target. Right now we can't use a credit card. We don't have much money. We—"

"Okay, I get it. We need a plan." A hitch of hesitation had her flipping open and closing the cover to Gray's cell phone. "What if she's not here?"

Gray flashed her a heart-stopping smile. "Noah jokes that his sister is too married to her job to find a human companion. What a pity. If Kingsley's a golden retriever, then Joanna's an Afghan hound—sleek, sexy and sophisticated."

"I heard that," an amused voice said.

Gray turned and beamed his charm at the tall woman who materialized behind the desk. Her long hair was the color of pulled taffy—the highlights no doubt salon bought. Her hazel eyes gave the impression of both nononsense sharpness and an eccentric sense of humor. Leaning across the desk, she pecked a kiss on Gray's cheek. "But since it's coming from you, I'll take it as a compliment."

"I meant it as a compliment. How are you, Jo?"

Her smile lit all the way to her eyes. "Married to my job and too busy for a human companion."

Gray leaned in to Joanna as if she were the center of the world, and Abbie tried to brush away the unwarranted barb of jealousy. How well did Gray know this Joanna?

"What a shame," Gray said. "Still riding?"

"Every chance I get. I recently bought a new Hanoverian from Germany. Coal-black. Strong, athletic and energetic."

Much like his mistress, Abbie surmised.

"You'll have to let me know next time you enter one of those musical horse-dance things."

"Dressage freestyle? Two weeks from Saturday."

"It's a date. How's Meredith doing?"

"My darling sister is still driving herself crazy trying to prove she's the perfect Realtor, perfect wife and perfect mother."

"And your folks?"

"Hiking through the wine regions of France."

"I hope I have as much energy as they do when I get to that age."

Joanna's laughter was as rich as her hotel. "I certainly hope not or there'll be no safe place on this earth. What can I do for you? Somehow I get the feeling you didn't come all this way at this hour just to chat with me."

His lips brushed much too close to Joanna's ear. "We need a room and some silence."

Joanna's eyebrows shot up. "You mean I get to know something that Noah doesn't?"

"Something that Noah can't find out."

"Ooh," she crooned, as if having something on her brother was a mouthwatering treat. Her long fingers flew over the keyboard of the reservation computer. "We're pretty full up, but I can stash you in one of the smaller suites. It has one king bed and a separate sitting area with a pullout."

"That's perfect, Joanna."

His smile practically made Abbie gag. *Pouring it on a little too thick, aren't you?*

"My treat, of course. I've entered you as Mr. and Mrs. Franklin." Joanna's smile glowed with delight. "Not quite as suspicious as *Smith.*"

"I owe you."

"Big-time." Joanna emerged from the back of the registration desk and crooked a finger at them. They followed her dignified couture-enclosed derriere to the elevators. She escorted them to the ninth-floor room, trying to pump Gray for information. He poured on the charm and gave her enough to think she knew more than she did but not enough to give Abbie's plight away.

Was he manipulating her, too? Was this another ruse? Get the runaway witness all nice and comfortable in a luxury hotel, then—wham—she'd wake up in protective custody in some underground secure room at Seekers, Inc.

She should make plans, too. When he was sleeping, she could slip out and disappear in the city. She could wander the subway and bed down in a homeless shelter. Seven more days. She could do it.

After a few more syrupy exchanges, Joanna gave Gray her personal number, told him to call if he needed anything and said goodbye. At the end of the hallway the elevator carrying her away *bing*ed. Gray turned around to face the inside of the room but didn't come in.

He stood in the doorway, a hand wrapped around each side of the frame as if he were holding himself back. The expression on his face was blank—as if talking to Joanna had used up his quota of charm for the day. His jaw sported a flinty set she hadn't noticed before, making her wish he'd take off his glasses so she could see some sort of softness in him.

"Are you going to stand there all night?" She gestured to the vast suite. "There's enough room for both of us."

A muscle in his jaw twitched.

He couldn't come in. The realization jolted through her, and she dropped onto the foot of the bed.

If he did, he couldn't go back. She was asking him to divide his loyalty. Seekers or her. He'd remained loyal to the mother who'd abused him. He'd remained loyal to the sister who'd denied him. And now by refusing to go to Seekers, Inc. with him, she was asking him to give her the one thing that wasn't an obligation but a passion of soul.

"Go home, Gray. You don't belong here."

He flinched. Of course, that was the wrong thing to say. He thought she meant here in this fancy hotel room. She'd meant in the magnet of death she seemed to attract. No matter how good he'd made himself look on the outside, the little boy in him still wore thrift-shop clothes and lived in the tired house on Peanut Row. None of that had mattered to her, but he'd never quite believed her—especially after she'd refused to go away with him thirteen years ago.

"You know I can't," he said. "I promised to bring you back and keep you safe. If you won't go to Seekers, someone has to watch out for you."

And Grayson Reed always kept his word.

She didn't want to see him hurt. She didn't want to need his help or his protection. But she did. Having one hunter on her trail was hard enough to deal with. Two equally determined ones would be too much.

Which left her no choice at all. She *had* to be sure of something, of someone, or she wouldn't get through this with her sanity intact.

She stared at Gray, at his ramrod-straight body, at his unflinching determination. At his unseen hesitation. Did he feel loyalty to her because he still had feelings for her? Did it matter?

A stab of sorrow bit into her breastbone. Absently she rubbed at the deep ache.

The trial started in seven days. Seven more days to hide. Seven more days to stay alive. *Please, for once, if someone has to die, let it be me.* "Come on in, Gray. Close the door."

He let go of the door frame. His hands hung at his sides for a long moment, then he stepped inside the room.

She wanted to cry.

Chapter Six

Gray would have to call in, of course, but he wanted a firm plan of action first—a way to let Falconer know that he was still performing his duty to Seekers, Inc., still a team player. The important thing was to keep Abbie alive to testify. In the larger scheme of things, the where and how of that wasn't as important. Falconer would understand.

Say that often enough and maybe you'll believe it.

He hadn't lied to Abbie when he'd said he'd found what he needed at Seekers. What was important to him was important to them, too. They shared the common goal of recapturing fugitives and putting them back behind bars where they belonged. Bending rules and cutting corners came with the territory. Something the Navy and the Service didn't always understand.

Seekers, Inc. had a ninety percent capture rate when the industry average hovered around fifty percent.

They were doing something right.

To buy himself some time, he ordered soup and sandwiches from room service. Abbie wasn't going to like the next part of plan B any more than he liked the idea of leading her through it.

While they waited for the food, Abbie puttered

around the room, gazing at the original oils of knights and their ladies bolted to the walls, trailing a hand over the polished mahogany arm of the gold-upholstered sofa and opening the doors of the solid-wood armoire hiding the big-screen television set.

Out of habit he snagged two empty glasses from the quartet on the silver tray on the coffee table, placed them on the windowsill and closed the curtains, shutting out the view of the harbor. Not that anyone would scale the smooth outside wall to get to set off his cheap alarm.

After room service left, he threw the security bolt and posted the trash can by the front door. No connecting doors, so he didn't have to worry about intrusion from the adjoining rooms. He turned to the inside of the room again. Maybe not such a good idea. The world now contained only him and Abbie. The fact she was sitting on the king-size bed, with its pile of gold and red pillows, wasn't helping any. He could tell himself all day long that Abbie was just a friend, but his body wanted her in a way that had nothing to do with friendship.

As if sensing the treacherous turn of his thoughts, Abbie got up and wheeled the room-service cart to the sitting area. She lifted the silver domes off the plates and placed them on the desk. "Where do we start?"

"With Vanderveer." Gray took a seat at the opposite end of the oblong table.

She munched on a long, skinny French fry that couldn't possibly have come from a real potato. "How is that going to help us with a plan to hide for the next week?"

Might as well plunge right in. "We need to know who's running after you."

"Easy. Rafe."

Potatoes—fried, baked or mashed—were to Abbie

what chocolate was to most women. He pushed his toward her. "He's not working alone, though. He's behind bars. Someone has to be doing his dirty work on the outside."

"How do we find that out?"

"Tell me about him."

She stared at him long and hard with her big honey eyes. Her trust didn't extend more than arm's length. She was still pissed at him for trying to bring her to Seekers. She feared betrayal. Used to be a smile would chase the shadows from her eyes and set their gold on fire. Now the look in them told him not even the most sophisticated of lie-detector tests would make anything he said sound like truth.

"I need to understand what Vanderveer's capable of," Gray said. "What Vanderveer's comfortable with."

She picked up another fry. "You want the whole sordid mess."

"Something like that." Gray concentrated on his sandwich. How could the chef have managed to turn something as simple as two slices of bread, roast beef, provolone and spicy mustard into something that needed a road map to figure out?

She swirled her fry in a blob of mayonnaise for a long time. "I don't know him that well."

The creep of red along her neck, her reluctance to look directly at him and her jerky movements denied her words. "You were never any good at lying."

"I'm not lying."

"Tell me what you know. It's the details that can make or break a case."

"It's not that simple."

"Relationships never are."

"No, they aren't."

Was that regret in her voice? Was she thinking back to when she'd walked away from him? He hadn't expected her to remain single or pine away for the one true love that got away. Not when she'd made it clear he wasn't the one for her. But he thought about her. Often. Too often. "I'm not here to judge, Abbie, only to understand."

She pressed her lips tightly together, and the crackle and pop of tension flickering in her eyes shot through him like a thousand honed knives. He didn't like feeling so damned twisted around her. *Come here, Abbie, let me hold you. Everything's going to be all right. I promise.* But of course he couldn't—hold her or make that promise—so he forced another bite of sandwich into his mouth.

Finally she blew out a breath and shook her head. "Rafe wants...I don't know. It's more than money. It's more than success. It's..." Frowning, she picked at the leaf of lettuce sticking out from the crust of her whole-wheat bread.

"It's what?"

"I don't know, okay. Stop bullying me."

Bullying? Where was she getting that? He was asking questions. Simple ones at that. They were nowhere near the hard part yet. "How did you meet him?"

Their stares met across the table. She needed someone to yank her out of the whirlwind her life had become, and he was only dragging her in deeper.

Her fingers squashed the soft bread of her sandwich nearly flat. "I didn't meet Rafe until after his father, George, died. He was at the funeral. His father wasn't even in the ground yet when Rafe informed my father that he was taking over where George had left off."

"Why didn't your father just tell him it was a no-go?"

"Money."

The root of all evil, if the catechism nuns were right. "So what happened next?"

"Rafe wanted a more hands-on approach. He wanted changes that would bring on short-term gain but would hurt the company in the long run. The cuts would affect the people who trusted Dad. Dad saw the potential damage and argued against the changes. But in the end there wasn't much he could do. Dad needed Rafe's money. Rafe knew my father's loyalty to his employees was his weakness and he worked it for all it was worth. The government contract was going to put Holbrook Mills on the map again and give Dad a chance to buy out Rafe." She made a face and pushed away the sandwich. "Then everything fell apart."

"How?"

She shook her head, sending the gold feather earrings at her lobes swinging in alarm. Tears were brimming, and her mouth opened as if breathing had suddenly become an arduous task.

When in-your-face didn't work, there was always the back door. "Bryn mentioned that your father died to protect you. What did she mean by that?"

"Not long after Rafe took over George's office, he decided he wanted me."

That piece of garbage had made advances toward her? His blood pressure spiked into the unhealthy range. "How?"

She shrugged a shoulder. "You know."

Gray was going to strangle the scumbag the first chance he got. He ripped into the roast beef as if it were prey. "Sexual?"

She sighed and dunked an infuser of chamomile tea

into the silver teapot. "He was charming at first. He made me smile, you know. But…"

"Go on."

"I'd just ended a relationship and didn't want to start a new one, not when my photography was finally taking off."

"He couldn't take no." Gray shoved aside the thought of Abbie in someone else's arms, someone else's bed, someone else's heart. She wasn't his. She'd never been his.

She dropped her gaze. "When I kept turning him down, he tried to intimidate me into marriage. He could make my father hurt, he said, turn him into dirt in his employees' eyes, drag his good name and reputation through the mud. He could make sure no client ever visited my studio. That…" She shrugged and her voice trailed.

"I got the picture." Gray sensed what was coming but couldn't help himself. He had to ask. "What did you do?"

"I agreed to an engagement."

Gray swallowed a vicious string of curses. Of course. Abbie hated conflict, hated causing waves, hated disappointing anybody. Especially her parents. How could she have offered herself to that piece of pond scum?

"I couldn't risk everything my father had spent a lifetime building," she said defensively and poured her tea. "I figured if I held him off long enough, then the contract would come through and Dad would buy Rafe's share of the company. Everything would go back to normal."

"Except it didn't."

Still refusing to look straight at him, she stirred honey into the hot tea. "He was trying to put the pressure on Dad for a marriage merger. That way he could have everything."

"And when your father refused, Rafe killed him."

Swallowing hard, she nodded. "After Daddy died, the scandal exploded, making it look as if he was the one selling classified information about Steeltex, not Rafe."

Tears pooled in her eyes. "The police found Dad's body in the pond at the mill. He had incriminating evidence in his pocket. The water had washed away all forensics. They said he'd killed himself in remorse."

Gray got up, yanked a tissue from the brass holder on the bedside table and dabbed at her tears. His fingers brushed the soft skin of her cheek and his libido soared higher than a rocket. Trying not to think of kissing her, of soothing her, of loving her, when she was so close and so sad, was like trying to ignore a blue elephant in the middle of the room.

He handed her the tissue, scooted back to his end of the table and chugged down his iced tea as if that was what he desperately needed. The ice cubes clinked against the glass when he set it back down. "What happened to put Rafe behind bars?"

The tissue became confetti in her lap. "After I took the picture, I ran. I was afraid he'd kill me, too. Bryn convinced me to go to the police. That photo helped persuade them that Dad was innocent. At least of suicide. They're still not convinced he wasn't involved with the treason."

Elliot Holbrook and treason simply didn't add up. If something illegal was going on at the mill, Gray had no doubt Vanderveer was behind it. "We'll find all the proof you need. Who's running the mill now?"

"Right now? The creditors are. They've appointed an interim chief operating officer. But Rafe wants control back. And I've instructed Dad's lawyers to do everything they can so he won't get it."

"Do you want to run the mill yourself?" She'd be good at it, and it would deepen her bond with Echo Falls. Why would the thought sink through him like an anchor?

She gathered the tissue confetti in the palm of one hand, then shook the pieces onto her plate. "I don't know. All I know is that it's a real mess and the employees are caught in the middle."

As much as he hated getting close to her, he crouched by her chair and held her hands. It was like holding a sparkler. His skin prickled and heated. "Abbie, I'm going to have to call the office. We need to get someone inside the mill."

She shook her head. "U.S. Army personnel have been through every inch of the mill. They took away truck-loads of paperwork. Production's been stopped and there's only a skeleton crew working right now. If there was anything incriminating Rafe, the Army would have found it."

"Not necessarily."

"My evidence put him in jail for murder. My testimony could keep him there for the rest of his life. He didn't leave anything behind that would hurt his case."

Nor could Vanderveer afford to leave Abbie alive either.

Gray dug his hands into his pockets to stop them from reaching for the spun silk of her hair. She wasn't his girlfriend. They'd burned that particular bridge thirteen years ago. She was his job. *Keep your head screwed on right. Don't screw up.* "Someone like Rafe has to keep records. It's the only way to prove how great he is—even if it's just to himself."

"Brynna can help."

"What?"

"Brynna—you know, your sister."

"I know who Brynna is." He strode back to his own chair. He knew who Brynna was all right. She was the sister he'd spent his childhood watching over and protecting. Not that she'd appreciated it. He dug into his chowder. It could've been talc for all he tasted. "What about her?"

"We should ask her to look into Phil's bank account."

"I have an electronic guru I can consult."

"Someone at Seekers?" Her hands pressed against the table as if she were about to bolt.

"Kingsley. Joanna's brother."

Abbie's chin cranked up a notch and her voice took on the uppity tone of a mistress displeased with her servant's attitude. "He's still at Seekers and he has access to every scrap of information that goes through there."

"Kingsley's solid." Gray would trust Kingsley over Bryn any day of the week. Kingsley had no agenda. Brynna always did.

"But what Kingsley works on might not be. You don't know who's working for Rafe there. Who could be watching over his shoulder."

Gray hooked an arm around the chair's back. *Keep cool.* "Using that logic, you shouldn't trust Brynna either. Vanderveer didn't have anything good to say about her in his letter."

"Brynna has problems, but she'd never side with Rafe. He's never going to let me go. She gets that."

Implying he didn't. *I get it, Abbie.* What he didn't get was her running from sure safety into the open, where she was one trigger squeeze away from eternal sleep. "Bryn doesn't want to have anything to do with me."

"She's hurt."

"I couldn't take her with me." He forced his hand to relax. How many times was he going to have to explain himself? He was barely eighteen when he'd left. What was he supposed to do with a sixteen-year-old brat who couldn't stand him while he was at sea? She'd have hated being alone and away from everything she knew.

Abbie cocked her head. "Do you know what happened to her?"

"How can I when she won't talk to me?" But he knew. Had always suspected. Nothing he could do about the roller-coaster dive his stomach took, except ride it out. "I was the resident butt everybody kicked, especially Mom. When I left, the position became vacant."

Though Abbie couldn't see his eyes, he silently pleaded for understanding. He'd had to leave. He couldn't have stayed where he wasn't wanted, where every day he had been told he was a loser just like his father, where he'd been expected to turn bad and end up in jail. *I sent money home so she wouldn't have to work for food the way I did. I offered to pay for college for her. I did everything I could for her.* "I didn't think Mom would turn around and do the same to Bryn. Mom always treated Bryn right."

"It goes deeper than that."

He tossed his hands up. "Like what?"

"It's not my place to say."

"You started the conversation." And he'd give anything to stop it from going any further. He was sweating like a racehorse, and the finish line still seemed a mile away. *I couldn't stay. I barely escaped in time.* He'd known it was time to leave when he'd found himself shoplifting a package of beef jerky to fill his belly because his mother had pilfered the paycheck he'd cashed and hidden in his room, and she'd spent it on booze. Jail wasn't where he saw himself, not even for three squares.

"We need Bryn's help. We need to find out about Phil. We need to find out if someone inside Seekers is working for Rafe. If someone is, then we can't trust anything anyone at Seekers says. And we can't do this alone."

She was right, of course. Kingsley was an electronics wizard and had resources Bryn didn't, but until Seekers was cleared, they were better off using outside help. And for all Bryn's anger at him, she would do her best to help Abbie. "All right."

Abbie bounced to her feet, reached for the leather bag on the desk and turned for the door. "Let's go."

"Whoa, not so fast." He held her back with a hand and ordered his thumb not to rub at the soft skin of her arm. After all she'd gone through today, the subtle scent of almonds and honey still perfumed her skin. "We can't go there. Too predictable. One of Vanderveer's flunkies is likely parked close and watching the house."

"She won't leave."

"What do you mean she won't leave?"

Abbie subtly moved out of his grasp and pawed through her leather bag as if the answer to the puzzle of the universe lay somewhere at the bottom. "It's complicated, Gray. Just trust me on this. We need to go to her."

"What's wrong?"

Holding a tube of peppermint lip balm between her fingers, Abbie hesitated. "Agoraphobia."

Gray swore. He should've tried harder to get Bryn out of there, to take her with him.

The sense of suffocating terror squeezing at his chest

existed only in his head. His lungs were fine, strong, healthy. He could run a mile in less than four and a half minutes. Faster than the rest of the team. He could handle a return trip to the old homestead with its halls full of painful ghosts and impaling guilt if it helped him keep Abbie safe. Hell, he'd survived both for years and he was still walking among the living.

He fished the piece of paper Joanna had given him out of his pocket and dialed the number.

Alarm rippled in her voice as she gripped his arm. "Who are you calling?"

"Joanna. We need transportation that nobody can trace back to us. I can't use a credit card to rent, and we don't have enough money between us to buy one."

Joanna promised to make arrangements and have a car waiting for him in the morning. Just as he replaced the receiver on the cradle, ending his call with Joanna, his cell phone—in Abbie's vest pocket—rang, making her jump.

"REED," GRAY SAID INTO THE cell phone, bracing himself for a verbal flaying. The rules at Seekers were loose, but Falconer still expected a certain protocol—for everybody's safety.

"Where are you?" Falconer's voice had a sharp edge of impatience to it.

"We ran into some trouble." A common enough excuse not to warrant too much attention.

"What's your ETA?"

"Seven days," Gray said and tried to make it sound like seven hours.

A long silence stewed between them.

"Bring Ms. Holbrook in. Tonight."

"No can do." No one was going to get to his golden girl if he could help it.

"Do I have to remind you what's at stake?"

Life. Her life. The lives of witnesses who helped the Marshals Service put scum in jail. The lives of soldiers battling for peace on foreign soil. "I understand. She understands. But there's also the small matter of surviving until the trial."

"We're equipped to protect her."

Falconer saw the Aerie as an impenetrable bunker. Gray saw Abbie's sanity-gnawing fear.

"You have a mole."

Silence became a black hole. "Not here."

"Give me a day to prove you right," Gray said.

"It's not time to play the hero."

"I'm no hero." *Welcome back to Echo Falls, coward.* "I'm protecting your asset."

"Twenty-four hours, then I'm sending in Mercer."

Gray cut off communications before Falconer could have Kingsley pinpoint their position. He pulled the battery out of the phone, effectively rendering the locator chip mute. He'd have to ditch it. He'd get a few hours of sleep, then they'd have to disappear from both Vanderveer's assassin and the Seekers team that had become his family.

THE NEXT MORNING, BEFORE dawn even thought about cracking, Gray woke up Abbie. She'd sat up for most of the night. Looking as zoned out as a drug addict in the grips of a chemical high, she'd watched a marathon of old Elvis musicals with the sound down low. She stumbled to the bathroom to dress. When she emerged, they left the room.

At the registration desk a perfectly groomed woman in a burgundy suit greeted them. With her black hair swept up, she looked almost as regal as Joanna and was much too perky for the early hour. "What can I do for you?"

"You should have a message for me." He smiled at her and she smiled back, interest glinting above simple politeness. "Mr. Franklin in nine-thirteen."

A quick check of the computer told her where to find the message. She reached under the desk, then handed him a fat envelope with the King's Arms logo. "Here you go. You have two."

He frowned. His fingers splayed the envelopes apart. Two? "Thanks."

He recognized Joanna's bold script on the top envelope. As he tore open the envelope, keys dropped into his hand. The promised rental car was sitting in the parking garage, second level, spot B-27. The second envelope bore the perfect penmanship of a grade school teacher and sent a snake of dread slithering in his gut. "Who left this?"

"I'm sorry, I don't know. It was already there when I came on shift."

The note read, "You had your chance. She turned you down. You can't win. She's mine. Ask her about our love child."

Chapter Seven

Abbie stood beside Gray as the descending elevator taking them to the parking garage hummed. The stark light of the small carriage emphasized the brows straightened into fierce lines above Gray's sunglasses. The taut set of his face could cower the biggest, baddest of bouncers into submission. A pulse throbbed at his neck above the collar of his silver polo shirt. Why? Where was the sudden burst of anger coming from? Joanna's note?

"You're going to blow a gasket unless you let out some of the steam raising your blood pressure. What did the note say to upset you?"

Watching the brass door as if at any second an army of aliens would try to zap their way through it, he ignored her. The B-level light came on with a *bing* and the carriage settled.

As the doors slid open, Gray said, "You'll be thirty next year. How come you're not married?"

Without waiting for her answer, he walked out and started on his panther-on-the-prowl maneuvers. Her jaw dropped as she trotted to catch up to him. "What brought this on?"

"Isn't your biological clock ticking like mad?"

Reflexively she moved her leather bag across her stomach. His tone of voice was definitely ticking her off. "Not particularly."

"Why not?" His voice and the discordant slap of their soles echoed in the concrete forest of pillars and dividers in the garage. Under the shield of his glasses, she suspected his eyes kept roving, searching for anything out of place.

"I have other things on my mind." She'd had one long-term relationship in college and another after. She'd failed miserably at both. Some people weren't meant for marriage, and she fell into that category. Through the eye of her camera she'd stumbled upon what she'd unconsciously searched for—a sense of truth, a deep connection, a peaceful calm. Something she hadn't found in either of those failed relationships.

"Why didn't you mention you were pregnant with Vanderveer's child?"

Her step faltered. How did Gray know? The note, of course. Rafe. Had to be. Rafe would use that weakness against her. "Because it wasn't important."

"You had his child."

Something in her heart contracted. "I miscarried after Dad died."

She'd barely known she was pregnant before she'd lost the baby. How could something that was too small to feel have caused such a thick catalog of emotion to flip through her in such a short span?

Pure hatred. At Rafe for manipulating her into a position she'd wanted to avoid.

Pure love. For the tiny seed that would grow into a baby—her baby.

Cold emptiness and deep longing. For that lost chance at motherhood. Her only chance?

Her chest heaved and she muscled the rising sob back to the empty cradle of her womb. It didn't matter. Really. What had made her think she could raise a child on her own? It was better this way. She could never take her hatred of the father out on the innocent child.

"Did he…?" Gray's steel-hard voice penetrated the bumper of pain surrounding her like a bruise. She hadn't realized they'd stopped. He searched the maroon sedan in the stall marked B-27 as if he expected to find a bomb, going as far as sliding under the car to look at its underbelly and flashing a penlight at hard-to-reach spots.

"Rape me?" She shook her head and held her bag tightly to her belly. "No."

"Then you…?"

Averting her gaze, she reached for the passenger door handle. "It's really none of your business."

"You're right."

Holding her car door open, he looked down at her expectantly. Not knowing what to do with the humiliation squirming through her body, she wrapped and rewrapped the strap of her bag around her hands. Silence pressed around her, becoming a vacuum that demanded filling.

"I was at one of those interminable business things with Dad." Her tongue was so tied, the words folded thickly in her mouth. "I drank too much and one thing led to another." She shrugged a shoulder carelessly, trying to dislodge the lingering stain of shame. "I don't even remember what happened, really, except that I woke up in his bed." With Rafe's face hovering above hers and his body possessively pinning her under him. *You're mine now.* And the smile he'd beamed had frightened her to the core.

"You don't remember?" The curl of Gray's hands

around the top of the car door tightened and his voice was as cutting as glass. "Did it ever occur to you that he might have drugged you?"

A time or two. But she hadn't felt drugged, just hungover. And she did remember drinking way over her quota. She rubbed circles on her temples with the tips of her fingers. The echo of a headache pounded through her brain. "I never said no."

"But did you say yes?" Gray's hand palmed away the wetness on her cheek, and the tenderness in his voice brought on a fresh wave of sadness. "Abbie—"

"It's ancient history. The baby doesn't exist." She'd lost it in a strange city, among strangers, and hadn't had time to mourn her loss before the WITSEC inspector had dragged her to another town and left her to fend for herself. That raw feeling of being torn apart threatened to overwhelm her once again. She reached for the handle to close the door. "We have more important things to worry about."

He tossed her the note penned on King's Arms Hotel stationery. A savage fierceness growled through his voice. "You're right. How did he find us?"

The single sheet of paper with the perfect handwriting trembled in her hands. Love child? A child had been created, but no love had been involved. "I—I don't know. Maybe Joanna told her brother. Maybe we were followed." This wasn't her fault. She hadn't asked for any of this. All she wanted was to stay hidden long enough to testify at the trial and regain control of her life. "How should I know? You were the one with the plan."

Gray settled in the driver's seat. "We can't go to Echo Falls. It's too dangerous. If someone tailed us here, they could follow us to Bryn's."

She cradled her bag on her lap and looked straight ahead at the concrete pillars and the dark shadows writhing in the brassy light. His plan hadn't worked. They were going to try hers. "Then I guess you need to make sure we're not followed."

GRAY CRANKED THE ENGINE TO life and backed out of the stall. How had Vanderveer's gofer managed to find them at the hotel? Corinne was safely tucked into a parking garage miles away. Even if someone had attached a tracking device he'd somehow managed to overlook, finding the Corvette would lead to a dead end.

Had someone from Seekers guessed that he'd use this hotel? Kingsley had made no secret of his background. Everyone at Seekers knew Joanna had taken over the hotel and Meredith the real estate business when the senior Kingsleys had retired. Had Joanna talked to her brother? Had someone at Seekers passed on the information to Vanderveer?

That someone had found them this fast made no sense. He'd been careful. No one had followed him.

He didn't like having to distrust people who'd become as close to family as he'd get. It was like being back in Echo Falls. Alone, except for Abbie. Abbie, who'd gotten pregnant with Vanderveer's child. Pregnant. With Vanderveer's child! How could she?

And why did the thought drive a bayonet of regret through his gut? He jammed the parking card into the slot and tapped his thumbs on the steering wheel while the barrier took its time rising. *None of your business, Gray.* He had no right to question Abbie about her choices. Hell, he'd never had the right. She'd turned him down flat from the get-go.

He nosed the car onto Rowes Wharf. The early hour and light traffic would make spotting a tail easy. He'd checked the rental for a tracking device and found none. No signs of tampering either. But that didn't mean squat. If Vanderveer's flunky knew they were staying at the hotel, she'd watch the lobby and follow them. No one had come down the elevator. But that didn't keep his nerves from jangling like a buoy bell in a storm. *She* was probably waiting outside. He adjusted his mirrors for the widest viewing angle, made a sweep of his surroundings and turned onto Atlantic Avenue.

He didn't want to bring trouble to Bryn. As much of a pain as she was, he still cared for her. But if he was going to have a chance at keeping Abbie safe, he needed information—and fast. Especially if a Seeker was involved in selling out Abbie.

As he merged onto the Mass Pike, his hands tightened around the steering wheel. No one was tailing them. But a shiver of warning zigzagged down his spine. Going to Echo Falls was a mistake.

THE THING THAT ABBIE HAD always liked about the Reed household was the noise. Her growing-up years had been marked with a need for silence. *Shh, Abbie, your mother's resting.* Even after her mother had died, silence at the house had become such a habit that neither she nor her father could bring themselves to break its sanctity. Conversations were held in her studio or at his office or in the car while driving—never at home.

The Reed home always bustled with uninhibited noise—the television blaring in the background, Gray stomping down the stairs or teasing his sister, Brynna singing along with the radio or shrieking at her brother.

Pillow fights and card games. Cookies consumed without a care about crumbs. And no adult supervision. There was a certain kind of peace among the chaos of their home, just as there was an insidious kind of chaos in the apparent peace of hers.

The atmosphere today in the Reed home had the weighty feel of a funeral parlor during viewing hours. The drapes were closed, shutting out sunlight and plunging the room into near darkness. Only the soft hum of the computers' brains and the slow ticking of a clock shaped like a giant magnifying glass—that Abbie had given Bryn when she'd received her P.I. license—stirred the thick silence.

Reference books spilled from two tall oak bookshelves in the front parlor Bryn had converted into an office. A bank of file cabinets occupied a wall. Two desks with a faux-granite finish and two computers filled most of the space.

Abbie and Gray sat in stiff folding chairs. Bryn perched on her rolling office chair like a bird about to take off, one of her desks a pointed barrier between her and the visiting intruders. All three were parked as far apart as they could get from each other. Queenie, the Yorkie, sat in Bryn's lap, a low growl rumbling her body like a lawn mower engine.

Gray and Bryn were both friends. Abbie didn't want to take sides.

"How's business?" Gray asked, hands hanging between his knees. His attempt at relaxation fell a shade off believable.

"I'm surviving."

The wall of ice around Brynna should take care of the greenhouse-warming effect for the next decade.

"In Echo Falls?"

"The Internet has made it a small world," Abbie said, trying to build a bridge between these two stubborn mules. "Brynna runs a lot of information searches. She's the perfect choice for what we need."

Brynna's eyes were cool and flat, the color of neglected silver. Her once-bronze skin had faded to paste-white, emphasizing the freckles sprinkled across her nose. She hadn't cut her hair in years, and the sandy locks were pulled back in a loose ponytail. Her round face was a study in sadness—one that would draw any viewer to tears if Abbie ever dared to capture it.

"Has anyone asked you to look for Abbie?" Gray asked, obviously giving up on small talk.

His particular brand of charm had never worked on Bryn anyway. *She needs you, Gray. Don't let her hardness fool you.* "Gray's trying to help me, Bryn."

Brynna shot the zipper of her faded blue hoodie to just below her stubborn chin. Hostile energy crazed around her like lightning. "Of course not. I wouldn't have betrayed Abbie."

"You might not have meant to." Gray softened his voice, but it still sounded like razor blades. "Did anyone ask for any information on anything that relates to the Holbrooks, the mill, the mansion or Echo Falls? Before or after her father's murder."

Bryn turned her back on them and pulled up the calendar feature on her computer. Her friend's temper licked too close to the fire of resentment, and her staccato answer sounded like the gunshots Abbie had heard much too often lately. "The Holbrooks' lawyers asked for an asset search. Nine months ago. For the bankruptcy proceedings."

"You don't need to justify your livelihood, Bryn."

"I'll need a copy of the report you gave the lawyer," Gray said, peering at the slash of light between the drapes.

Bryn looked at Abbie and Abbie nodded. "I'll print you a copy."

Abbie could have kissed Gray for the patience and respect he showed his hurting sister as he outlined the information he wanted about Phil Auclair, the WITSEC inspector who'd miraculously survived three attacks, and Hale Harper, the newest Seeker. For pretending Bryn hadn't ignored him for years. But then, Gray's compassion even for the bullies who'd picked on him was one of the things she'd admired about him.

"When do you need this by?" Bryn asked, her attention focused on the notes she was taking.

"As soon as possible."

Bryn blinked once, wheeled to the other desk and reached for the phone. Using the name BMR Financial Systems, a corporation she used as a front, Bryn requested a credit check on Phil Auclair with the three major services. Next she impersonated an insurance company and inquired about Phil's driving record and the cars registered to his name. She logged on to a site of a company that collected public records and entered Phil's name and searched for any lawsuits, marriages and divorces—anything that could be used against him to win his cooperation.

Watching her march through the steps of her search with dizzying speed and pick out what they needed was as if watching a circus juggler at work. She made it look easy. Abbie glanced at Gray and silently urged him to give his sister credit for what she'd done right.

A subtle shift transformed the rigid lines of Gray's body from guilt-leaden to predator-primed. He rose from his chair as carefully as a tiger sighting prey. He sidled to the window he'd eyed since they'd arrived and scoured the street outside through the crack in the drapes.

Then, as cool as can be, he turned to Brynna. "Can I borrow a pound of sugar?"

GRAY EASED OUT THE BACK DOOR and melded with the cool shade of the two-foot-wide dirt alley between row houses. The old toolshed, the shape and size of a telephone booth, stood backed up to the sagging panel fence that separated Peanut Row from Mechanic Lane. The shed had once held a push mower, a snow shovel and his sports equipment. Now all that inhabited it was of the arachnid and rodent persuasion. He surveyed the street, taking in the raw neglect of a place without hope—the wealth of weeds on the postage-stamp front yards, the crumbling mortar on the brick steps and the bare wood showing through old paint.

Like his own rental parked across from Spinner's Tavern, the white Taurus loitering on the opposite side of the street looked too clean for this neighborhood of dusty pickups and rust buckets. No one seemed to be sitting inside the Taurus, but he couldn't ignore the stared-at feeling that had him wanting to brush down the raised hairs along the back of his neck.

Nobody hung on Peanut Row unless they had to. The odds were good the Taurus was here looking for Abbie. Was it here because they'd been followed from the King's Arms Hotel? Because of the mole at Seekers? Or was it here because staking a lookout at the one place Abbie was likely to seek help was the smart thing to do?

Spiders never feasted at his neck unless there was a

reason. Even though the driver's seat looked empty, he'd bet a pair of Prada glasses that those invisible eyes were parked in the bucket seat. Steeltex would explain the phenomenon.

Gray figured he had three choices. He could go back and get Abbie and try to slip out unnoticed. Evading the tail wouldn't take much work, but it wouldn't ground it either. He could hike three doors down to the tavern, start a diversion and pour sugar down the gas tank while the tail was otherwise engaged. But that required a certain amount of cooperation from unstable sources.

Or he could bank on the tail not wanting to be made. Getting caught wearing a Steeltex suit was a ticket straight to jail. That would mean losing Abbie's tail. And that would not please the bully paying the bills. He cracked a grin. Sometimes the smartest thing to bring to a gunfight was a knife.

One thing he'd learned while stalking prey in unsavory territory was that nobody fooled with crazy people. He'd cultivated a twitch just for the street. And that had allowed him to catch up with more than one dirtbag on the lam.

He sneaked back into the house and grabbed the fatigue jacket that hung on the peg beside the door. His father had left it behind decades ago and nobody had ever moved it. Dust coated the shoulders, but he didn't wipe it away before donning the coat. He snatched a kitchen towel that looked like a faded red bandanna. He slashed holes at the knees of his jeans, then smeared alley dirt onto his clothes and face for that chic-bum effect. Tying the towel over his head, he debated over his shades. With regret he stuffed them into the coat's breast pocket.

The unaccustomed brightness had him blinking. He settled on the slitted look. It went with the crazies and it would keep the tail from pegging his eye color.

Using the backyards as cover he made his way to the tavern. He slipped inside through the alley door and nodded at the bartender as he made his way to the front door where, holding a knife up one sleeve and the plastic bag of sugar up the other, he staggered into the sunlight.

"Turn it down!" He looked straight at the Taurus, cut across the street seemingly as if he hadn't cleared traffic, then pounded his fists on the hood. "Turn your freakin' radio down! They'll hear us." He made his gaze dart around as if little green men were about to land and brought his voice down to a harsh whisper. "They can hear you through the radio," He pressed his face against the driver's-side window and peered inside. Nothing but a miragelike shimmer, as if whoever sat in the driver's seat had leaned away from him. "It's a conspiracy. They're tuning in to our thoughts."

A dark line appeared as if in midair. It streaked down like a line of sweat around a face. Interesting. "They take them out and put their propaganda in."

He raced around to the passenger's side and sawed off the antenna with his knife. Jumping up and down, he hollered as if he'd just won a race.

Lucky for him the Taurus didn't have a locking gas cap. Lucky, too, that this model had the tank on the passenger's side. Because this was the iffy part of the plan. Get the sugar in before whoever sat there quite knew what was happening.

Carrying on like a loony hearing voices, he ranted himself to the gas cap. He flapped the small door open as he bent forward proclaiming doom, then twisted off the cap. He raised the knife high, threatening violence against the unseen attackers. Then with a downward thrust of the knife, he sliced a corner off the plastic bag. As he pushed the makeshift funnel into the gas tank, he brought the knife's point against the window and started scratching out a mad doodle. "Protection," he rasped. "The eye will keep 'em away. They're afraid of the eye."

When the bag was empty, he stuffed it in his pocket and closed the small door. Pretending to hear a new set of voices, he jerked his head toward an empty truck parked on the other side of the street. "Hey, you! Yeah, you in the pickup! I said turn down the radio!"

He repeated his act, minus the evil-eye carving, at three more cars before disappearing between two houses. Keeping an eye out for the Taurus, he made his way back home. He ditched the coat and towel in the shed, put his glasses back on and went in to collect Abbie.

"How long is your search going to take?" he asked Bryn, scraping the dirt off his jeans.

Her gaze never left her computer screen. "A couple of hours for the basics. A couple of days for the rest to come in."

Reaching out a hand to Abbie, who looked at him as if he'd just arrived from another planet, he said, "We need to go."

"Leave a number, and I'll get back to you," Bryn said.

Gray hesitated. "Do you have a cell phone I can borrow? I can't use mine or I'll get tracked."

Bryn's fingers stilled on the keyboard, and he couldn't help wondering what he'd said to warrant the ripple of fear across her shoulders. "Give me a minute."

Once Bryn left the room, Gray turned to Abbie. "I wish you'd tell me what's going on."

"I can't. I promised. But whatever you're thinking…" Abbie shook her head. "What Bryn is doing—it's good, okay?"

A leaden feeling settled in the pit of his stomach. He didn't have much choice but to accept. Right now Abbie's safety had to come first.

Bryn handed a cell phone to Abbie. "Once you activate it, it's good for only thirty minutes of talk."

"Thanks," Gray said.

Ignoring him, Brynna strode to her desk and went back to work as if nothing had happened.

"Bryn?"

"What?" Impatience cracked whip-sharp.

"Come with us."

"No," Brynn said with the finality of a slammed door.

"Are you ever going to forgive me?"

"I'll let you know what I find."

As he traveled the hall to the back door, his mother's voice seemed to ooze from the brittle wallpaper. *You're a runner just like your father.*

And he was proving his mother right, because he was about to run out on Bryn yet again. At least she had a high-tech security system protecting the house. He'd also spied the Beretta in the top drawer of her desk.

As he opened the back door, Bryn's voice drifted down the hall. "You got a place to stay?"

"I'm working on it.

She came out of her office looking like a waif in her loose jeans and baggy sweatshirt. Magpie Bryn, who'd always liked shiny objects, wore not one piece of jewelry. *Where has your smile gone, Freckle Face?* She flung a business card in his direction. The only thing on it was a phone number. "Mo'll take care of you. She's used to runaways."

"Thanks." He couldn't risk using her contact, but he wasn't going to throw back the olive branch she'd tendered in her face.

"For Abbie."

Of course. "Watch your back, Bryn. This guy's dangerous."

"Nothing I can't handle."

"HOLD OFF ON PICKING UP THE chocolates," Rafe told Pamela when she checked in.

The drone of traffic buzzed in the background. He longed to get into his titanium-gray, three-liter, six-cylinder Z4 Roadster and open up the engine as fast as she would go. He longed for rack of lamb served on fine bone china. He longed for Stevie Ray Vaughan blasted through Bose speakers and curvy white limbs spread on red silk sheets.

"But I'm just about there," Pamela whined, shattering his fantasy.

"The lawyers are working something out. I can open the box myself." Satisfaction bubbled deep inside him, and he struggled to keep his emotions in check for the bullet-headed, brawny-armed guard listening in on his conversation.

He couldn't wait. A day. Maybe two. How could they resist his ruse when he dangled a bigger prize than he was in front of their noses?

Oh, sweet Abrielle, I'll get to taste you again before I squeeze the life out of your soft center. Just as she'd squeezed the life out of his future.

Chapter Eight

"What's taking Bryn so long?" In the drab motel in Fitchburg that smelled faintly of must, Gray paced the length of the ratty brown carpet. Not only was the hair at the back of his neck bristling like a dog on the defensive, the rock at the pit of his stomach was growing into a boulder.

Abbie perched on one of the twin beds, watching *Whatever Happened to Baby Jane?* on a grainy television channel. "Maybe she found something interesting and she's tracking it down. She's good at what she does."

Or maybe Bryn was making him wait on purpose just to get even. Except he didn't think she'd do that to Abbie. He glanced at his watch. It had advanced exactly two minutes since the last time he'd checked it. He thumbed open the phone Bryn had given him and made sure it was turned on. When he couldn't stand the suspense anymore, he dialed Bryn's number and got her voice mail. Swearing, he headed to the scrap of faux-marble counter outside the bathroom and brewed a second pot of coffee.

Better than drowning his worries in beer, right? Damn if the thirst for something stronger wasn't there.

It burned a straight line from his throat to his stomach. Hands flat against the counter, he didn't dare look at the mirror backing for fear he'd see his mother's eyes staring back at him.

He concentrated on the coffee dripping into the pot and made himself wait until it had finished its last steamy burp before trying Bryn's number again. Nothing.

"Call me," he barked at the beep. He downed a cup of coffee that left him wired but unsatisfied and deepened the groove his pacing was carving into the carpet. "Something's wrong."

"Her voice mail catches her calls when she's working," Abbie said in a voice that sounded robotic. "She never answers when she's working."

"For you she'd call back. She knows how important this is."

Abbie tore her gaze from the black-and-white snow on the tube and stared at him. "You don't think…"

God, he hoped not. "No, you're the target. Bryn can't tell them anything." Except where she'd sent them. Not that it would do anyone any good, but neither Bryn nor their hunter knew that. He'd hoped Vanderveer's flunky would get out of the neighborhood before the sugar seized. But what if she'd gone after Brynna?

Abbie's eyes grew wide, and he imagined the faces of the dead deputies and the dead cop paraded in her memory. She didn't believe him either. He wanted to erase the horror from her mind. Not that she'd thank him for crossing the line of propriety and kissing her into oblivion.

"You're right," Abbie said, her gaze zeroing back on the TV. "Bryn doesn't know anything. I'm not there, so she won't get hurt."

"Yeah." He sounded as sincere as a car salesman.

Frowning, Abbie tucked her legs in closer and stared at the tube. He recognized her coping mechanism for what it was, but it still bugged the hell out of him.

On the other hand, he didn't want to have to deal with a barrage of questions and dire possibilities that would only make him feel impotent. He was usually good at playing turtle, at waiting patiently, but right now he'd rather be doing *something* than standing here worrying.

For the second time he attacked the copy of the report Bryn had given the Holbrooks' lawyers, dissecting it down to the last period. Nothing there came as a big surprise. Holbrook had lived his life like an open book. What you saw was what you got. And what you got was someone ethical to a fault. That sense of ethics had cost him his life and—if the report was right— a good chunk of his fortune. Abbie's future was protected by a trust no one could touch—not even Vanderveer—but her father had barely scraped by. Did Abbie know?

The only thing that made a blip on Gray's radar was Bertrice Storey's name as a beneficiary in Elizabeth Holbrook's will. If Vanderveer or any of his flunkies had seen a copy of the report, they would've known where to find Sister Bert. Was that why they'd run into Vanderveer's hired gun on the island?

Gray tried the phone one more time. Still no answer. Enough caffeine jolted through his system to light up all of Echo Falls. The last thing he needed was another cup of coffee. But he poured one into the black ceramic mug anyway.

He was going to have to call for help. No getting around it. He couldn't risk going back to the house in Echo Falls, but he couldn't take the chance that Brynna was hurt either. If anything had happened to her... No, he wasn't even going to go there.

He'd call Kingsley. Just like his sister Joanna, Kingsley *was* his job. He wouldn't do anything to undermine the electronic show he got to run his way at Seekers. Plus the Boy Scout didn't have a single skeleton hanging in his closet that anyone could use to pressure him. Seekers and his family were his world. He had two sisters. He'd understand. And if there was a mole at Seekers, Kingsley would want to ferret him out. If Gray called him on his cell, he could bypass Falconer. Maybe that would buy him time and protect Kingsley's position.

Do it before you change your mind.

Breath drawn, he scooped the phone from the counter and punched in the numbers. He couldn't stand still in the puddle of frustration backing up around him, so he paced.

"Can you talk?" Gray asked when Kingsley answered.

Without missing a beat, Kingsley answered, "No, but when can you deliver?"

"The day of the trial."

"I need it sooner."

You and me both. The next six days were going to drag on much too long. Especially when he didn't know who was after them and he couldn't see his prey coming. Not to mention the fact that Vanderveer's poison might have infected their family. "Someone from Seekers isn't batting for the home team."

Falconer's and Liv's voices lilted and fell in conversation in the background. Kingsley's command-center chair squeaked a restless tempo. "That's not possible."

"What do you know about Harper?"

"I'm pretty sure I gave you the right part number, but I'll double-check."

That's what he liked about Kingsley—the guy was quick. "I need another favor." Gray leaned against the counter and vented a breath. They all thought he lived the life of a carefree bachelor without anyone to answer to. His confession would blow his image big-time. "Can you check on my sister?"

Kingsley's chair stopped creaking. "I didn't know you even had one."

"Long story. She tried to help me and that might have gotten her a visit from Vanderveer's flunky. She's not answering her phone and she never leaves the house." For Abbie she'd pick up the line.

"Okay, give me the data and I'll look it up."

Relieved, Gray gave Kingsley Brynna's address, her phone number and his. If the fact that his sister lived in Echo Falls registered curiosity, Kingsley didn't let it show. But then, family was big with Kingsley. He'd do anything for his sisters, his parents—or his fellow Seekers. More than Gray could say about himself. "Call me as soon as you've checked on her."

"Will do."

Gray hung up and went back to wearing down the carpet. Bryn was all right. She had to be. She'd lost track of time. She'd done that all the time when they were kids. How many times had he had to go run her down somewhere? She'd always looked at him angry for showing up and surprised at the passage of time.

He poured another cup of coffee and stared at the black liquid. How much caffeine would push him into overdose territory? How long would it take Kingsley to get to Brynna?

THE MOVIE HAD ENDED A FEW minutes ago, and Abbie flipped through channels trying to find another film to distract her buzzing mind. If she thought about Bryn, about Rafe, about Gray, she would go crazy. Part of her realized this evasion wasn't healthy, but the other part couldn't take another ounce of pain. Chilled with cold sweat, she huddled beneath the polar fleece of her vest and wished for something other than stiff motel sheets for solace. June be damned, her body shivered with January-like furor.

The television barely got five channels, and none of those came in very well. The rest just hissed and crazed her nerves. News, news and more news. She couldn't handle news. She couldn't handle anything negative. She simply couldn't add the weight of Brynna's possible death to her already overloaded shoulders. She would break and no one would ever be able to put her together again.

Flick. She should have listened to Gray when he'd told her it was dangerous for them to go to Bryn. *Flick.* But no, all she'd thought about was getting what they needed without forcing Bryn out of her comfort zone. *Flick.* How much comfort would she get in that broken-down house if someone forced their way into her sanctuary? Her peace would be violated all over again. *Flick, flick, flick. Oh, God, Bryn. Forgive me.*

Gray tore the remote from her hands. "Okay. That's enough."

"Give it back." She grabbed for the remote and missed.

He pitched the remote across the room, where it skidded to a halt against the baseboard under the counter between the bathroom and the closet. He crouched beside her and grasped her wrists. "No, Abbie. Enough is enough."

"Gray, please…"

Please what? Let me numb myself into oblivion? Save me from myself? She didn't even know what she wanted, except out. Out of here. Out of this mess. Back in her own studio with its painted backgrounds and lights and cameras and kids—yes, even the shrieking, bawling ones who didn't want their picture taken. Back in her darkroom developing magic from negatives.

The shouts of children playing in the pool outside stippled the air. A car rumbled by in the parking lot, valves knocking. The radio, with bass maxed, boomed by, making the window throb to its primitive beat.

As she fixed her gaze onto Gray's face, the noise receded, gripping the room with a hollow silence. The taste of fear was metallic in her dry mouth. Tears cramped her chest and climbed into her throat. "I can't —"

"Yes, you can."

Gray was the one real and solid thing she could count on right now, so she let the heat of his fingers warm her skin. *Don't let go. Whatever you do, don't let go.* "How long will it take your friend to get to Bryn?"

Gray looked as worn and as haunted as she felt. He might act as if he didn't care, but his family—as fractured as they were—had once meant the world to him. He'd tried so hard to hold it together and blamed himself for its failure. If Brynna was hurt, a part of him would die, too.

"Wintergreen is about an hour from Echo Falls," he said, and it sounded as far as the moon.

"It's been more than an hour since you called."

"Getting away was probably a bit of a problem. Kingsley's going to keep our secret. For now." Gray's grip on her wrists loosened and her hands fell into his. The heat of his palms zinged into hers.

"What if *he's* the one in Rafe's pocket?" she asked, a needle of ice digging into her spine.

"No."

"He would know you well enough to think you might go to his sister's hotel."

Gray shook his head. "Even if he had, he would have sent Mercer, not Vanderveer's hired gun."

"What if—"

"No. Not Kingsley."

"I don't trust anyone from Seekers."

Gray cocked his head. "You're trusting me."

"That's different. I know you."

"And I know Kingsley. He wouldn't let Vanderveer touch anyone he cared for."

Gray rocked back on his heels, creating a canyon of space between them, breached only by the bridge of their touching hands. "What haven't you told me about Vanderveer?"

"There's nothing else," she said more sharply than she'd intended. Numbness crept back into her limbs and she glanced at the television, yearning to lose herself in the simple plot and pageantry of an Esther Williams movie. "I just can't—"

"Of course you can." He sat beside her on the bed and urged her head onto his shoulder. He smelled good, like soap and fabric softener, and it reminded her of home. "You always noticed everything. You and Bryn could get to the bottom of a secret faster than a tabloid journalist."

She couldn't help the small smile. There was no problem she and Bryn couldn't solve—except their own, of course. For whatever reason, the kids at school had confided in her and Brynna, especially their relationship problems. The Doctors of Dating. Which in itself was a joke. Neither she nor Bryn had dated much. Abbie because she'd had a crush on Gray since she could remember. And Bryn because she hadn't wanted to become attached to anyone from Echo Falls. She'd planned on leaving town as soon as she'd graduated from high school.

Then her mother had become sick, anchoring her to the hated town. And her mother's last boyfriend had turned to Bryn for what he couldn't get from her mother. After that cruel blow, nothing had been the same. Bryn had thought she could get rid of the feeling of violation by entering the police academy and becoming the law. But breaking a fellow trainee's nose for making advances toward her had gotten her kicked out for behavior unbecoming an officer. She'd shrunk into herself and never made it back out. Abbie had wanted to tell Gray so many times over the years. But Bryn would have seen the broken promise as betrayal and she'd already suffered so much.

"Tell me about Rafe's staff." Gray's voice buzzed in her ear, bringing Abbie back to the present she so wanted to avoid.

She closed her eyes and concentrated on Gray and the soothing heat of his shoulder, his hips and his thighs. "Rafe put in long hours. He had plans. A vision, he called it. From the gossip around the mill, he barked orders and expected everyone to hop into action before the words were out of his mouth. He couldn't keep a secretary."

"Why not?"

"Most didn't consider verbal abuse part of the job. To tell you the truth, the atmosphere got so tense there that I avoided going anywhere near the offices. If I needed to talk to Dad, I'd meet him after work at the house or at my studio."

"Who did Vanderveer bring aboard?" The tips of Gray's fingers brushed across her shoulders as he repositioned his arm along the headboard.

She snuggled closer, greedy for the warmth that peeled from Gray's body in waves. "The plant manager, Donald Townes. I remember Dad not liking his choice."

"Why didn't your father like Donald Townes?"

She shrugged, savoring the contact of Gray's hard muscles against her shoulder. "Something about attitude." Don hadn't fit the friendly family atmosphere her father preferred.

"What about women? Other than his secretaries, did Vanderveer hire any?"

Gray's voice was hypnotizing, couching the memories she didn't want to revisit in a hazy cotton that made them tolerable. "I don't know. After Rafe took over his father's position, I kept away from the mill. I was trying to build my business and avoid Rafe's attention."

"Okay, we'll look into the manager. That may be how he got some of the Steeltex for his personal use."

She turned her gaze to him. The mirrored lenses of his glasses reflected her own face back at her. Skin the color of ashes. Deep hollows that sucked in her cheeks. Eyes glassy and dull. She reached up to remove the glasses. He jerked his head back and grabbed for her wrist. "I can't stand seeing myself in your lenses."

He blinked but let her finish removing the glasses. Without looking, she threw them on the table between the beds. She'd always loved the warm silver of his eyes, the way she could read the race of his thoughts in them, the way it seemed as if she could see straight down into the glow of his soul. The way he'd made her feel with just a look, as if the world revolved around her. That look had flowed a warm river through her, alive and powerful—as if she could navigate any stretch of rapids and win. She needed that feeling now that her fractured soul was hanging on to nothing but the thin thread of hope.

"Gray." Her knuckles scraped the prickly shadow of his beard. She'd wanted to kiss him since she was thirteen. She'd practiced for the anticipated moment with her pillow. She'd given him overture after overture, but he'd never taken any of them. She'd thought he was a gentleman. Then she'd thought he wasn't interested. She'd even tried to make him jealous by going to the sweetheart dance with Mark Conway sophomore year.

When out of the blue Gray had asked her to marry him, every cell of her body had screamed, *Yes, yes, yes!* But a roll of fear had bowled through her brain, knocking her back a step, and *no* had come spewing out of her mouth. *I'm only sixteen. We've never even kissed. How can I go away with you? How would we live? Where would we stay?*

The kiss that would have sealed their promise died unborn because of the fear she couldn't express. Something had shattered in his eyes, and that break had echoed through her heart. She'd turned away from him and stumbled home to cry an ocean of tears.

The silver staring down at her now was intense, darkening with desire before her eyes. Her heart thudded hard and a tingle squirmed low in her belly. This wasn't smart. She wasn't young and naive anymore. She'd grown up, hadn't she? She should know better. He was

Brynna's brother. A friend. Nothing more. Brynna was her best friend. Brynna would see this as betrayal. And there was so much hurt between all of them. Why add more chaos to an already full slate?

Because he was here, and she needed to feel the surge of power his keen, smoky gaze could stir. She didn't want to think about Brynna hurt and alone in her house, of another person possibly killed by Rafe because of her.

Fueled by the twin flames of terror and temptation, she leaned forward and pressed her lips to Gray's. Warm. Wonderful. He tasted of coffee and something infinitely more potent.

Her name rasped from between his lips, half like a prayer, half as if he were in pain. "Abbie, I—"

She slid her legs over his and raked her fingers through his short hair, tipping his head back. He closed his hands over her shoulders and made as if to push her back.

"Maybe we—" he started, but she cut him off by deepening her kiss.

Fantasy hadn't come close to the real thing. Warm. Solid. Giving. She pressed herself nearer. The boom of his heart thumped against her breasts.

"I think—"

"I don't want to think." Thinking filled her imagination with blood and death. If she didn't think, she could ride through the terror. She nipped at his earlobe and ran her tongue along his jaw.

Cold—that's what James, her last boyfriend, had called her. She wasn't feeling cold now. She was burning from her scalp to her toes. Her blood was sizzling, her pulse sparking. Every atom in her was alive, wild with power. And the guttural sounds in Gray's throat made her giddy. She scraped her nails down the soft hair along his nape and over his shoulders. He quivered and something in her thrilled.

"Abbie—" He sounded breathless.

"Shut up." Her lips curved over his. "It's television or you." She skimmed the tip of her tongue along his upper lip. "I choose you."

Just as she swallowed his protest, the phone rang, and the cold returned.

Chapter Nine

At first Gray thought the shrill jangle was the smoke alarm going off. Then his conscience reminded him that this path would take him straight to hell. Except that this particular brand of torture sure touched him like heaven.

The woman of all of his fantasies, his golden girl, kissing him, touching him, wanting him. How was he supposed to resist that? Her honeyed tongue plunging into his mouth. Her clever hands setting his skin on fire. Her full breasts pliant against his chest. His willpower frittered away faster than dry wood. She had him breathless and on the edge of insanity. He was made of flesh, after all, not steel. And she was so hot, so soft, so delicious.

But he was a coward. Because when he finally realized the cell phone was ringing, reason pierced through the haze of hot lust, leaving behind the slick film of sweaty fear. He'd almost broken his personal code of conduct. He'd almost given in to temptation. He was supposed to protect her and instead was becoming one more person whose trust she had to question. He'd almost let his weakness for her get the best of him.

Still tasting the lingering sweetness of Abbie's almond-and-honey skin on his tongue, he slid off the bed and strode to the counter where he'd left the phone and ripped it off the top of Bryn's report. "Reed."

"It's Noah."

The hesitation in Kingsley's voice had every nerve in Gray's body on alert. "How's my sister?"

"Bad enough to require emergency care. Not bad enough she didn't fight me over calling an ambulance."

Relief sagged his shoulders. That sounded like Bryn—never knowing what was good for her. Thank God she was alive. "What's the prognosis?"

"Concussion. Some bruising. No broken bones. She needed a couple stitches on her scalp. She was passed out when I got to the house, so they're going to keep her overnight for observation."

"She'll need protection." Vanderveer and his minions weren't going to get close to her again. "Not the Aerie."

"I've got it covered. When she's released, I'll take her and her yappie little dog to my parents' place—kicking and screaming, if I have to. My parents aren't home, but their housekeeper is, and she'll take care of your sister. Marta's looking forward to having someone to fuss over."

Marta was better than a pit bull at guarding what she considered her territory. Gray hadn't realized how much tension bunched in his muscles until Kingsley lifted the burden of guilt off his conscience. Bryn was going to be all right. She was going to be safe. "How did the intruder get in?"

"The back door was forced open."

Over the steady beeping of machinery, Bryn mumbled something.

"Hang on." Kingsley put a hand over the receiver and came back on a few moments later. "She says to tell you she was beaten by a ghost and to beware of shadows.

She says to tell Abbie to stay away from the hospital and go have a latte."

"Latte? What the hell is all that about?"

"They have her drugged. She needs rest." Kingsley hesitated. "I'll have to tell Falconer about the incident at your sister's."

Yeah, Gray had figured as much, but giving up a step was worth it to make sure Brynna was okay. "Thanks for the heads up."

"I won't mention where she's staying. Just in case. I took Brynna's hard drives home to see if I can recover anything."

That, too, was inevitable. He and Abbie would have to leave this motel to avoid Mercer, who'd track them down much too soon. "Let me know what you find."

"About Harper…"

"Yeah?"

"He's Falconer's cousin. He was DEA."

"Was?"

"His wife and kids took a bomb meant for him. They all died."

Gray swore.

"Grief doesn't mean betrayal," Kingsley said. "Let me dig a little deeper."

Grief might not mean betrayal, but it sure made powerful motivation. If Harper wanted revenge badly enough, would his grief make him give up Abbie for information? Gray didn't know him well enough to say. Another reason to cut and run without leaving a trace. The time on this phone and this hiatus had all but expired. "I'll call you."

After he'd put down the phone, Abbie, wringing her hands, asked, "Bryn's okay?"

"She'll be fine." He hated seeing worry spin in Abbie's eyes. He much preferred the hot fire that had set them ablaze earlier. What he wouldn't give to remove the obligations between them and have her melt into his arms again. He scrubbed a hand over his face. *Stay out of the gutter, hotshot.* "They'll keep her overnight for observation. Then Kingsley's going to take care of her." She would be under the protection of a brother Seeker. Her world and his would collide. Would she understand then why he'd had to leave?

"What was that about a latte?"

"Bryn told Kingsley she wants you to go out and have a latte."

Color raced up Abbie's face. She swung her legs over the edge of the bed and her hands crimped the thin comforter. "Are you sure?"

He started to reach for her, then shoved his hands in his pockets. "It's the drugs. She's talking about ghosts and shadows."

Steeltex. Vanderveer's flunky had gone back to the house all decked out in her Steeltex suit.

"No, not the drugs. It's help." Abbie thrust her feet into her shoes, grabbed her bag and raced toward the door. "Let's go."

"Wait a minute!" He lunged after her, barely catching her vest as she flung open the door. "Where do you think you're going?"

"Out for a latte."

"We can't—"

Abbie cut him an impatient look. "Bryn managed to send a copy of the information she'd found before she was attacked. We have to go retrieve it."

"You can't access your e-mail account."

She shook her head as if he were a dull child she

needed to indulge. "Bryn showed me how to set up a third-party anonymous remailer account. That's how we talked to each other when I was in WITSEC. Lattes. Cybercafes." Her smile beamed as if for the first time since he'd found her she had real hope. "No one can trace it."

IN CAMBRIDGE, AT THE MUFFIN Top Bakery and Cyber-Cafe with its red-and-white awnings and white metal ice cream tables, Gray plunked down five dollars for an hour's worth of computer time. He insisted on adding a couple of carrot muffin tops and coffees to their order so they would fit in with the patronage. As soon as he'd picked a table, Abbie latched on to the computer bolted to the table and navigated the Web to her anonymous accounts.

"There it is," she said triumphantly. She'd had to check three separate locations. Bryn had suggested that multiple addresses would give her more freedom to connect. This anonymous way to talk to her friend had proved her salvation. Abbie didn't know how she would have survived the year of isolation without this fleeting contact with Bryn. "There's a file attached."

She clicked open the file and scrolled down, trying to make sense of all the information Bryn had collected. Gray flopped an arm around the back of her chair as if they had all the time in the world, which served only to make Abbie nervous. The more relaxed he looked, the more tension strung his body.

"What's wrong?"

He shrugged. "A bad feeling."

"Let me download the file so we can look at it later." She pulled on a chain hanging around her neck. A flash drive dangled from the chain. She tugged on the flat, fin-ger-size disk and connected it to a port.

"Where did you get that?"

"Bryn. She showed me how to transfer my digital photos onto it." Bryn was also the one who'd encour-aged her to try digital photography. If she hadn't, then Abbie wouldn't have caught Rafe's murderous deed in action. And the police would never have believed that her father hadn't killed himself. Rafe had planned his clean up too well.

"The pictures you took of your father are on there?" Gray pointed at the stick she'd furiously guarded through the past year of mayhem.

This was what Rafe wanted to murder her for.

She gulped and nodded.

"Is there a copy?"

"The police have one and so does Bryn."

Gray's face took on a pensive look. Behind his mir-rored lenses, his eyes were once more unreadable. "Her office was tossed. It's probably gone. And if Rafe has the locals in his pocket, it wouldn't surprise me if that particular bit of evidence vanished." He tapped a finger against the table. "Make sure the files don't mix."

She dragged the file to the flash-drive icon and checked that the green light was on, signifying active transfer. Bryn had explained to her that in court the original photo file could prove crucial. "I'm not com-pletely helpless."

"Never said you were." Gray squeezed a warning on her thigh, and a moment later a woman wearing light gray yoga pants and a purple T-shirt that said Breathe stopped at their table.

"Excuse me." The woman's mass of red curls was

caught in a stubby ponytail high on her skull. A black tote bag dangled from her shoulder. "Abrielle? Abrielle Holbrook? Sue. Sue Collins. You took my daughter's picture two years ago. Hillary? I get so many compliments on it."

Of course she remembered Hillary, with her big, blueberry eyes and strawberry curls. A soap bubble had so captured the two-year-old's attention that Abbie had frozen a moment of pure joy on film. "You must be mistaken."

Gray grinned and the woman saw nothing else. That easy charm worked every time. "My wife and I are on vacation. We're e-mailing a cyber postcard home to California. Aren't these cybercafes great?"

"Oh, I'm so sorry. Really, your wife looks just like this photographer who took the most awesome picture of my little girl. They could be twins."

"No problem."

The woman backed away, blinking as if to focus blurry vision. She continued to the counter, where she purchased a dozen muffin tops. Twice she looked over her shoulders at them. Gray draped an arm around Abbie as if this kind of intimacy was his right. Not that she minded. In the air-conditioning his heat was welcome, grounding.

"What now?" Abbie asked as she returned the flash drive to its chain around her neck and slipped it beneath the silk of her blouse.

He polished off the last of the muffin top and drained his coffee. "We need to go shopping and find ourselves a new home."

"Shopping?" She hated shopping on a good day. This was definitely not a good day. She stood and hooked the strap of her bag over her shoulder.

He plucked at the collar of her robin's-egg short-sleeved blouse. "You stand out too much. We need to dress you down."

"Me?" She eyed him up and down, taking in his dress shoes, khakis and silver polo shirt. He was right. It wouldn't do for another Sue Collins to recognize her. Not when they needed to lie low for five and a half more days. "What about you?"

"Two blue-light specials coming up." He smiled down at her, igniting warmth that spread from her center out like a lazy summer day. Sliding an arm around her waist, he guided her toward the street where they'd left the rental parked. And for a second it seemed as if all was right with the world.

Until his hand tightened against her waist and he kept walking right by the car.

"WHAT'S WRONG?" ABBIE WHISPERED into his ear.

Smiling as if she'd just told him a joke, Gray leaned close. "Two tails."

Her head started to jerk back over her shoulder. He stopped it with what would look like a caress of his cheek against hers. "Don't look back."

"Two? Are you sure?"

Mercer was easy to lose in the shadows, but he wasn't wearing Steeltex, and Gray had worked with him often enough to recognize his style. Gray figured the reason Mercer hadn't pounced on them yet was the tall, thin woman who was working hard at looking like a simple shopper but couldn't quite hide the predatory tension of her body. Nice to put a face on the ghost licking at their heels. How had she found them? How had Mercer? Had he caught up with Vanderveer's pawn and followed her?

Gray had tossed Bryn's phone and hadn't followed a predictable path. What was he missing? How could anyone have latched on to them so quickly? Hell, *he* didn't even know where he was going. How could someone else? "One tail at nine o'clock across the street. He's one of ours. The other one's behind us. She has to be Vanderveer's."

"She?"

"Looks like it."

"That's why you were asking if he'd hired a woman. You knew the person following us was a woman."

"Not for sure." Until now. "Brown hair in a braid. Tight safari suit. Backpack."

Like a champ, Abbie followed his lead with the carefree-lovers playacting, pasting on a smile that warbled on the edges but still shot right to his gut. He'd rehearsed for this role a million times in his mind, but never had he imagined it would come true under these circumstances. "So, what do we do?"

"We pretend we don't know they're there. I want to give Mercer a chance to study Vanderveer's gofer and take her down. It'll give us one less thing to worry about." Gray didn't need to worry Abbie by mentioning that once the tail was stopped Mercer would resume his hunt for them. By then Gray hoped to have holed up somewhere safe. No action meant no triggers for Mercer to follow.

"Then what?"

He stopped and whirled her into his arms and looked deep into her worried honey eyes. God, he wanted her. He wanted her safe. He wanted her his. *It's all pretend. It's all a game of survival.* The kiss he was about to plant on her was business. Part of the show they had to put on. No, the softness of her lips wasn't frying his brain.

That was lack of sleep. Her hands around his neck weren't blistering his skin. That was the two-o'clock sun beating down on him. The sweet molding of her body to his wasn't turning him rock hard. That was his usual state around her anyway.

Liar.

He broke the kiss and held her for a long moment—as if danger wasn't licking their heels, as if she hadn't run from him all those years ago and belonged in his arms. An ache pinched his heart. He kept her close and started strolling down the street as if he had no particular care in the world. "Then we disappear. Again."

"That part doesn't seem to be working out too well."

He pressed a kiss on the top of her head. "I don't know what's going on, but I'll keep you safe until the trial."

He led her into a shop that sold retro merchandise. They stopped by lava lamps with amber bubbles that matched the color of Abbie's eyes. Sun struck her hair, highlighting the gold, and her sweet smile made him long for all the missed years. If he'd done things differently, he could have woken up to that glorious sunshine of a woman every morning.

But this was a job, and if he let Abbie distract him too much, he'd fail. Gray clocked the movements of both their stalkers. The woman picked up an ashtray and put it down without really looking at it. Mercer hovered outside in the shadows.

Gray led Abbie in and out of shops as if they were tourists with an afternoon to wile away. Her hand fit into his as if it were made for him. She seemed to intuit his every move, following as smoothly as if they were dancing down the sidewalk. Vanderveer's tail and Mercer trooped right behind.

Roses and candlelight. That's what he'd give her if he could, instead of this footrace with danger.

Gray pictured a map of the subway in his mind and planned a route. He ambled in one door of a magazine kiosk and sauntered right out the door on the opposite side. "Time to find out how well your fancy shoes hold up."

"Where to?" She swallowed hard.

"Won't know till we get there." He tucked her in closer to his side. Vanderveer was going to pay for every second of hell he'd put Abbie through.

ABBIE GRIPPED GRAY'S HAND like a vise, afraid to let go of the one thing that was keeping her from complete terror. They raced into the T station and down the steps. Tails. Two of them hot on their heels. How could anyone have found them?

Gray shoved tokens into the turnstile and hurried them into the rush-hour crowd gathered on the platform. A slap of heat and exhaust engulfed them. Even the blowing fans couldn't fight with the underground humidity or quite dispel the polluting fumes.

How clever of Rafe to send a woman after her. Abbie would have never guessed. Probably would have trusted her. This woman wouldn't dare shoot in the thickness of this crowd. Would she? She'd already killed four people. What was a few dozen more? But here in this crowded subway station she'd have no chance for a clean getaway. To kill and steal the flash drive, Rafe's assassin would have to get up close and personal. As long as they kept distance between Rafe's tail and them, they'd stay safe.

A rumbling along the dark tunnel announced the arrival of a train. After it braked to a stop, Gray waited until the last possible moment and feigned a leap inside. Rafe's tail took the bait but managed to jump out before the doors closed. Gray propelled Abbie to the stairs that would take them to the other side of the platform and they caught an inbound train.

Rafe's tail jumped in two cars down. This wasn't happening. They weren't sardined in a train with an assassin only a few feet away. In spite of the heat, Abbie shivered.

The train started with a jerk. The steel wheels *click-clack*ed along the rails in time to her fast-beating heart. The car rolled from side to side, brushing Gray's hip against hers like a match head against a striker with each roll. The smell of sweat and clashing perfumes of the tightly packed crowd clouded the air, nauseating her.

She couldn't move without bumping into someone's arm or leg or briefcase. Trapped. They were trapped. A bubble of panic rose and ballooned in her chest.

Escape. Flee. How?

Gray's hand squeezed her. "We're okay."

Abbie nodded and forced herself to breathe in the fetid air. They weren't caught in an ambush. Rafe's tail couldn't get to them. Nobody was going to die.

No time for complacency. Be prepared. Don't just sit there like a rat in a trap. Look for a break. Taking a cue from Gray, she scanned her surroundings.

Her heart sank when she spotted the brown hair combed back into a severe braid at the back of the head. Pushing through with sharp elbows, she was making her way toward them. Determination shone in her eyes. Abbie's heart couldn't help its jungle beat of fear.

Gray's thumb stroked the back of her hand, reminding her she still had a lot to live for. He, too, had noted the woman's movement and he urged Abbie forward through the gauntlet of bodies and into the car ahead. "When the train stops, push your way out and head right back in at the next car."

"I'm not going alone." She wasn't going to allow him to face this assassin by himself to save her. Not after what she'd done to Brynna, the three deputies and the young police officer.

"I'll be right behind you."

The train screeched to a stop. The doors whooshed open. Gripping his hand even tighter, she didn't give him a chance to go solo. Passengers crammed the doorway, then disgorged like a herd at market, fanning out toward exits. She and Gray were swept along with the human cattle. Scrunching himself down to meld, Gray kept them in the thick of the crowd and sidestepped them into the next car. Abbie grabbed the overhead rail and swiveled forward to search the crowd.

"That woman's a tick." She followed their every move as if she were glued to them, forcing them to keep scrabbling against the tide of people.

Rafe had warned her.

You won't ever be free from me, Abrielle. I won't ever let you go. I'll be in your dreams and in your nightmares. I'll follow you wherever you go.

This woman was proving him right.

At the next stop Gray urged Abbie out.

"Stairs," he said and shot toward them as if he planned on leaving the station.

Parallel to the last car, he yanked her close and said, "Jump!"

They hopped into the train just as the doors were closing.

"Did we lose them?" Abbie asked, breathing hard, anxiety banging around her chest.

"Looks like it." But Gray's gaze kept scouring the crowd as if he, too, feared that their pursuer would reappear inside the subway train, right next to them.

On the platform the woman, staring at them with a steely expression of wrath, spewed silent curses as the train sped away. Then she noticed the dark and dangerous-looking man striding toward her. Their second tail—the Seeker Gray had mentioned?

The subway train entered a dark tunnel, snuffing out the image of both tails running. Would they catch up with them?

There was no place to hide. The knowing lodged in Abbie's throat and threatened to choke her.

As she and Gray sprinted across the T lines from red to green to blue, then yellow, she held on to only one thought. *Stay alive.* For the next minute. For the next hour. For the next day. She couldn't let Rafe win. *Stay alive.*

At the North Station they bought a commuter train ticket.

"Were are we going now?" Abbie asked as they climbed into the northbound train.

"To the end of the line."

With a terrible jarring the train lurched forward. Away from Rafe's assassin. Away from the Seeker sent to bring them in.

A thought pried into her conscience. She tried to shake it loose. But once it sank its claws into her brain, she couldn't flick it away.

Her hands curled around the edge of the seat to stop them from shaking, and she pivoted her head to look at Gray. His features were sharp, unreadable, on alert. The outside landscape strobed by on the mirrored lenses of his glasses.

He'd evaded one of his own Seekers teammates.

Helping her had cost him everything.

For him, turning back was no longer an option.

Chapter Ten

The motel room they found in Lowell was situated in the kind of neighborhood where no self-respecting woman went, especially after dark. Beyond the stack of derelict row houses, storefronts and rusty chain-link fencing ran a railroad yard with its jumble of tracks and cars. Further out snaked the sooty waters of the Merrimack River. The air stank of fuel and neglect. The graying sky added to the dreary atmosphere.

The stairs creaked as they climbed to the second story. Gray did his guard-dog circuit around the room—not that anyone would want to hide in a place like this. It smelled of cigarettes and sex and the cloying spray of canned disinfectant. Abbie sat gingerly at the foot of the bed, reached for the remote and pointed it at the television set bolted to a metal frame in the wall. No response. Great. She shed the new white espadrilles that had already blistered the back of one heel, hiked a foot to her opposite knee and massaged her aching arch.

On the way from the train station they'd stopped at a discount store. Within its aisles they'd found everything they needed to pass unnoticed in this blue-collar neighborhood—from sandwich fixings for dinner to jeans and T-shirts.

Gray had asked her to change clothes in a dingy gas-station bathroom. He'd thrown her silk blouse and her rayon pants in a Dumpster. Okay, she could understand the need to blend. Clothes were easily replaced. Then he'd asked for the rest of her things—her gold-and-silver watch, the gold feather earrings she'd worn since Deputy Marshal Kushner had died, even her leather bag. They had sentimental value, but she could replace them all.

She'd balked when he'd asked her for her mother's wedding ring. Heat had fired in the pit of her stomach, crackling with destructive urgency.

Abbie rubbed at the naked finger on her right hand and fought back tears. The sparkling-diamond-and-smoky-topaz creation her father had commissioned especially for her mother now lay under a patch of earth near the railroad fence. She just couldn't bring herself to throw it into a Dumpster. How could Gray make her give up the one thing that kept her mother close to her? She didn't have to wear it. She could have hidden it on the chain that bore the flash drive. When all this was done, she'd dig the ring back up. Rafe would not succeed in destroying all of her past.

Then Gray had done the unforgivable. He'd asked for the camera Bert had loaned her. The fire inside her flashed to five-alarm proportion.

"It can't be bugged. It's not mine. It's Sister Bertrice's. Rafe's robot didn't find us until *after* Bert loaned it to me." Her body had bunched tight, a need for violence making her muscles ache.

"We can't take a chance."

Just knowing the camera was there in her bag had given her a sense that she still existed. Now, with its film ruined and its body lying amid fast-food restaurant refuse, the fire had died and a lethargy had weighed her limbs.

"You okay?" Gray barely turned his head as he pawed through the black duffel he'd bought to stow the socks, underwear and change of clothes, but his mirrored gaze went through her like an X-ray.

"I'm fine." Having given up on coaxing the dead television to life, she stared at its blank screen to avoid looking at Gray.

"Something was giving our position away," Gray said, his voice flat and even, as if he were afraid to set her off once more. "It had to be something you had on you. We had to get rid of everything."

"I know."

"Abbie."

"What?" Irritation whooshed out as she flung herself back onto the bed's pseudo-Navajo blanket pattern. The store-stiff jeans and T-shirt chafed at her skin. How exactly had she gotten herself into this mess? There was an end, wasn't there? A little more than five days to the trial. She could survive that long. For Dad.

"That was phase one," Gray said, his voice so gentle, it set fear scurrying through her as if she were racing just ahead of a hurricane.

She slowly turned her head toward him. She blinked once, a Novocain-like numbness settling into her body. "Phase one?"

Out of the duffel bag he lifted two boxes of hair dye and a pair of barber scissors. "A couple of shades lighter for you. A couple of shades darker for me. We have to look as different from us as we can. We have to blend."

Why was it so cold in the room? She jerked up and cranked off the growling air conditioner. "We'll just stay here until the trial. If we don't go out, no one will know where we are."

"We can't take a chance we won't have to move again."

Numb. She was numb. From her face to her feet she couldn't feel a thing. "You made me get rid of anything Rafe could have possibly tagged with a tracking device. There's *nothing* left. He can't find us. Although frankly I have no idea how he could have rigged a ring."

"Technology's smaller now. All it takes is a microdot."

She rubbed the heels of her hands over her eyes. "I didn't even see a speck of dirt on any of the things you made me toss."

"Just because you can't see it doesn't mean it isn't there."

She sat on the edge of the bed and wrapped her arms around her tucked-up legs. What could she say? How did you fight against the invisible? "I have no choice, do I? I have to keep fighting him." Or die.

"There's always a choice. You could turn yourself in at the U.S. Marshals office in Boston."

She shook her head. "No, we don't know how Phil's connected to Rafe."

"There are other agencies."

Other agencies with staff that could die if she sought their help. "No, you're right. There's no other way."

Gray was giving her options, letting her take charge. He'd always believed in her, made her believe she could do anything. *Photography as a career? Why not, Abbie? Look at the life you give even inanimate objects.* She'd already decided she wanted to live. Now she had to follow words with action.

She pried the box of dye out of his hand and frowned at the back, not really seeing anything but a fuzz of print. "You go first."

"Yours will take longer."

"Right."

"Have you done this before?"

She shook her head. "Not since Brynna and I dyed our hair blue for the homecoming pep rally freshman year. And that was wash-out stuff, not permanent."

"The only way to lighten is to go permanent."

"Here goes nothing." Desperately trying to avoid the penetrating scrutiny of his gaze, she ripped open the box. He was risking so much for her, she had to put on a brave front. She dumped the contents on the dresser and read the instructions twice. Gray disappeared into the bathroom and came out with one of the thin towels provided.

"Ready?" He donned the set of rubber gloves included in the kit.

Her throat too thick to talk, she simply nodded. As he shook the bottle of chemicals, her heart rate kicked up.

The first cold squirt of gunk hit her scalp. She scrunched her eyes closed and held her breath. Gray's strong fingers worked the dye from the roots to the tips, and the gentle massage soothed her in spite of her fears. Reaching for his hand to feel safe was getting to be a bad habit.

"It's a shame to hide such glorious hair." Wistfulness wafted on his voice.

I love the way your hair is streaked with sunshine, Abbie. She could still picture a seventeen-year-old Gray blushing red after his admission on a warm July afternoon at the quarry. He'd kicked into the water to hide his embarrassment, but the warm feeling of his artless candor had stayed with her for a long time.

A lump formed in her throat. "If my hair turns orange, you're paying to get it fixed."

"It won't turn orange. I bought a reputable brand."

He worked a comb through her hair to spread the gunk and smooth out the clumps, then he put the plastic bag included in the kit over her hair and secured it with a clip. The heat and stink of the chemicals reacting had sweat running down her back—or maybe it was plain old fear.

"Want a sandwich?" Gray asked after he shed the gloves and set the timer on his watch.

She shook her head. "I'm not hungry right now."

He pulled two decks of cards from the duffel and offered her a crooked grin. "If I remember correctly, you owe me a Spite and Malice rematch."

Why not? It wasn't as if she had anything else to do. And he was trying hard to make this ordeal as easy on her as possible. If she concentrated, she could pretend she was sitting in the Reeds' kitchen, munching on cookies and laughing as she beat the pants off Gray. Maybe then she could pretend that every deck wasn't stacked against her and Rafe didn't exist. "Are you sure your ego can take another whipping?"

He shuffled the four jokers into the stockpile and placed the pile facedown off to one side of the bed they were using as a table. "Cast iron, honey. Can't be dinged."

"We'll see if you're still singing the same song in half an hour." She accepted her twenty-six cards and turned the top one faceup.

Nerves had her stomach churning and her heart

bumping. The chemicals and her inability to eat made her light-headed. She hunched her shoulders and tried to concentrate on her cards, instead of Gray's strong fingers as he played his turn. He'd always had nice hands. She hunched her shoulders further to hide the heat creeping up her cheeks because her crazy brain had just flashed her a picture of Gray's hands on her bare skin. Crazy, this whole mess had made her totally insane. The last thing they both needed was to make this situation even more complicated.

For the next twenty minutes she misplayed, miscalculated and misread the cards. The sexy stubble of Gray's jaw distracted her. His playful teasing when he managed to better her hand distracted her. His nearness on the bed, with the inevitable bump of knees and fingers, distracted her. And when Gray's watch beeped, she realized that Gray being Gray had kept the fog that usually clouded her brain when she was afraid from shutting off her mind.

Jitters returning with a vengeance, she slid off the bed and patted the plastic cap on her head. "I'm gonna wash that man right out of my hair."

If only it were that easy.

Gray cocked a finger at her. *"South Pacific."*

"Yeah," she said, surprised he would know.

In the narrow shower stall, bumping elbows against the turquoise fiberglass, she shampooed until the water ran clear. The sound of water gurgling down the drain swirled away her tears—and a little bit more of her essence.

Steam fogged the mirror, but Abbie refused to wipe it away. She didn't want to see the results. She dried herself in a hurry and put on the itchy clothes.

"Your turn." Putting on a brave face, Abbie reached for the second box of dye.

Gray twirled the lone hard-backed chair to face her and patted the seat. He armed himself with the barber scissors and a comb. "Not yet."

A ripple of dread arrowed down to her stomach. "No, please, Gray. I can't lose any more of myself."

"Just enough to change the look of your style." He tipped his head and sadness misted his smile. "Remember, you get a chance at payback when it's my turn."

Defeated, she let herself fall into the chair.

Feet flat on the threadbare carpet, hands stiffly in her lap, back ramrod straight, she psyched herself up for the first slash of scissors.

Don't think. Don't feel.

What are you willing to do to survive, Abbie?

Anything.

As long as Rafe lost.

As the steady snip of scissors clicked around her, she focused on her breathing. *In. Out. Don't think. Don't feel.* At regular intervals, a snow of hair cascaded down her arms and prickled her neck.

Finally Gray said, "All done."

Body encased in ice, Abbie rose, shook off the snippets of too-blond hair and walked to the bathroom, carefully placing one foot in front of the other.

Hands braced against the cold porcelain of the sink, she inhaled a long breath. *Be brave, Abbie.*

She forced her gaze up and worked up the courage to look into the mirror.

Hello, stranger.

Where was she? Who was that?

The stranger in the mirror frowned at her. Four inches were missing from the foreign blond hair. The shaggy cut gave her a hard edge that made her look as if she could chop her way through a field of ninjas. Alias undercover.

She cranked her head to the right, then to the left. If this was supposed to make her feel safe, how come she wanted to run? How come she wanted to bury her head in the sand? How come she wanted to cry?

She reached for a strand of hair. *It's for Daddy.* Someone had to restore his good name. *It's for you.* To get her life back.

Once Rafe was put away in the deep, dark dungeon of a maximum-security prison, everything would be all right. Her hairdresser could fix this. Everyone in Echo Falls would understand that her father wasn't the criminal who'd sold them out but the man who'd given his life to save their town. And she could return to her normal eras and her studio. Everything would go back to normal.

Just a bit of patience, Abbie. That's all you need. This is nothing.

Really, she had a lot to be grateful for. She wasn't alone. She had Gray, who was risking his job and his life to protect her. Once this was over, he would disappear from her life, but for now he was here when she needed him. She was alive. And once she testified, Rafe would lose what was most important to him—a town under his control.

But no amount of pep talk helped. As she stared at the stranger in the mirror, a terrifying darkness all but swallowed her.

Gray walked into the room and stood behind her. He wrapped his arms around her. His face softened as he rubbed his stubble-roughened cheek against hers. "You look beautiful."

She speared his gaze. "I can never go back, can I? I can never be the person I was." She pulled on a strand of hair. A hollow wind howled inside her. "There's nothing left of me."

"There's everything that's important. Just because you can't see you doesn't mean you aren't there." His lips brushed her cheek. Her heart did a slow roll. She leaned into the embrace, desperate to connect with something solid, with something warm, with him. "I see you, Abbie. I'll always see you."

Tears filled her eyes, and their image in the mirror merged and blurred.

ABBIE HAD FINALLY FALLEN asleep. The arch of her bare foot on the edge of the bed was curiously vulnerable. Gray wanted to take it in his hand and rub away the red marks left by the ill-fitting shoes they'd bought. Dangerous thoughts. *You can't protect her if you're drowning in feelings.* Gray freed the comforter from beneath her legs and covered her. She kicked away the cover as if it would slow down a possible escape.

He lifted a pair of socks from the duffel, sat on the edge of the bed and carefully slipped the socks over her feet. Against his better judgment, he let his palm linger against her arch, savored her pulse against his palm.

To punish himself for his weakness, he headed to the bathroom. There he assessed the damage to his carefully polished image. The brown of his hair was drab. The cut uneven. Abbie had apologized endlessly for the untutored results. He'd told her it was perfect. No one would look at him twice.

He'd asked Abbie to give up all she'd taken with her from her previous life. The least he could do was lose the shades that would peg him as her escort before anyone could get close enough to recognize him.

An oily sensation swam in his gut. He'd worn sun-glasses since he was fourteen. Since Bobby Fehr had seen the fear in his eyes and taken advantage of it.

Gray reached up and slowly peeled the shades from his face. The bright light from the fixture above the sink made him blink.

He was once again fourteen, short and scrawny—a runt. Muscle and height hadn't caught up to him until he'd turned eighteen. On the first day of high school he had stood on the concrete apron by the front door of the mustard-yellow building, waiting for the first bell, as the welcome letter had instructed the freshmen class.

Bobby Fehr, a sophomore, had swaggered out of no-where, zeroing in on Gray as if he'd had a target tattooed on his forehead. A ring of students had gathered around them. Excitement had buzzed. Gray had tried to move away from the bull seeing red. He tried to talk his way out, but Bobby had been looking for a fight and noth-ing was going to stop him. Gray had already had enough experience with this type to know the signs, so he'd thrown the first punch and had tried to make it count. It had. Bobby had gone down like a sack of cement.

All day the spiders had fed on Gray's neck. All day his body had been primed for payback. The blow had come as Gray had been walking out the front door, al-most tasting freedom. Bobby's size-thirteen foot had jacked Gray's legs from under him. Gray's face collided with concrete, and two triangles of tooth enamel and his blood now decorated the apron. And even though Bobby Fehr's father had been the town dentist, Gray had had to wait until the free clinic came around a few months later to get the teeth repaired.

School had proved a lonely place where he couldn't let his guard lapse.

And now, staring at his darkened hair, butchered hair-cut and uncovered eyes, he saw that young boy again—always off balance and trying to hold himself up.

Leaving himself this exposed was dangerous. Showing emotion was lethal in this business. Especially when it came to Abbie. He'd always felt too much for her. He couldn't let her see that his feelings for her still ran deep. She didn't need to deal with his failures on top of everything else.

His job was to keep her safe. Nothing else.

Her father had been right. He couldn't give her what she needed. He slammed a fist against the lip of the sink. "Yes, you can. You can give her your skills. You can keep her alive. You can get her to court. There's more at stake than Abbie here. WITSEC. Steeltex. The U.S. Army. Seekers. They all depend on you getting Abbie safely to court." His feelings for Abbie came way down on the list.

He scooped up the pair of shades from the rim of the sink. His fingers itched to settle them over his eyes. Instead he tossed them into the garbage can.

With a resolute flick he turned off the light, strode into the room and took up his post on the chair.

Just because someone overcame his past didn't mean he could escape it.

"READY?" GRAY ASKED AS THEY settled into a computer cubicle at the library in downtown Lowell the next morning.

"As I'll ever be." Abbie scooted her chair closer to his, and her sweet scent went straight to his head. Shadows had deepened under her eyes and her cheeks had hollowed as if her sleep hadn't proved restful. After they got out of the library, he'd make her eat whether she wanted to or not. She had to keep up her strength.

Clearing his throat, Gray focused on the screen and the contents of the file Bryn had forwarded to Abbie. He was amazed at the amount of information his sister had managed to gather in such a short time. She could give Kingsley a run for his money. Unfortunately not much of the news was good. Maybe Vanderveer *had* tossed out a couple of crumbs of truth along with the slab of lies.

Phil Auclair was now part of the multiagency task force headed by Seekers, Inc. He was the liaison between Seekers and the USMS. One of his bank accounts showed a steady accumulation of funds in eight-thousand-dollar increments over the past four months. Real-estate records showed he and his wife had made a deposit on a piece of land in a retirement resort in Florida. Coincidence that the deposit came two days after the last attack on Abbie while she was in WITSEC custody?

Brynna confirmed that Hale Harper was Falconer's cousin and had until a year ago worked on a DEA task force in Texas. Bryn had included an article covering the car bombing of his family. In the past six months his bank account had seen a steady decline in funds. But *A* plus *B* didn't equal *C*. Harper's withdrawals nowhere matched Auclair's intakes. Harper was now working at the heart of the federal building where witnesses were processed. A click of a button would provide him all of Abbie's information. But the lines between him and Auclair or him and Vanderveer didn't connect. Which didn't mean the connection didn't exist, only that Gray couldn't see it—yet.

Gray had had Bryn run a check on everyone on the team—just to prove to Abbie that Gray could put his trust in the people he'd worked with for the past two years. Apart from Harper, everyone looked clean.

Gray had also asked his sister to see if she could pull up any information on mill employees who answered directly to Vanderveer.

And there, bold as brass, flashed a picture of a woman called Pamela Hatcher, Raphael Vanderveer's personal assistant—the woman who'd chased them in Boston yesterday.

"I took that photo," Abbie said, leaning in close to him so her voice wouldn't carry. Her breath was warm against his ear. He tipped his head closer to catch every last wisp. "At the press conference announcing the winning Steeltex bid. I don't remember seeing her there. But I remember seeing her before. At the mill."

He pointed at the woman dressed in a brown tweed suit, standing on the dais behind a group of men, shaking hands. "She doesn't really stand out. Look at how she's dressed."

"Her whole demeanor is different than the woman who's following us, but I should have recognized her."

"Obviously she didn't want you to. Whoever she is, she's good." Gray clicked the file closed with more force than it needed. What he really wanted to do was strangle Pamela with his bare hands so she could never harm anyone again. "Someone who sees killing as a sport."

With shaking fingers Abbie returned the flash drive to its holder on the chain around her neck. "And I'm next on her list."

Chapter Eleven

Rafe sat like a model prisoner across the table from the colorful platoon of testosterone-laden law-enforcement thugs vying for his cooperation. He'd already dismissed every rank of officer from state to federal as beneath his worth. All he had to do to gain their assistance was twitch the right string.

The one person who fascinated him was the man they called Falconer. His stare penetrated as if he could see through all the layers that made Rafe tick. Yet Rafe could read nothing in the dark gaze and stone face—as if the features belonged to a one-way mirror. But the condescension came through loud and clear. This Falconer was just like his father. No matter what Rafe had done, George had looked through him as if he didn't exist.

I will not *be ignored again.*

Rafe measured and weighed his opponent. Smiling, he turned and played the rest of the federal puppets like a master. "Of course I understand. I want nothing more than to clear this whole misunderstanding. Abrielle is a fragile woman who is very loyal to her father. She manipulated the photograph to protect her father's image.

Any child who loves a parent would do the same. I'm simply asking for a chance to prove my innocence."

"You'll have your day in court next week, Mr. Vanderveer." That was the lawyer trying to sound oh-so professional. Too bad the thousand-dollar suit didn't come with sweat-absorbent lining. The black stains under his pits were a dead giveaway to his eagerness for results. "We need something now to prove your goodwill."

"Once you have Marko al-Khafar in custody, you'll realize I wasn't selling anything of value." Not that the Chechen rebel could give them any answers. Or at least not the ones they sought.

"First we need to catch him." That from the local twerp who was doing his best to impersonate the voice of reason.

"It's very simple," Rafe said, laying out his plan for the eager imbeciles. "Bring me a phone. I'll contact my source. I'll promise him the piece of Steeltex technology he's been pining for. Once the buy is set, your team of experts can follow me to the rendezvous point and collect your prize." He smiled because he'd learned that it put people at ease. "Everybody wins."

"No go." This from the eagle-eyed Falconer, who still stared at Rafe as if he were as transparent as onionskin paper.

The bald marshal, who'd pegged himself the leader of this little gathering of morons, motioned for an underling, who came scurrying from his post along the vomit-green wall. "Bring a phone."

Falconer crossed his arms over his broad chest. "I suggest we hold off on this decision."

The marshal's jaw twitched like a fish on a line. "Let's see if he can make good on the first part of the plan."

"You're making a mistake," Falconer said.

The marshal's jowls quaked like a volcano about to blow. He reared off his chair and gestured Falconer outside the room. Of course, neither could know that simply moving out of ear range didn't mean Rafe couldn't hear their conversation. Not with that plate-glass window on the door framing their war of wills. He'd learned to read lips from his deaf mother. Really, how gauche of them not to have uncovered such an important detail.

"The plan is too risky," Falconer said, keeping his cool.

The marshal's shiny pate turned a bright pink. "It's the best chance we have to find out how much damage he's caused."

None, my dear sirs. I've sold defective merchandise to defective nations with defective ideals. The loss goes to the foreign rebels. Really, they should see that he was helping them. The sooner all these mujahideens killed each other off, the sooner the world could return to peace. *I'm doing you all a favor.*

"Raphael Vanderveer isn't trustworthy." Lob, Falconer.

"None of these pukes are, but we have to start somewhere. This Chechen is part of a group that receives help from foreign terrorist groups, including al-Qaeda. We get al-Khafar, we can start connecting the dots back to the point of origin." Volley, the marshal.

"Do you really think he has any intentions of leading you to his source?"

"What else can he do? It's not like we're taking the chains off and sending him out into the world with a promise to come back on his own. We're going to hang on his tail every inch of the way." Rage pretzeled the marshal's body at an odd angle.

"He has a plan or he wouldn't cooperate so willingly."

"He can plan all he wants. He won't have a chance to breathe crooked until he's back behind bars."

"I can't sanc—"

"That's right, Falconer, you can't." The marshal straightened as if he'd just remembered he was in charge. "You have no jurisdiction in this operation."

The marshal strode back into the room, slamming the door on Falconer's retreating back.

Sweet victory.

AFTER LUNCH GRAY CONTACTED Kingsley via a throwaway phone. Pillows propped against the headboard, mouth tight with strain, Abbie leafed through the printed pages of Bryn's report hoping to make connections. "Any news?"

"Falconer's out to skin you alive when he finds you."

Gray squirmed uncomfortably against the hotel-room wall. "Five days. We're almost there. How's Brynna?"

"Except for the bruises, she looks fine."

"But?" Why was there always a *but* when it came to Brynna?

"Let's just say Marta isn't used to someone who's so self-contained."

Gray's guilt cranked up another notch. He should have done more to get her out of Echo Falls. He should have tried harder. That he didn't know how bad things had gotten for her wasn't an excuse. She was his kid sister. "She's been in a world of hurt for a long time."

"It shows." Kingsley's chair creaked. The click of computer keys filled the background. Was Kingsley trying to locate the call? "What's with you and your sister anyway?"

"Ask her and—if you get an answer—then tell me." Gray rubbed at the pain blooming at the base of his neck. "Can you run financials on Brynna?"

Kingsley's hesitation weighted the silence. "Personal or business?"

"Both." Gray bit out the word, remembering Vanderveer's insinuation about Brynna's financial problems in his poison letter. Since when had a scumbag's lies meant anything to Gray? He wiped a hand over his face, then everything in him stilled except for the overloud beating of his heart. He'd cared about what went on in bullies' skulls since he'd resorted to a forced laid-back attitude and shades to deflect regular poundings. Gray turned away from the disturbing thought. Vanderveer didn't matter. The check on Brynna's financial state would simply prove him wrong. Brynna was many things, but she wasn't a criminal. She wouldn't betray Abbie.

"Listen," Kingsley said. "Vanderveer's making a move. The task force allowed him to set up a meet with Marko al-Khafar, a U.S. national with Chechen roots he's been doing business with. Falconer thinks Vanderveer's going to use the opportunity to escape."

No surprise there. Cramming Vanderveer's vast ego into a prison cell had to hurt. "Watch out for a woman named Pamela Hatcher. She's his secretary and personal gun-for-hire. At the very least she's killed three deputy marshals and a cop in Maine."

"Mercer's on her. She flew right under the radar when we first looked at her."

Her average background had made her a perfect choice for Vanderveer's mission. "Steeltex makes her invisible, for one. For another, she's a drab mouse until she dresses up like Lara Croft on a mission. I have no

idea how she's doing it, but she's been on our trail since
day one." But if Rafe had called her back for his escape
attempt, it gave him and Abbie a window to act. "Did
Mercer manage to crank cuffs on her?"

"No, she nabbed an MBTA cop and played the scared
female well enough that Mercer was stopped and
brought in for questioning. By the time he straightened
everything out, he'd lost her track."

Gray swore. He'd hoped to have one less worry chasing him. Instead he'd doubled his trouble. "When is
this meeting of Vanderveer's taking place?"

Kingsley cleared his throat. "Need-to-know. You
don't."

"Even if I could fix it so al-Khafar takes offense at
Vanderveer's offer? Without al-Khafar's help, Vanderveer's chances of getting away clean shrink."

Kingsley's chair creaked in time to his thoughts.
"How are you going to do that?"

No freakin' idea. "A man's gotta have his secrets. Especially with a mole in the house."

"No mole, Reed. I've been through everything with
a magnifying glass. I'd bet my new mixing board Harper's clean. He's in pain, but he's coping. He's got a lead
on the inside informant at WITSEC."

"Who?"

"He's still following tracks."

Pretending he's giving, but not showing his hand,
Gray thought. "One of Auclair's bank account shows
heavy deposits in the past few months."

"Yeah, we're on that. Falconer's out interviewing
Auclair's wife." Kingsley gave an appreciative whistle.
"Your sister's got some nose for digging up information.
Almost as good as mine."

Coming from Kingsley, that was the height of compliment.

The squeaks of Kingsley's chair stopped abruptly. "Tomorrow at dawn." He lowered his voice. "Falconer's in the nest."

"Thanks for everything."

"Call me tonight at home and I'll give you the details." Kingsley let out a long breath. "I hope to God I'm doing the right thing and didn't get snookered by your Hollywood charm."

"Boy Scouts have a nose for truth, right?"

"Right. Hey, watch your back. I don't like where this is going."

Neither did Gray.

ABBIE DUMPED BRYN'S REPORT on the bed, scattering its pages. The news Gray had just shared with her hit like a blow to the solar plexus.

Tomorrow the U.S. Marshals Service was going to allow Rafe to walk out of his jail cell and into the world. Tomorrow Rafe was going to take advantage of these people's ill-placed trust and escape. Four days before his trial? What was the Marshals Service thinking?

She gulped and one hand clutched her throat.

Would Rafe come after her? Finish what he'd started himself? Would he look into her soul with his dark, cold eyes and kill her as he'd killed her father? "I can't stand it."

Voice ripe with disgust, she faced Gray. "I know I said I didn't want to leave this room until the trial, but I think we need to."

From the chair where he sat, Gray's sharp silver eyes assessed her. "And just where do you want to go?"

"I don't know." Trying to draw her scattered thoughts into a clear composition, she capped the jar of peanut butter and shoved it back on the dresser.

"I'm not going to let you put yourself in the path of danger. That's crazy."

"As crazy as sitting here just waiting for Rafe to show up?" As crazy as waiting for Rafe to kill Gray before he ripped the flash drive off her neck and disposed of her body?

"Staying put is a good idea," Gray said quietly. "It leaves no markers."

"He's going to escape." She combed her fingers through the short spikes of her hair and yanked at the ends. "You know he will. He's greasy enough to slip his shackles. He was greasy enough to let them think the idea of taking him outside prison walls was a good one."

Gray rose, came toward her and cupped her elbows in his hands. Only self-restraint kept her from sagging into his solid arms. "Abbie, listen to me. Vanderveer won't get near you. I won't let him hurt you. Trust me."

Trust me. He'd said those words thirteen years ago. If she'd believed him then, if she'd followed him out of Echo Falls, would her father still be alive? Would a child of Gray's fill her arms instead of her dreams? Would he still love her? She'd give anything to turn back the clock and have Gray wear his love for her as openly as he had that day long ago. But she'd said no, and now she had no right to ask him to sacrifice more.

Gray skimmed her jaw with the edge of his thumb, regret and something tender winding through the gray of his eyes, begging for compliance. "All I have is one Glock and a spare magazine. We have no idea what we're up against. How many people Vanderveer's bought. I'm just one person."

She wanted to comply, really she did. She pivoted away from his touch, away from the yearning to have him hold her and protect her. This was her fight. She had to take control.

She needed to face Rafe, not lie low and wait for him to pop up like a monster in the dark and knock her down as he'd already done to so many of her protectors. "What we need to do is undermine Rafe's plan. Just like you told Kingsley. We need to shake Rafe's confidence. We need to turn his contact against him."

Think of Rafe. Of how to stop him. Of betrayal.

She rounded on Gray and grabbed handfuls of his T-shirt. "Let's razzle-dazzle him."

Half of Gray's mouth quirked up. "Billy Flynn. *Chicago.*"

She tugged playfully on the T-shirt lumped in her fists, not sure if he was teasing her as he used to do about her taste in entertainment. "For a guy who claims to hate musicals, you sure know your shows."

He tilted his head to one shoulder, and the silver of his eyes shimmered all the way to her toes. "Keep talking."

Disturbed by her desire to lean forward and see if that shimmer gave his skin an electric taste, she ran her tongue over her dry lips and looked over his shoulder at the geometric pattern on the curtains. An idea developed as if she'd exposed it to photographic paper and placed it in a developer. "Rafe is like Billy Flynn. What he says and what he does are two different things. Winning is more important than truth. So, what we do is play the game by Rafe's rules. We give this al-Khafar person the illusion of truth. Just like Rafe does to everyone else. We turn ally against ally. When al-Khafar doesn't show for their rendezvous, Rafe loses face in front of the task force he's supposed to wow. They smell betrayal, so they keep the chains tighter and he has no chance to escape."

Concentrating, she bit her lower lip. "What would this al-Khafar consider betrayal?"

Gray shrugged. "Vanderveer selling the same secrets or better secrets to the enemy."

"Right. You said al-Khafar was a Chechen Muslim rebelling against Russia."

"He's a U.S. citizen raising money for a rebel group in Chechnya. At least, that's the rumor. No one's caught him in the act. So?"

She released the T-shirt bunched in her fist, and her fingers automatically stretched out toward the warmth of Gray's chest. "So, if we send al-Khafar a picture of Rafe shaking hands with a Russian official, then he would naturally react with anger and seek revenge."

The more fervor crept into her voice, the milder his became. "And how are you proposing to accomplish that feat?"

A smile bloomed on her lips. She had the skills. For once she knew what to do and how to do it. "Magic. All I need is my studio."

Gray shook his head and a note of panic skated along the edge of his voice. "Abbie—"

His objection to her every idea was starting to tick her off. She reached for the canvas tote on the dresser. "The nice thing about digital photos is that you can manipulate them so well that no seams show. All we have to do is find a picture of a Russian official and clone it with Rafe's. I have plenty of stock of Rafe.

Apparently paranoia does pay off. And with the recent terrorist activity in Russia, finding a picture of someone incriminating on the Internet shouldn't prove too hard."

Gray tagged her hand and held her back. "Even if we could manage all that, how do you plan on delivering this photograph to al-Khafar?"

She attempted a smile and hoped the stiffness didn't show. "Well, that's your contribution to the plan. You can think about it while I'm creating the composite."

His grip on her hand tightened. "Out of the question."

"Rafe's going to be too busy—"

Gray shook his head. "No. We're not going anywhere near Echo Falls. Remember what happened to Bryn?"

"How can I forget?" The mistake would plague her the rest of her life. "Then we'll need to find another studio."

"I'm not walking you into danger."

"Fine, I'll go by myself." Heart thumping, she headed toward the door. How had she ended up like Rafe—manipulating people, photographs to get what she wanted when always before she'd sought truth? But survival demanded a different set of rules.

Hard fingers digging into the flesh of her arm, Gray stopped her dead in her tracks. "You are *not* going to go off on your own."

"You're hurting me."

As if she'd slapped him, he instantly let go. He prowled the room with feral intensity, muscles sleek and tense, ready for battle. By the window he stilled, lifted the edge of the curtain and swore. Then he faced her with his grimmest expression. "We have company."

"Pamela?" Abbie rubbed at the goose bumps trooping up her arms.

Fury and frustration filled his long, fierce stare. He gave a stiff nod. "Standing outside the office."

Pamela here? How had she found them? They'd tossed everything. No one, not even Gray's Seeker friend, knew where they were. "How are we going to get out of here?"

Gray yanked on her wrist and aimed her toward the bathroom and its tiny window two floors off the ground. "We need to find some wheels."

THE CALL CAME RIGHT ON schedule. Pamela practically purred with delight. "I have the chocolates in my sight."

"Very good." One less detail to take care of after his great manipulation. The sooner he retrieved the evidence Abbie carried, the sooner he could move on to more pleasurable distractions. Rafe was counting down the hours until he could taste fresh air again. The rasp of crickets and the drone of tires on asphalt murmured in the background like a siren, making him lick his lips in anticipation. "Where is it?"

"At a processing place. I have what I need to take care of the problem."

Processing place? Her studio? What was Abbie doing there? "Keep it boxed." To sample, he first had to escape. "Were you able to reach the interested party?"

"Of course." Pamela sounded insulted. Maybe his spy girl was becoming a tad too big for her boots. That was when mistakes happened. And he couldn't afford any mistakes in the next two days. Soon he wouldn't need her anymore. Perhaps his inside source would want to trade one life for another.

"Have you taken care of all the details for the party?"

"Everything's in place and waiting," Pamela said.

"The right party will get the right morsel. Caterers are like that."

And false leads fed to morons made tasty snacks. "Pamela—"

"If I'm going to meet my schedule, I need to get going." Something like nails against a hard surface clicked in the receiver.

"*My* schedule, Pamela. To the letter. Nothing can go wrong." He *had* to get it right on the first try. The task force would have him on a tight leash. He hated depending on others for something this vital.

"I've got everything covered. Trust me. By nightfall the order won't be a problem for you anymore."

"Pamela, about the chocolates, I want to open—"

The buzz of a disconnected call filled his ear. He shot up, tumbling his chair backward, and slammed down the receiver. The bitch had hung up on him. Had she developed a taste for blood in the past few months?

If you cheat me out of this pleasure, he vowed, *it will be your last.*

If it weren't for his desire to improve people's lives, he wouldn't be in this position now, and he could handle Abbie and her evidence himself.

Pamela would not ignore him and live.

No one would.

Chapter Twelve

Gray eased up a slat on the blind in the window of the Serendipity Gallery, owned by a friend of Abbie's. He didn't like its isolated location outside of Shelburne Falls. With only one road in, a clean getaway from the old brick home and its barn gallery could prove difficult. On the other hand, driving down the narrow country road, he hadn't caught sight of anyone on their tail.

Of course, that didn't mean anything. Especially when the spiders were feasting on his neck. If Pamela had put on Steeltex, she was invisible—especially at night. He'd done everything possible to evade pursuit before, and Pamela had still found them.

Outside the gallery, talons of black clouds scuffed a ripe moon. Crickets and frogs and mosquitoes chirped and croaked and buzzed in a relentless cacophony that made hearing footsteps next to impossible—especially from someone intent on stealth. The promise of rain hung on the horizon like a threat. The thick, humid air clung to his skin in an oily film. No breeze breathed relief in the stuffy air of the barn office.

"Is Pamela out there?" Abbie asked in a strained voice as she booted up her friend's computer.

"I'm assuming she is even if I can't see her." He caught a glimmer of wetness in Abbie's eyes. She surreptitiously knuckled the evidence away. Then her graceful fingers stuttered over the computer keys until they found home again. Bigger men would've folded by now, but Abbie soldiered on. His teenage princess had turned into a full-fledged warrior. In spite of his intention to keep his hands to himself, Gray squeezed her shoulder as he walked by her, then scanned the property once more.

Abbie's friend, Serena—of the flamboyant *S* and no last name—was off at a show, but had told Abbie to make herself at home and given her the location of the key hidden in the stone wall. Security wasn't Serena's highest priority—as evidenced by the dark property and the primitive security system. Someone had mostly kept up with mowing the large lawn. Weeds and overgrown bushes populated the flower beds, instead of the riot of annuals and manicured greens he imagined should grace them. That made for plenty of places for a conniving tail to hide.

He'd hoped to spend the night at the gallery, but given the way he couldn't shake the center-stage spotlight sensation, staying here wasn't safe either.

Inside the gallery a serpentine of partitions hung from the plank-and-beam ceiling by chains and wound around the main floor, offering a taste of everything from paintings to tapestries to photographs. A series of long, narrow windows were cut into the barn siding to offer natural lighting during the day. All were equipped with shades made of wooden slats aged a weathered silver.

Gray prowled from window to window, drawing down shades as he went. His gaze roamed the darkness, searching for anything out of place. With Pamela surely skulking about, he had to stay alert. "How long will this take?"

"Depends," Abbie said, clicking her way across Serena's desktop computer.

The glow of the computer screen softened Abbie's features. Was that how she looked when she worked on her projects—focused and radiant? All those years ago when Abbie had said no, when she'd chosen to stay in Echo Falls rather than follow him, he'd told himself she'd made the right decision. Her life should be filled with beautiful things—Holbrook mansion, her photographs, a wealthy husband, children. Things he couldn't give her but that had given him solace. If she was happy, then he was happy for her.

But she'd had few of those things. She'd even lost a baby. Another man's baby. A man who hadn't loved her. A man who now wanted her dead.

He found himself playing What if? as he'd done on so many long nights. What if he'd tried harder to change her mind? What if she'd come with him? She'd be safe from terrorists. Her father would be alive. They'd have a snug little home with a play set in the backyard and children playing and laughing and a big, goofy dog. They'd go hiking, canoeing and camping. They'd go to the aquarium and the zoo and the circus. They'd go to summer theater in the park, afternoon matinees and school plays. Together as a family, he and Abbie and their kids. They certainly wouldn't be here, looking over their shoulders, waiting for Pamela to shoot them between the eyes.

He cleared his throat and shifted his stance. "Depends on what?"

"On what photos I find and how hard they are to composite."

His glance slid to the hollow of her throat and the even beat making the silver chain jump, and found his own pulse leaping with a sudden desire to kiss that tender spot. After the trial, then what? Could he let her walk away again? Did he really want to spend the rest of his life chasing after scum and bedding down in cheap motels more often than at his own house? She deserved better, didn't she? She deserved a husband who came home every night. "What about your flash drive? You have photos of Vanderveer on there, right?"

"I do."

She pulled on the chain, popped off the flash drive that lay nestled under her T-shirt and inserted it in a port. She chose a photo of Vanderveer shaking hands with a U.S. Army representative and imported it into the Photoshop program. Abbie had caught Vanderveer with a jackal smile and greed that practically beamed dollar signs in his eyes.

He bent down for a closer look. His hands instinctively curled around the narrow wings of her shoulders, so fragile beneath his fingers. How could her hair still smell of honey and almonds when she'd had to make do with cheap shampoo? "Good choice."

"Next we have to find a picture of a Russian official that will make al-Khafar burn with rage." Abbie clicked on the icon that connected her to the Internet.

She Googled "Russian Generals" and got mostly history sites. She hit pay dirt with a CNN news account of a Russian general's visit to Washington, complete with a picture she could capture and use. "There we go. All I need to do now is cut out the general and layer him in Rafe's photo. I'll have to flip-flop the general around so he's facing the right way."

"Will that be a problem?"

"Shouldn't."

Gray shook away the ticking-clock sensation in his head. But the unwavering alarm hammered his chest and multiplied his worry for Abbie's safety. "How long is that going to take?"

"A lot longer if you stand there breathing down my neck."

He straightened and swiveled toward the window, hooking a slat from the wooden blinds with his finger. He wanted a whole lot more than just breathe down her neck. He didn't want to stand here looking out for a gun-for-hire. He wanted Abbie, and no amount of telling himself that he shouldn't was going to change that. "Will al-Khafar know who this man is?"

"According to the news article, Vladimir Soldatov has recently come back from a tour of duty in Chechnya, where he was sent by the Kremlin to control separatists. During his term, Russian troops were often accused of abusing and abducting civilians deemed terrorists. Human rights weren't high on his list of priorities. He was sent to the U.S. to testify before a congressional panel on terrorism, more specifically on the al-Qaeda connection to the terrorist activities in Chechnya and its U.S. connection. If that doesn't set al-Khafar off, I don't know what will."

Gray's fingers twitched reflexively over the Glock holstered beneath his polo shirt. Lighting and composition and whatever else went in a photo should fill her mind, not terrorists and murderers. "Hurry."

"Quality takes time, and we need quality to fool Rafe's contact."

And time was a commodity they were short on. Gray

paced the length of the gallery, going from window to window and scouring the grounds to keep her safe while she created the composite. All these damned windows, even with the shades down, made him feel as if he were on display.

As he cut between two panels, something familiar caught his eye, making him stop. The prints on this section of wall pictured a host of people he recognized from around Echo Falls. Familiar but different. He was seeing buildings and people as if he'd never spent the most miserable part of his life there. Women working in the mill, children playing in the schoolyard, men fishing off the stone bridge. Every aspect of life from the awe-inspiring to the gritty gave a revealing, emotional and multilayered look at the town he'd seen through the skew of his pain. The vibrant images made words unnecessary—intrusive even—and touched something in his soul. What view was real? His or the photographer's?

Not just any photographer. Abbie. These were Abbie's photographs. Even without the discreet description he would have known her work.

"Diane Arbus said something to the effect of, 'A photograph is a secret about a secret.'" Abbie's voice startled him out of his musing. The shy, soft look in her eyes as she sat behind the computer took him back to summer afternoons at the quarry, when she'd practiced flirting and fired his teenage hormones into overdrive. She could still turn him on with just a look. After thirteen years that ability should've faded.

"I can see the secrets in the faces," he said before he could stop himself. Heat rushed up his neck, and he quickened his step to the window. What would she see in him? What would her camera catch? Would her picture reveal the truth he hid with shades, the secret he was doing his best to hide from her—from himself? "You caught something in every one that isn't obvious at first glance. You do good work."

"I did." Pain darkened her eyes, and she sliced her attention back to the computer.

His hands fisted. He wanted to wrap them around Vanderveer's neck until it cracked for putting the hurt in Abbie's eyes.

"You will again." If nothing else, he could give her back that part of her life. Echo Falls and her studio.

His gaze scanned the grounds growing darker by the minute as clouds swallowed the moon. He searched deep into the shadows for signs of Pamela. Abbie belonged on her father's grand estate. She belonged in her studio making magic. She belonged in the small town that held her heart. If she'd come with him, if she'd left her world behind to follow him, would her photos exude so much soul? Saying no had been the right thing for her to do.

A growl of thunder rumbled in the distance. The crickets and frogs ended their concert, as if a conductor's baton had cut them off midbar, and a weight of expectation hung in the air. The spiders at his neck went crazy. Was the sudden silence marking the approaching storm or Pamela's arrival? "Are you almost done?"

Her top teeth scraped at her bottom lip as she adjusted the brightness level of the merged layers of her composite. She leaned back, a pleased expression on her face. The smile lit her eyes and warmed his insides. "There. What do you think?"

He bent toward the screen, knocked a little off center again by her sweet scent. There right in front of him in full, perfect color, Raphael Vanderveer stood shaking hands with a uniformed Russian general. He couldn't help it, he leaned his temple against hers. He wanted more, but this would have to do. "Wow! That's great."

Would it be enough? Perception. Face value. Too many people judged things that way. But illusion still made for a dangerous pawn.

Lightning strobed at a distance. A roll of thunder grumbled in return. A slow pelt of rain knocked at the window. Was Pamela out there, waiting for them to come out?

"The ball's in your court," Abbie said as she transferred a copy of her masterpiece onto the flash drive. "How do we get this to al-Khafar?"

By racking up a heavy debt. If this didn't pay off, he was burning bridges he could never rebuild. "I call Kingsley."

THE PHONE NUMBER KINGSLEY had given him was no doubt untraceable. It rang nineteen times before someone answered with a curt, "Yeah."

"Marko al-Khafar?"

No answer.

Adrenaline tripping through his veins, Gray kept his tone quiet and even. "Vanderveer is setting you up."

"And who are you that I should trust your word?" the voice scoffed.

"A friend."

"A man in my position has no friends."

"Ask yourself how I could get this number except through your contact himself."

Silence strained the connection. "Who are you?"

"It's safer not to say."

"For who?"

"Both of us."

Another pause jacked up the tension knotting Gray's muscles.

"Why are you calling?" the voice asked.

Perspiration oozed from his pores as if he were in a sauna, but Gray kept his voice smooth. *Never let them see you sweat.* "This man you call an ally has no intentions of selling you anything except a long trip to a maximum-security prison. The U.S. Marshals Service plans on escorting him from his jail cell to your rendezvous at the warehouse. A task force'll be waiting there to cuff you."

"How do I know you tell the truth?"

"I have proof. Do you have an e-mail address?"

"I want nothing from you."

"You've heard of Vladimir Soldatov."

Silence again. Then a curse and a spit.

"Vanderveer sold you defective technology. Water short-circuits the conductive fibers. The recent fix, he saved for Soldatov."

"I'll give you one chance to prove yourself."

Clutching the phone between his jaw and shoulder, Gray snatched the pencil and paper Abbie handed him.

The voice rattled off an e-mail address, then hung up.

"What did he say?" Abbie asked, eyes wide and anxious.

"To send our proof. Use one of your remailer accounts. I don't want your friend caught up in this."

She nodded and got to work. "What do you want me to say in the e-mail?"

He tapped the back of her chair. "Get up for a second."

She stood and hovered, then mumbled something.

Gray finished the message, then clicked the send button.

The message-sent pop-up had barely flashed on the screen when a spear of lightning crazed the sky. The answering crack of thunder ripped open the seam, shaking ground and glass in a sonic boom. Power died, instantly dropping the room into pitch-black darkness. Lightning and thunder struck again simultaneously like woolly mammoths butting heads on top of the building. The sulfur scent of spent ozone charged the air.

Then underneath came an updraft with the undertones of something stronger.

He snatched a Maglite from the desk. Searching for the source, Gray stood, angled the light to the floor and flashed it around the gallery's perimeter. All those damned wall panels shook and rattled like ghosts on their chains. Stairs to the attic. Front door. Bathroom door. Back door. Darkroom door. Supply closet door. Photography chemicals were flammable, and Abbie had said Serena dabbled in the craft.

"We need to get out of here."

Before he could move, a loud *whomp* did a three-sixty around the gallery. The red glow of flames flashed across the windows of all four walls, chomping on the fuel of dry barn wood like a starved beast. The sudden light blinded him. Heat poured around every opening, swamping the room.

Pamela.

Every instinct in him screamed, *Run!* Then his hand reached back and caught nothing but air. "Abbie!"

No answer.

"Abbie!" Where the hell was she? She'd been right there beside him before the power had gone out.

His heart pounded in his chest. Acrid smoke irritated his lungs, stung his eyes. Had Pamela nabbed her during the commotion of the primary explosion? "Abbie!"

How long before someone noticed the flames to sound the alarm? In the middle of a thunderstorm, what was one more explosion?

A tiny voice reached him from up above. "Abbie?"

Another mewl, like a kitten in distress. What the hell was she doing up in the attic?

He charged up the stairs two by two. Heat clambered up right behind him and flames chased him. He slammed the door on both, shutting off all light.

"Abbie!" He coughed and brought his T-shirt up to cover his nose and mouth.

"Here!" She choked on her words. "I'm stuck."

Gray took the penlight from his pocket and frantically flashed it across the attic. He spotted her hunkered down beside an old trunk, one leg swallowed by the floor to midthigh. He sprinted to her. "What the hell are you doing up here?" Fear for her sharpened his voice. "What was worth your life?"

Beside her the canvas tote bulged with a camera, flash and lens.

"This is the first camera I bought myself with my own money. Serena borrowed it. You made me give up everything else. I wanted something that was mine. How did I know lightning was going to strike the building?"

"Not lightning. Pamela." Lightning would've hit one spot, not sparked the whole perimeter of the building. He shoved the flashlight in Abbie's hand. "Hold it steady so I can get you out."

As he worked furiously to free Abbie's leg, his breathing rasped in his ears. Sweat drenched his face and back. Scouts of smoke slinked from the cracks between the planks of the floor. Flames stretched greedy fingers under the attic door.

"Give it a go," he said, putting pressure against a board he couldn't dislodge.

Teeth gritted, she pulled on her leg. Denim ripped on the snags of splintered wood, but she kept tugging until she was free.

"Are you okay?"

She nodded. Clear rivers of tears streamed across sooty cheeks. He smeared the wetness with the back of one hand. "I'm sorry, Abbie."

"Let's get out of here."

"You're bleeding."

"I'm okay."

"We can't go down the way we came in." Not the way the flames had chased him up the stairs. He took the flashlight from her and swept it around the walls.

"There's a window on the road side of the building."

With a strong and steady grip she guided his hand. He almost shouted with relief when he spotted the gleaming panes of glass. Shutters battened down the window.

"Hands and knees," he said, leading the way. "Follow in my track."

If the floor held his weight, it would hold hers. He made his way across the rickety attic, knocking over a light on a tripod stand, cursing Pamela and Vanderveer. He unlocked the window latch and pushed against the sash to open it. It wouldn't budge. No time for finesse.

If Pamela had orchestrated this incident, then she

was waiting outside, admiring her work. She'd see them escape. No getting around it. But alive and on the run was much better than fried and dead.

"Cover your head," he said. With a series of swift kicks he blew out both the glass and the shutters. Damp air poured into the opening and he gulped it in. Flashlight pointed to the ground outside, he studied his landing area.

First the motel, now the studio. "You're sure making me jump through hoops today."

Her laugh beside him was rocky with terror. "That's it, Gray. You've finally caught on to me. I've been wanting you to catch me since I was thirteen. Why do you think I kept diving off that quarry ledge?"

His heart did a flip. Really? "Well, today you're getting your wish. Twice. Let me get down to the ground, then, just like at the motel, go out the window and let go. Don't think. Just do it as fast as you can."

Weapon drawn, he climbed out the window, let himself drop and hit the wet grass rolling. Without taking time to catch his breath, he crouched and searched for Pamela by the fire's glow.

As Abbie hooked her canvas tote over her shoulder and clambered out the window, he positioned himself to catch her. Coughing, she let go.

He stopped breathing and prayed like he'd never prayed before. And when she landed square in his arms, he clung to her hard so she wouldn't feel his arms shaking. "I've got you, Abbie."

"I never doubted you would."

The trust in her golden eyes had him thinking he could move any mountain. Until a shot blew out the barn wall behind them. He shielded Abbie's body with his and nudged her forward. "Let's go."

·A sick sensation slithered through Gray's gut as he led Abbie deeper into the dark. This hit had been close— too close.

They rounded the corner of the barn and made it to the car. Gray fired the engine, then punched the accelerator. "Get down and stay down. It's going to get nasty."

The car swerved in the mud slick caused by the rain. He straightened it out and found the driveway.

Rain had neutralized the cloaking quality of the Steeltex, and Pamela stood in the middle of the driveway, framed by two stone pillars, like cowboy at a showdown, weapon drawn and pointed straight at them. He flicked on the high beams and aimed square at her. Right below the mirror a bullet punched through the windshield.

Chapter Thirteen

They were out in the middle of nowhere. They were out of gas. They were out of cash. Rain poured down the windshield like a silver curtain and dripped onto the dashboard through the hole blown in by Pamela's bullet—just before Gray had clipped her with his fender as she'd tried to jump out of the way. After hitting her he'd called 9-1-1, but he hadn't stopped to help her and felt not even a twitch of remorse about it.

Technically they weren't lost. Gray knew exactly where he was. They were west of 91 and a few miles out from Green Goose Lake—much too near Echo Falls for comfort.

"What do we do now?" Abbie asked, apparently fascinated by the spreading pool of water on the black dashboard.

Gray drummed his thumbs against the steering wheel. "Didn't Coach Beasley own a cabin on Green Goose Lake?"

Abbie brightened. "Yes, she does. Remember, she took the whole track team there for a cookout after M.J. Cooper won the state championship banner for the mile my freshman year? And there's still a week of school, so it's likely empty."

His gaze zeroed in on the dark stain her blood had spread around the gash of denim on her thigh. "Are you up to walking?"

Without waiting, she grabbed her canvas tote and scrambled out the passenger's side. "I'm up for anything that puts distance between us and Pamela."

With Abbie's help Gray pushed the car off the road and hid it as best he could in the trees. With daylight someone would notice it, but tracing it back to him would be next to impossible. And if the gods were smiling on him, Pamela was in no shape to follow them.

He shouldered the duffel with their belongings and wrapped his free arm around Abbie. Too late to keep her dry. But this was more for him than for her. He needed to touch her to reassure himself she was okay.

"Do you think she's dead?" Abbie asked in a hushed voice as they hiked up the road. Rain slicked her too-blond hair close to her head and pasted her clothes to her skin, making her look small and fragile.

"I hope so." One less worry.

She shivered. "I know that's horrible, but I hope so, too."

"It's not horrible. She wants to kill you. Scum like that deserves to have her civil liberties deprioritized to the maximum."

Abbie shrugged. "She's still a person."

That was Abbie, always thinking there was something good in everyone. Even him. Who was going to watch out for her once the trial was over?

COACH BEASLEY'S CABIN WAS just as Gray remembered it. Not the King's Arms Hotel, but the A-frame was dry, the kitchen pantry was stocked with nonperishables and, once he turned on the pump and water heater, the water was hot and running.

The open loft upstairs held three sets of bunk beds. No way he was going anywhere near those beds with her. He'd sleep guard downstairs. The couch was long enough to accommodate his height. Better if he wasn't too comfortable anyway.

The bottom half of the building consisted of a kitchen separated from the living room by a butcher-block counter. A mudroom off the back side of the house next to the entrance camouflaged the door to a long, narrow bathroom complete with shower stall and washer and dryer.

Given how they'd just missed being fricasseed by Pamela, he opted to skip building a fire in the stone fireplace. Instead he lit the thick jar candles on the counter and coffee table. Their scent of clean cotton would soon take care of the damp, closed-up smell. He heated canned soup and rounded up some crackers while Abbie showered. For one night he'd like to give her the illusion she was safe.

She came out of the bathroom wearing a baby-blue sweat suit that had to belong to Coach Beasley. The sleeves and pants were a few inches too short, showing off small wrists, defined calves and arched feet and making her look once more like the gangly teen he'd lusted after.

Still lusted after.

"I made soup," he said, proud he could pour the chicken and noodles straight into the bowl, given the tight fit of his damp jeans.

"I'm not really hungry."

"Eat anyway. To fight Vanderveer you need your strength."

"You're right." She accepted the bowl and spoon he gave her but made no move to actually eat the soup. "I'm going to run a load of laundry later. Let me know if you want to throw stuff in there, too."

It seemed intimate somehow, mixing laundry. Not trusting himself to speak, he escaped to the shower. When he came out, she was sitting on the plaid couch, the empty soup bowl on the side table and a cup of tea steaming in her hands.

He wasn't going to touch her, he told himself as he crossed the room wearing only the sweatpants he'd found on the dryer. He was just going to get close enough to reassure himself she was okay. That she wasn't reliving the trauma of the fire at the gallery. She already had enough ghosts peopling her conscience; she didn't need any more. Especially not Pamela's.

For now they were at a standstill. Vanderveer's rendezvous with al-Khafar wasn't until dawn. They'd done their best to foil the meet. If Gray was lucky, Pamela was dead. At the very least that clip had to have broken bone. Seeking medical attention would slow her down. "You're safe here tonight."

"I know." Abbie sipped from her cup, frowning as if the contents displeased her. "Do you ever wonder how things might have turned out?"

"Like what?"

"Like you and me."

All the time. Too often. He crouched beside her, heart knocking hard inside his chest. But how could he admit this weakness to her? She needed someone strong right now, not a guy who was still hanging on to a fantasy decades old. "I—"

"I'm sorry. I didn't mean to put you in an awkward

position." She tucked her legs close into her and sipped at her tea.

"No, it's all right." She was scared. Thinking back to a time when life had seemed full of promises was normal.

She shrugged, eyes blinking fast as if she were beating back tears. "I'm not usually so needy."

No, Abbie usually took care of everyone else's needs before her own.

"It's tonight," she said, rolling the cup between her palms. "It's everything. It's making me wonder about the road not taken."

Was it possible? Did she regret saying no? She'd deserved better than him. She still did.

"Abbie…" His throat went dry. He drew in a breath, wanting….what? To take her back? To take her forward? He didn't know, so he settled on what he knew to be true. "I loved you, you know."

She lifted her gaze from the steam of her cup and connected. "Then why did you always keep your distance? You always sat alone—at the quarry, at lunch at school, on the bus when we went to track meets."

He rocked back on his heels and joked, "Someone had to make sure that equipment bags didn't fall over on the bus."

"You could've joined, you know." Her golden eyes remained rock serious.

He gave a slow shake of his head. "It wasn't really an option, Abbie. Didn't you ever notice that anyone who talked to me ended up getting the stuffing kicked out of them?" He skimmed the back of his fingers across her cheek. "Except for you. Everyone liked you. And everyone knew you included everyone—even a loser like me."

"You weren't a loser. You worked too hard to end up a failure. Anybody with two ounces of brains could see that."

He stared into her eyes, into that sea of goodness. "Abbie of the golden heart."

"I was afraid," she said, staring back, a certain sadness crimping the sides of her eyes. "That night when you asked me to marry you."

"You were afraid of me?" Surprise rocked through his voice, pushing him to his feet.

She set the cup of tea on the side table and raked her top teeth over her bottom lip, deep in thought. "Have you ever had that happen? Wanting something desperately but being afraid of it, too?"

More often than he cared to admit. He sat beside her on the couch, hooking an arm around her shoulders. To comfort her. She needed comfort. "Maybe once."

Crazy, really, the way she'd pursued him like a crazed fan but had always feared taking that last step and admitting her infatuation. "You were so…intense."

"Comes from always having to watch all sides at once." He pressed his nose against her hair and inhaled—as if the scent of soot and rain and dime-store shampoo was the most exquisite perfume he'd ever smelled. "You didn't love me."

Of course she had. But the size of that love had frightened as much as it had addicted her. She shook her head. "It's not that. My heart was too full. And I don't know…it scared me."

"You have the biggest heart in all Echo Falls."

A sad smile flitted on her lips. She leaned back against his cocooning arm and looked into his eyes as clear as mirrors. "People think you're this relaxed guy.

They look at you and they think of lazy days at the beach. That's what you want them to think. That you're not a threat. The truth is that you're intense. You play for keeps."

He tilted his head, appraising. "I wouldn't say that. If I did, I'd still live in Echo Falls."

Was that a bit of yearning in his voice? Had he wanted to stay? She should have asked him to wait for her for a few years, until she'd graduated from high school. By then she'd realized what a horrible mistake she'd made, but it was too late. "How many relationships have you had since you left home?"

He shrugged. A careless toss that tried to pretend male pride wasn't involved. "My fair share."

"Real ones. Long ones."

His gaze narrowed as he studied her more closely. "A few."

"How long did they last?"

A crooked grin revealed the beginning of his unease. "What is this? The Inquisition?"

"How long?" she insisted. She jostled his shoulders when he hesitated, at once jealous he'd let anyone else into his heart and furious she hadn't had the courage to stake her claim to him.

"A while." A hint of sadness again behind the light tone.

"What happened?"

The hold of his arms around her shoulder loosened as if he would let her go. "It's ancient history, Abbie."

"I'm trying to prove a point," she said, holding on tight to the waist of his borrowed sweatpants, refusing to let him sway to another topic. "What happened?"

He leaned his temple against hers, and she couldn't quite focus on his expression. "One couldn't handle the long deployments when I was in the Navy. The other couldn't handle my odd hours when I was in the Marshals Service."

She let out a triumphant bark. "*They* called it off. Not you."

"It was mutual, Abbie. I don't see where you're going with this."

"You're a keeper, and I wasn't ready for a lifetime. I was only sixteen. I wanted to say yes, but I was afraid."

"We were just kids," he agreed and shrugged as if her refusal had meant nothing to him. But the heaviness of the pain she'd caused still clung to him.

She looped her arms around his neck, placed her cheek to his heart and listened to the regular rhythm of his life force. "I didn't know who I was or what I wanted to be when I grew up. I wasn't ready to be a wife. Forever." She shook her head. "It sounded so *big*."

"Abbie—"

"Even back then you were a keeper, but no one in town would take you seriously. Bryn thinks you left because you're a runner like your father. I think you had to go because you needed something that was yours and nobody here would let you have it."

"Including your father."

Her father, for all he gave his workers, saw only the outward marks of failure on Gray—the drunken mother, the absent father, the ragged clothes. What he'd never quite believed was that Gray was destined to greater things than repeating old patterns. Until special operations Gray had participated in had started making the news. "Dad would think differently today. You've grown into a fine man, Grayson Reed."

"Nobody was good enough for Elliot Holbrook's princess."

"You found what you needed at Seekers, and I took it away," she said, taken aback by the sharp arrow of pain truth brought. "I'm sorry about that."

"I'm responsible for my decisions. I knew the odds going in. Falconer's a fair man. He'll listen to my side of the story."

And if he didn't? The hole in her heart seemed to grow with every beat. "You took the risk anyway."

She kissed him, a soft, slow, repentant kiss. An apology, that was all. He deserved that much. He was a friend. He'd put his life on the line for her.

He slipped her legs onto his lap, pressing her body closer to his, returning her kiss hungrily. She wound her arms tighter around his neck. His skin was warm, the bone of his shoulder solid, the muscle strong. He tasted like soup—homey and healing. He smelled of Ivory and that outdoorsy musk that was uniquely his.

How long had it been since she'd felt this safe, this whole? Slow pleasure melted and unwound, spreading until her bones had no more substance. Just for a moment she'd allow herself to savor this closeness. Until she realized how starved she was, how much she wanted him to hold her, to kiss her, to love her. Then she pulled away and stood up.

"I should get some sleep." And get ready for whatever came tomorrow when Rafe escaped and sought revenge.

"Abbie—"

Gray's fingers cupped one elbow, spun her back to him. She gasped at the naked potency of his desire. She wanted to capture that look in his eyes on film, let the world see the real Gray—the keen intelligence, the river of emotion, the depth of strength. The slow heat of pleasure that had so relaxed her started to tighten into a sharp yearning.

"I'm lost, Gray. So lost. They took everything away from me—my past, my home, my career. Where do I belong? Who am I?" She shook her head. "Leaning on you because you're familiar…it's a mistake."

Tenderness softened the hard edges of his face as he rose. "You're right here, Abbie. All the parts that count—your spirit, your heart, your compassion—they're inside you. No one can take those away unless you let them."

He'd know, of course. He'd lived through the experience in Echo Falls. And he'd survived. Look at what a wonderful man he'd forged himself into strong, sure, solid. He fought for justice, for the people who couldn't fight back…like her.

He pressed his forehead against hers, the silver of his eyes warm and determined. "I'm going to make sure you get as much back of the rest as you can."

"What if—"

He pressed a finger over her lips. "What if you survive? What if you testify? What if Vanderveer never sees the light of day again? What happens then?"

The thoughts whirled in her mind, a dust devil she didn't dare look through. Because whatever the future brought, Gray's presence in it was still an empty space. "I don't know. I want…I thought I wanted everything back as it was."

"But now?"

A sinking feeling weighed her like anchors. "Now I want more. I want different." *I want you.*

"Then reach out for it."

"There's no road map." *I'm afraid to take a wrong turn again.*

His teasing smile had her forgetting the logic of her fears. "That's half the fun of traveling—seeing where you'll end up."

"What if I end up alone?" *What happens when you leave again?*

"Honey, as long as you let your sunshine glow, you'll never be alone. You can't help it. You draw people to you. All you have to do is sit down on a park bench and some stranger'll start telling you their story and you'll want to take their picture and before you know it, you're fast friends."

"Sunshine?"

"Golden sunshine." The reflection of it in his eyes made her blink at its brightness. "Just be who you are, Abbie. The woman with the sunny smile who can talk to anybody and make them feel good. The woman who listens and lets the speaker find his own solution. The woman who points a camera at someone and lets them see the best of themselves."

"I do that?"

"Did you ever doubt it?"

Every day, when everything and everyone pulled in a thousand different directions, and she couldn't be sure which was the voice of her heart.

"When did you stop dreaming, Abbie?"

She buried her face against his throat, let the strong beat of his pulse reassure her. "The day my father died."

"Then it's high time you started again. Because if you don't, then Vanderveer wins no matter what happens."

Gray's energy and his faith in her had her imagining possibilities once more. And when the shock of seeing a future for herself dissipated, an eye of calm centered her. That feeling of inner peace came only when she lost herself in her work, in her art, observing life behind the lens of a camera. Why had she never aimed it in her own direction? This sure and focused feeling now, in a man's arms, was new to her. Grounding. Empowering.

Her past was stolen, made to disappear as if it had never existed. Her present was a rocky road that seemed to have no end. Her future was nothing more than a dim light. The constant along that line was Gray. He shared her past. He shared her present. And if she let herself open up to the possibility, he could share her future.

"Gray." She straightened and met his gaze straight on. "Let me take your picture."

"Me?" Color creeping up his neck, he started to pull away.

With a flick of her hand on his chest, she pushed him into the cushions of the couch. "Yes, you."

"Abbie…"

She dug into the canvas tote and pulled out the camera she'd taken from Serena's attic. The first camera she'd bought for herself. The one that had truly made her believe she could earn a living taking photographs. The compact number fit nicely in her hand. Serena hadn't liked the manual focusing ring because by the time she thought she had her subject focused the expression she'd wanted was gone.

Abbie lifted the camera to her eye. She framed her composition. She adjusted the aperture and depth of field so the background of fieldstones would blur, showing off the strength of Gray's cheekbones, the hint of dimples on his cheeks, the soft curve of his lips, the bottomless depth of his silver eyes. "Let me show you the best in you."

He looked stiff and formal, posing like a model at a shoot. Not for long. She bit down on her lips, holding in the smile bursting to get out. "Gray?"

"Hmm." He leaned back against the couch, throwing an arm carelessly over the folded quilt tossed over the plaid cushion, so blatantly uncomfortable with her attention that her heart softened. Light and shadow played over the planes and angles of his face. Only one thing was missing.

Finger ready on the shutter release, she whispered, "Let me seduce you."

Chapter Fourteen

"What?" Gray's heart jackhammered in his chest, making him wonder if he'd heard right. Seduce him? Abbie? Was he in heaven or in hell?

The camera in her hands flashed at him midstun. What had she captured? Too much. Way too much. The thought sobered him instantly.

"You said I should reach out for what I want." She leaned over him as he sat paralyzed on the couch and kissed him deeply, pouring out all the sunshine that resided inside her into him, frying him as the fire at the gallery almost had.

Then she whispered, "I want you. I've always wanted you. Even when I had to let you go."

The cogs in his mind weren't quite catching right and he couldn't put together a thought that held. "No, Abbie—"

Her smile against his lips winged straight to his groin. "You know, for a guy, you talk too much."

He wanted to take what she was offering. He wanted—But he couldn't. Not until he was sure this wasn't just his fantasy going out of control. Not until his responsibility toward her was done. Not until she was safe and back in her home, in her world. And then she would realize that he didn't fit. He couldn't go back to Echo Falls any more than she could leave it. Nothing had changed. And he wouldn't take advantage of her in this vulnerable state—as much as he wanted to. This was Abbie.

He must be crazy. Certifiable. He was turning down a night with the golden girl of his dreams. *Keep this on a professional level.* Getting Abbie to the trial alive and able to testify—that was the important thing. His job.

Focus on that. Hands off, hotshot. Now back away.

He lifted his hands at his side in surrender, and she took it the wrong way.

Her golden eyes gleamed. Her smile, with its knowing feminine power, set off a chain reaction of raw male response. He cursed, but it didn't do him any good. His hands reached for her. His mouth opened for her. His blood sang for her. He was out of his mind crazy and he couldn't seem to work up enough outrage to get a grip on sanity.

She seduced him with her sweet determination. She seduced him with her intoxicating desire. She seduced him with her hands and her lips and her body.

Palms pressed firmly against his shoulders, she worked her way down his chest, then his ribs. She stroked his hip, his thigh. When she reversed directions and wrapped her fingers around him over the borrowed sweats, he jerked, stopped breathing, stopped thinking. He was helpless to do anything except sink into the pleasure.

Answering her touch with his own, he plunged his hands under her sweatshirt and slow-skidded his palms over every one of her ribs. Her pupils grew wider with every inch of territory he explored, drawing him a step closer to sheer insanity. Her mouth opened as he let his palms rest over her bare breasts, balancing their erotic weight. He couldn't help it, he groaned. He lifted the sweatshirt up and over her head and frowned at the fading bruise on her chest staring down at him. Frowned at the flash drive dangling on its chain, a blatant reminder of everything that was at stake.

He rolled Abbie onto her back on the wide couch, swiped the flash drive out of the way and traced the ugly yellow-green mark with a finger. He bent his head to her chest and kissed the bruise. She'd earned it when he'd tackled her on the island, when the dying sun had caught the steel of Pamela's weapon, warning him of danger.

"You saved my life that day," she said, her voice honey-warm as she guided his hands to her breasts once more. She tangled her fingers in his hair, then moaned in appreciation when he stroked her nipples with his tongue.

"Or maybe you saved mine." The knowing rang through him so clearly, he froze. Why hadn't he seen the obvious before? "Pamela shot three deputy marshals through motel windows. She hit a cop on a running boat." All those times she'd positioned herself far enough to get away cleanly. And she hadn't aimed at Abbie until he'd run up behind her. Pamela had made a clean shot each time, missing him only because he'd tackled Abbie. "But she's missed you all of those times."

"Tonight she shot at both of us." Abbie brushed her fingers at his temple and looked at him as if he could give her everything she wanted.

"That shot through the windshield hit my backrest."

"Oh, Gray. I should never have let you stay." She brought his head down to meet hers and kissed him again. He should object. He just couldn't remember why.

"It wouldn't have mattered," he said. "I couldn't let you face danger alone."

She made him feel warm inside, as if he'd been out in the cold too long and unaware of the ice growing on him. He hadn't closed himself off. Not really. But a guy like him had to put a barrier between him and the world. Abbie made the protection seem unnecessary. As if all she saw, raw and artless, pleased her.

Her hot breath teased his ear. Her hands stroked down the length of his back. One leg hooked over his, pressing his rock-hard cock against her sweet center. The layers of fabric had to go.

He was out of control. Some part of him realized that. Everything became sensation. Somehow what clothes remained came off. He moved, he tasted, he touched, answering her hunger with his. At her urging, he pushed himself into her, slowly, exquisitely fitting her to him. Sheathed in her welcoming warmth, he held himself very still, fighting once more for control.

He'd wanted this for so long, imagined it a thousand different ways. But his mind could never have conjured this unbearable humming of his being like a string drawn too tight, this need so deep it hurt, this love so strong it tortured. Smiling her honey-filled smile, she lifted to meet his thrust, and they settled into a rhythm that brought the whole world into sharp focus.

"Abbie." He was breathless, mindless, helpless. She filled him to overflowing with something he couldn't even name. Was there something bigger than love? If there was, it was Abbie. Not the Abbie of his fantasy but this warm, open, trusting Abbie who looked at him as if he was all she needed. He trembled from head to toe, desperately wanting to pleasure her before he fell apart.

Murmuring in her ear the madness of what she was doing to him, he rocked inside her until she tightened around him. A low cry tore from her throat. She stilled, then shuddered beneath him, gasping as she took him deeper.

The tight coil in him unleashed and spiraled, whipping him right out of this world and into another where all vistas contained Abbie—the golden glow of her honey eyes, the sweetness of her soft smile, the total surrender of her acceptance. A deep groan rumbled in his chest, clawed up his throat and rasped out as he arched up, pulsing inside her.

Right here, right now, he didn't have to be a hero, he simply had to be. For tonight, he was enough. And that was a gift he hadn't even known he'd needed.

Lungs pumping hard, body still quaking from the pleasure they'd shared, he rolled his weight off her and spooned her against him. He shouldn't have let himself be seduced by his golden girl.

The cost was too high.

She'd gone and imprinted herself on his soul.

What would become of him when she went back to Echo Falls?

He tasted the almond-and-honey sweetness of her skin and tumbled the quilt from the back of the couch onto their entwined naked bodies.

She was right. He played for keeps.

For him there would be no other.

He closed his eyes against the inevitable pain of having to let her go a second time. Morning would come too soon. He kissed the top of her head and whispered, "I won't let anything happen to you."

HER MIND WAS FOG. A GOOD FOG. A warm, fuzzy fog. Even better than a movie-marathon kind of fog. She marveled at how well she'd slept, even with the awkward sharing of the couch. For the first time in over a year her dreams hadn't been riddled with nightmares of Rafe and murder—just that wonderful, welcomed fog of contentment.

She loved the feel of Gray, smooth and hard against her. The feel of his hands on her. The weight of his leg tossed over hers, his arm around her waist. She loved how he'd dissolved her worries, her fears—*her*—with his tender attention. Too bad she couldn't bottle this moment and save this closeness, this connection, forever. Then she'd never have to wake up alone again.

For the past year every day had brought nothing but pain, grief and fear. Other than the few messages she'd shared with Brynna, there'd been no one to talk to, to hold, to care for. And every day she'd grown more and more isolated, feeling removed from the world as if she no longer belonged.

Until Gray had bowled back into her life.

She loved him. Always had. Always would.

But as a lance of light speared through the curtains and onto the braided rug on the floor, restlessness invaded her like a summer storm. She was growing too dependent on him. Sleeping like this, sheltered in his arms, felt too good.

How was this different from the life she'd fought to make her own before the mess with Rafe? If she was Gray's, then what would become of her? He'd asked, and she'd willingly given him everything. True, she was the one who'd started the seduction—and enjoyed every second of it.

But nothing had really changed.

She still didn't know what she wanted for herself, out of her future. Did she want Gray simply because he connected her to the scattered parts of herself? Because he was the one person she thought could actually save her from Rafe?

Unable to stand the track of her thoughts, she slipped out of Gray's arms and the cocoon of quilt. A hot shower failed to settle her thoughts. She donned an oversize sweatshirt left behind on the dryer, while her and Gray's clothes spun dry. Then she headed to the kitchen to scrounge up some breakfast, calling herself three kinds of fool.

She couldn't walk away from him because she needed his help to get to the trial alive and defeat Rafe. But even if she didn't need him, she doubted she would leave. Even with all of the doubts traipsing through her mind, she didn't want to let Gray go. Not yet.

The kettle's sharp whistle reminded her that Rafe planned to escape today, that her selfishness could very well put Gray in danger again.

For a few more hours they were safe here and Gray was hers. It would have to be enough. Carrying a mug of coffee and a mug of tea, she went back to the couch, to Gray, to a long goodbye that would have to last a lifetime.

THE CAR WAITED RIGHT WHERE Pamela said it would— outside the gate of this complex of warehouses, hidden behind a billboard that also camouflaged the underground exit. Rafe found the key and the plastic bag with a change of clothes butted against the left front tire without a problem and started the engine right up.

Most people would call him lucky, but luck had nothing to do with his success. Fate was too fickle a friend to trust in a situation like this. Attention to details— that's what put him a cut above.

He was a master artist—just like his namesake. Raphael was known for allegorical figures of Law, Philosophy, Poetry and Theology and for his exquisite harmony and balance of composition. His own mother must have had a premonition of her son's great destiny when she'd named him after her favorite Italian Renaissance painter. History would remember Raphael Vanderveer just as it remembered the original Raphael.

Though Rafe longed to open up the engine of even this subpar government sedan, he glided into Boston traffic as if he belonged there. Cup of coffee on the dash—just as he'd ordered; no one had to know it was stone-cold—he was simply another commuter on his way to the salt mines. The steel bracelets at his ankles and wrists were an unfortunate aberration until he could get to the tools in the trunk. But no one would notice. So few people bothered to get out of their own heads.

Despite al-Khafar's no-show, the task-force morons were still shooting it out with phantom snipers. During all the commotion, he'd slipped a shiv under his lone keeper's bulletproof vest and used the dead man as a shield to simply fade into the background. In the maze of warehouses his laid-out route took him underground and out to freedom. Rafe couldn't help chuckle at the irony that his getaway car belonged to the U.S. Marshals Service motor pool.

His inside contact had balked at such a bald move,

but a deal was a deal. Especially when it guaranteed a worry-free retirement.

Pamela had done good, setting up the automatic training snipers. Too bad he couldn't keep her around much longer. Using the government's own training technology to rev its agents' adrenaline was a stroke of sheer genius.

Just like dozens of other commuters fighting solar glare on this Friday morning, Rafe reached for the cell phone, charged and ready, in the cup holder.

"Where are they?" he asked without preliminaries. Only Pamela had access to the number he'd dialed.

"I'm hurt. Thanks for asking."

Rafe didn't bother responding to her childish pique.

"They're in a cottage on Green Goose Lake."

"Nicely done."

"Do you need me to draw you a map?"

Again he ignored her, seeing in his mind's eye the ugly twist of sarcasm on her face.

"We have a problem," she said. The edge of a tantrum leached into her voice.

Rafe waited. Patience was his virtue.

"Al-Khafar is demanding an explanation."

"For what?" If the twit couldn't come claim his prize when summoned, what did he have to complain about?

"He wants an explanation of your meeting with General Soldatov."

"Soldatov? I've never met anyone named Soldatov."

"He's a Russian."

Well, that explained the anger, but it didn't change the situation.

"Al-Khafar has a picture of you shaking hands with Soldatov," Pamela said. "The picture is dated a week be-

fore your arrest and a week after you told al-Khafar that
the data he wanted wasn't available yet."

"I see." What had Abbie done to him this time? She
was going to pay for this in spades. "Take care of him."

"I can't."

"Why not?"

"I told you. I'm hurt. Reed hit me with his car. My
hip's broken."

Pamela had definitely outlived her usefulness. "Fine.
I'll take care of it myself."

FRIDAY TURNED INTO ONE OF those perfect days where
the temperature wasn't too hot or too cold, where the
sky was an eye-hurting blue and the sun seemed to add
a touch of gold to everything it touched. Outside, the
green water of the lake gleamed, inviting summer swim-
mers to cool off and play. Tree leaves gossiped in the
breeze like teenage girls. The country road wound
around the lake, quiet and serene, empty of all traffic.

But in spite of the perfection of waking up to Abbie
kissing him and riding him, every minute that ticked by
cranked the ligaments on the side of his neck tighter.

Weekend cottages dotted Green Goose Lake, and
this afternoon the owners would start arriving to make
the most of the perfect weather. Would someone notice
the Beasleys' uninvited guests? Would the Beasleys
themselves show up? Track season was over, even if
school wasn't.

Then there was Vanderveer.

Gray's call to Kingsley went unanswered, but if the
op was on, then that wasn't surprising. Every man was
needed to ensure success. He wanted to hear that al-
Khafar had failed to show at the rendezvous. He wanted

to hear that Vanderveer had failed to impress the task force. He wanted to hear that Vanderveer was once again safe behind bars.

Then there was Abbie.

Familiar pain cracked his breastbone. Her remoteness since breakfast as she folded clothes, repacked their bag and neatened the cottage twisted him inside out. The sane side of him said her anxiety was because of the situation with Vanderveer. The vain side of him took that same silence and molded it into rejection—as if he hadn't done enough to reassure her that he could keep her safe.

Then again, maybe she understood that his promises held as much hope as determination.

He'd thought he could handle this —loving her, then letting her go—but he'd forgotten how big a piece of his heart she already owned. He rubbed hard at the pain stringing the tendons along his neck. His heart started racing. His feet couldn't keep still.

When it came down to it, he wasn't a complicated man. He had simple tastes—meat and potatoes, iced tea, classy clothes, classic cars and loud rock and roll. He loved his job. He liked the guys he worked with. And when he wasn't working, he enjoyed sweating and seeing how far he could push his body.

But when it came to Abbie, everything turned complicated.

Only because you're making it complicated.

The key was to break things down to their basic components. The important thing was keeping Abbie safe.

Concentrate on that and everything else'll work itself out.

And what they needed now was a plan. Letting his

love—oh, God, *love!*—interfere would only lead to disaster. They couldn't stay here much longer. Once the weekenders started arriving, keeping hidden would definitely fall into the complicated category, and simple was always better.

There was still the problem of no cash and no car.

Gray glanced at his watch. The meet between Vanderveer and al-Khafar was set for dawn. Six hours ago. If everything had gone right, if al-Khafar had believed Abbie's composite, if the task force had kept a tight leash on Vanderveer, then the situation was over and order restored.

Gray punched Kingsley number again. Once more he got the voice mail.

In the kitchen Abbie, angelic surrounded by a halo of sunlight, kneaded biscuits to go with the can of stew she was heating for lunch. His stomach took a dive. What if he couldn't keep her safe? What if he did fail her?

"After lunch we need to go out and scout." Gray couldn't leave her alone in the cottage. There were too many variables he couldn't control. "If we can find a couple of cans of gas, we can get the car going again."

"Then what?"

She dusted her floury fingers. From the other side of the counter he reached for one hand, entwining her fingers with his. That simple touch made his heart stutter. "Then we find another place to stay."

"What about—"

To his left a window cracked. A canister crashed to the plank floor and rolled toward him. *Flash-bang.* Where the hell had that come from? He shoved Abbie behind the counter. Aluminum powder burst from the bottom of the canister. It hung in the air, then flared like a peacock's tail five feet in diameter before combining with the room's oxygen and exploding.

A bright plume of light blinded him. The acoustic pulse deafened him. The sonic wave knocked him on his butt, stunning and disorienting him. The still-burning flash landed on his pant leg and burned like a son of a bitch. "Abbie!"

Another flash-bang exploded, flooring him a second time.

He tried getting up, skidded like a drunk, unable to tell which side was up. He couldn't see a thing. His ears rang as if he'd gone ten rounds with a heavyweight champion. "Abbie!"

He made it to his hands and knees, solid floor beneath both. He bumped his head against the island counter and patted his way to the other side. Nothing. "Abbie!"

A third device bowled him down.

By the time the smoke cleared, by the time his vision started to return, by the time the ringing in his ears went down a hundred decibels, the back door yawed open and Abbie was gone.

Chapter Fifteen

Abbie's body tumbled around as if she were falling down an endless, black, narrow hole.

She came to a stop with an abrupt halt and something hard digging into her side, arms and legs stuck together yet askew. Just as quickly she was jerked forward again and pitched against another hard surface. The smell of sweat and gasoline slammed into her. A trunk. She was locked in the trunk of a moving car. Her mouth, wrists and ankles bound with duct tape.

Rafe. Oh, God, he'd escaped. He'd found her.

He'd done what he'd said he would.

Now he was going to kill her.

Eyes wet with tears, she fought against the duct tape.

Gray! The last time she'd seen him, he'd been holding her floury fingers, looking as if he wanted to kiss her again, and she'd been thinking how she wanted him to. The whole world had seemed bathed with gold before it all exploded.

Was he here, too?

Like a turtle on its back, she frantically rolled her way around the tight space. But there was nothing. Not even her tote bag.

Gray!

The bomb? Had it hit Gray? Was he hurt? A bloody vision of all the death she'd caused swam through her mind—the three deputy marshals, the young cop, her father—and her tears redoubled. Her worst fear was coming true. Protecting her had put his life in danger.

She'd told herself Gray was different. That he was strong. Smart. That he couldn't die as all her other protectors had. Last night she'd reached out to him. He'd loved her back. What had she thought would change with the passage of time? She hadn't needed to find herself all those years ago. She'd belonged with Gray. She'd loved him then. She still loved him. And now that they'd found each other again, they couldn't just leave their relationship like that, without knowing where it could go.

Her breath stuttered in her lungs, impeded by the duct-tape gag. *Gray, please, be alive.*

She had to survive. She had to get away. She had to make sure he was all right. She hadn't told him she still loved him, that she was sorry for hurting him, that she wanted another chance. That this time she'd follow him to the end of the world—no questions asked—if it meant she could be with him.

The hum of tires on asphalt spun at a good clip. They must be on the highway. Route 2 or Highway 91? Which direction? Where was Rafe taking her?

As long as the car was moving, he held the advantage, but once the car stopped, once he raised the lid of the trunk, she'd have an opportunity to take him by surprise. He would expect her to cower, not fight. He'd never seen her strength—not the way Gray had.

She wriggled her way to the edge of the trunk and

patted all around the lining for something—a sharp edge, a tool—to cut the duct tape. Even after her eyes adjusted somewhat to the darkness, she could spot no neon trunk-release handle. This had to be an older model, not Rafe's own car.

Her hands stilled against the rough carpet of the trunk and the beat of her racing heart filled her ears.

What if it wasn't Rafe who'd kidnapped her? What if he'd sent Pamela instead? Or muscle? Maybe this was just an interim ride.

It didn't matter. She resumed her frenzied search for something sharp enough to tear through duct tape. No matter, she wouldn't alter the basic plan. It was good. If she caught the driver by surprise, she still had a chance to get away, to get back to Gray.

On the top part of the trunk, the pointed end of a screw scratched her fingertips. She positioned the duct tape on the miniature cutter and sawed with all her might, scraping as much skin as tape. Sweat ran in rivulets down the side of her face, stinging her eyes. Heat sapped her energy, weighting her wrists as if cement cuffed them. Lack of air made her lungs burn with her exertion.

Gray's face floated in the mist of her mind, joining the parade of ghosts already haunting her conscience. She refused to give up. She had to have the chance to tell Gray all the things she'd been afraid to say last night.

With one last jab at the screw, she freed her wrists. She ripped off the mouth tape, winced and gulped in air. Then she attacked her ankles.

Now what? *Now you prepare for action.*

Deciding that the illusion of captivity might buy her an extra second of response time, she restuck the tape around the hem of her jeans and the cuffs of her sweat-shirt. If she coupled her wrists and ankles, whoever opened the trunk would think her still tied. Seeing her like that, he'd likely put his weapon away because he'd need both hands to haul her out.

Rafe wouldn't kill her. Not right away. Not until he got the flash drive. Her hand reached for the slim stick hiding beneath her T-shirt. She couldn't let him get it.

Hands more mobile now, she tried to orient herself. On *Oprah,* she'd once heard of a woman who'd escaped her captor by kicking out the taillight and catching another driver's attention. Patting her way around the edge of the trunk, she located the taillights on the passenger's side. A hard metal piece housed the mechanism. She swore. This wasn't fair. Why was the car too old for a trunk-release handle but too new for a flimsy taillight housing?

So, you're going to give up. Just like that?

She kicked at the metal housing, imagining Rafe's face with each blow.

The driver began a side-to-side movement that tossed her around like a rag. Because of the noise? Still, she fought for some sort of purchase and kicked until the housing caved. The dent had popped off a piece of the plastic light, bringing in a shaft of day. With a swallowed *yes!* of victory Abbie yanked the flash drive from the chain and dropped it through the hole, praying for a miracle. She stuck one finger as deeply into the hole as she could and wriggled it, hoping it would attract another driver's attention.

Maybe nobody would find the flash drive, but it wouldn't end up in Rafe's hands either. And if she was lucky, then someone would turn it in to the police.

Sweat slicked her body. Her arm, twisted in an odd position, ached.

Was no one else out there on the road? How long had they been moving? How far were they going? She closed her eyes and relived Gray's hand being ripped from hers, falling, the whole world bursting white, then vanishing into black. Gray had to be all right. Tears climbed up her throat once more. *If you're going to do Gray any good, you have to stay strong.* She sniffed back the tears and concentrated on her plan.

In her head she rehearsed every step, seeing herself perform with calm and power. When the car slowed, she would position herself on her back so that when the trunk opened, she could punch at her captor with her legs. A self-defense instructor on some television talk show had once said that women's legs were their strongest point. Her captor would fall to the ground. As he tried to scramble up, she would run, fast and far. She saw it all executed like a perfect ballet.

Ironic really that the hours she'd spent watching television, retreating from the nightmare of the past year, were now going to help save her.

This time she was going to win. This time, Rafe would be the one getting hurt.

The road under the tires bumped more roughly. A sharp turn unbalanced her and threw her against the sides as if she were a loose bag of groceries. Bracing her hands against one side, she rode out the bumps that jostled her up and down and side to side.

The car slowed, then stopped. She rolled onto her back. Her heart jumped in her chest. The driver turned off the engine. Her blood whooshed in her ears. The driver's door creaked open. Her pulse went haywire.

This was it. Breath held, heart boomeranging inside her chest, she bent her knees and waited for the trunk to open.

STILL STRUGGLING WITH disorientation, Gray grabbed the cell phone and punched in Kingsley's number. His weapon was gone. Abbie was gone. "He's got Abbie."

"Who's got Abbie?"

"Vanderveer. He set off flash-bangs to knock me down and kidnapped her right under my nose while I was flopping like a fish. He's got her. *He's got her!*"

"Okay, okay. We'll find her. I've got to let Falconer in on this. We'll find her."

"Yeah, right, thanks." Kingsley was right, of course. Panicking wouldn't get him any closer to Abbie. He had to use his strength. Outside he oriented himself, looking for what was left behind. Shoes. Men's shoes. Not boots. Not Pamela. The tracks moved awkwardly toward the road, twin trails dragging behind them. Abbie? Unconscious? Dead? *Don't go there.* She was alive. He would know if she was dead. He would feel it. He rubbed at the ache in his chest and kept deciphering the track. He followed the trail to a thicket of trees two cottages down. They ended where tire tracks began.

"Where are you?" Kingsley asked.

"Green Goose Lake."

"I'll send Mercer down to pick you up."

Gray stalked the tire tracks to the main road, where they turned south.

"Where would someone with an alphabet soup of law enforcement after them go?" Gray asked more to himself than because he expected Kingsley to come up with an answer.

"He'd stick to side roads," Kingsley said.

"He'd have a safe house ready and waiting."

"Somewhere with options. Somewhere not easily visible."

"Yeah, murder's a private thing."

"Somewhere along 91, where he could head north to Canada or south to Connecticut or even escape by boat if he had to."

"That's over two hundred miles of territory. There has to be an easier way."

Gray examined the lake road. Its mouth opened on Route 10. He and Abbie had left the beater he'd bought with what was left of their money along Route 10.

"Pamela," Gray said. "I clipped her good. I didn't play Good Samaritan, but I dialed 9-1-1. If she broke a leg, she couldn't have gotten away before the ambulance reached her."

"I'll call up hospitals around Shelburne Falls and see if any woman was admitted with a leg or hip injury from a car accident."

"She might not use her real name."

"I figured as much. Mercer's on his way."

If Pamela had gone to the hospital, her car was still near the Serendipity Gallery. Gray started running. "Tell him I'm on my way to Shelburne Falls."

"What for?" Kingsley asked.

"Answers." Because he couldn't just sit here and wait while Abbie was in danger. He had to find her.

Gray had gone into every job knowing that the violent people he chased might turn on him and something might go wrong. He put himself on the line and accepted the odds because he was driven to do so. But not Abbie. She hadn't signed on for this. His stomach knotted at the thought of Vanderveer getting his hands on her. If Vanderveer hurt one hair on her head, if Gray lost his second chance with Abbie because of that piece of garbage, he swore Vanderveer would pay. Big-time.

SOMEONE TURNED THE KEY ON the lock of the trunk. As sunlight crept into the opening, Abbie blinked but kept her aim centered at the black shadow in the middle. As soon as the trunk clearance gave her enough space, she thrust her legs out and connected with air.

Something hard pounded against her temple. Pain exploded, scrambling her brain and making her see stars.

"We'll have no repeat of that, shall we?" Rafe said as he yanked her out of the car by her hair.

Pain tore through her skull, pounded. She couldn't quite balance on her feet and sagged. Rafe wrenched her up again. Gray's face floated on a wave of dizziness. His smile encouraged her. She couldn't pass out. She had to keep fighting.

Kick. Do something. Don't just take it like a sitting duck.

But brain and body couldn't seem to coordinate their messages, and all her effort gained her was a floundering of arms and legs.

Rafe's hand grabbed her neck and squeezed, lifting her until her vision went hazy and her breath raspy. "Enough of that, do you understand?"

Wheezing, she nodded.

Hand still wrapped around her windpipe, Rafe jerked her toward the house, forcing her to scuttle beside him with her head at an awkward angle. Her hands couldn't punch effectively. Her legs couldn't kick without tightening the squeeze.

For a second as they headed to the cottage she thought all they'd done was drive in one long circle around Green Goose Lake. This cabin could be a twin of the one they'd borrowed. Then the details focused. A twin with nicer clothes. The house was bigger. The lake was wider. The lot was spacier and more wooded. From here she couldn't see the road, which also meant no one could see her at the mercy of a madman. He could do whatever he wanted with her and no one would see or hear.

A brick grill sat on the deck. Fairy lights ringed the stairs and the railing. A patio table of redwood with six matching chairs and a hunter-green umbrella waited as if a party was just about to start. All that was missing was the people.

No witnesses. Just the way Rafe liked to do murder.

Her father had died for her, for the town he loved. But she wasn't ready to sacrifice her life. Not while she could still fight.

She was going to wait for an opportunity. She was going to get Rafe. Then she was going to make him pay for all he'd done to her, her family and her town. She'd make Rafe suffer until he wished he was dead.

Her anger gave her courage, and she desperately tried to hang on to it and let it cover her fear.

She tripped on a stair and gagged when Rafe's grip on her throat didn't loosen. She grabbed onto his white dress shirt so she wouldn't hang herself on the noose of his fingers, and he dragged her up the rest of the way. Once inside, he shoved her to the ground. She skidded on a bruised hip until the floor of polished maple slats gave way to terra-cotta kitchen tile and her head cracked against a kitchen cabinet.

Hands clutching at her throat, she gasped for air and

coughed, unable to do anything to defend herself against the monster standing at her feet.

"Where is it?" Rafe asked, hands on hips, looking down at her as if she were vermin.

Her throat worked, but only a strangled sound came out.

He made a great show of putting on latex gloves, as if he were dealing with something dirty and he had to keep contamination to a minimum. He dumped the contents of her canvas tote onto the counter and started rifling through the items, discarding things with a careless swipe of his hand. She pushed herself up only to have Rafe's foot shove her back down.

"The question is simple, Abrielle. Where is the photo?"

Her tongue felt too thick. Blood seemed to coat her throat. Her words spit out in an unintelligible tangle. All the while she frantically searched for something to use as a weapon. The knife block was too high. The decorative stone painted with a curled-up fox was too far. Even the ceramic dog bowl was out of her reach. Her hand splayed on the tile and she used the suction to pull herself up and away from her tormentor.

Rafe grasped the hose attachment on the kitchen sink and turned it on full blast into her mouth and up her nose. She sputtered, trying vainly to scramble out of the way. "Last chance, Abrielle. Where is that photo?"

"Studio," she croaked, choking and backhanding the water dripping from her face.

"See, now, that wasn't so hard." He crouched beside her and laid a hand on her shoulder as if he were a benevolent uncle. Then he started pinching the clavicle and scapula. The right shoulder. The clavicle he knew she'd already broken. "Now tell me, where is the photo?"

"Studio." Teeth jamming her lips tight, she fought his grip and the spreading panic the thought of more pain unleashed. "I don't have it with me. It's at my studio."

"Now, what did I tell you, Abrielle? I want the truth. I had your studio searched and it wasn't there."

She worked her throat against the pain of bone near its cracking point, lubricating her lie so it would sound like the truth. "Hidden."

"Where?"

"Please let go."

"Answer first."

"I'll have to show you. You'll never find it."

"No, sorry." A little more pressure and the bone bowed. "Tell me."

"It's in a hidden panel. Under the floor. I'll show you."

He eased up, loosening his grip so fast that Abbie actually felt the clavicle spring back into place. She rubbed at the bruise, willing the nausea back down.

"Okay," he said, his dark, dead eyes piercing hers. There was nothing there. No emotions. "We'll move on to question number two. Remember that the truth will save you a lot of pain, and I've learned the art of pain this past year. Are we understood?"

Afraid to speak, she nodded.

"What did you send al-Khafar?"

"I tell you, you kill me."

"You don't tell me, you die anyway."

She gulped. Not yet. She had to stretch her time here with Rafe. Give the task force hunting Rafe a chance to find him. Either way, Rafe wasn't getting out of this alive.

"Studio," she said. "I can show you what I did there."

He patted her cheek, and she gritted her teeth against his touch. "You must think me stupid."

She shook her head. "No, I'll give you whatever you want."

His finger skimmed the underside of her jaw. A lecherous smile oiled his lips. "Everything?"

She stared at him, not daring to answer.

He hauled her up by the front of her sweatshirt and dumped her unceremoniously into a kitchen chair.

Using duct tape he tied her legs to the chair legs and cuffed her hands behind her back. He dragged the chair to the edge of the wall and left her there like a naughty child. "Don't move."

He turned away and reached for a cell phone, pacing the length of the counter separating the kitchen area from the living room.

Keeping half her attention on Rafe, she scanned the living room. She struggled to free her hands, but the tape was wound too tight. Each time she turned her head, a searing pain lanced up and down the sides of her abused neck. She couldn't stand. She couldn't run. All she could do was bend forward. But she wasn't going to just sit there and wait for Rafe to kill her.

Pay attention, Abbie. Look. There has to be something you can use.

To her right, on a shelf unit filled with paperbacks, a stereo system and a pile of board games, she spied a small digital camera. If she could reach it, she could do to Rafe what he'd done to her and Gray—blind him with light. Would that be enough to reach for the gun tucked in his waistband?

Rafe had a lot riding on the two photographs burned onto the flash drive. The one of him killing her father wouldn't make or break his case—just make it more difficult. The one of him with the Russian general could cost him a lot more.

If she didn't show him how she'd done the composite, he would have no proof he hadn't betrayed his contact. She edged the chair until she could slip her bound hands through the back bars. Stretching her shoulders and arms as far as they would go, she reached for the small camera on the shelf. Too far. She rolled her shoulders back until the strained clavicle threatened to pop out of its socket. The bruise on her right side throbbed. Breathing in short, shallow pants, she managed to work through the pain.

Her fingertips finally brushed against the chrome body. Millimeter by millimeter she drew it closer. She tried for a side scoop. Her tense arm jerked, knocking the camera off the shelf.

No, not now. Not when I'm this close. She rounded her spine backward and forced her hands down farther, catching the end of the cord with the crook of one finger.

Breath held, she glanced at Rafe, who was still engrossed in his conversation.

Then excruciatingly slowly she wound the strap around her fingers until the body lay square in her palm.

Rafe cut his call and turned to face her. Keeping unflagging eye contact with Rafe, she held on tight to the camera.

"We're going back to Echo Falls." He caressed her cheek and bent down for a kiss. At the last second she swerved sideways. And while his lips seared her cheek, she skewed her bound hands to one side as if catching her balance and slipped the camera into the kangaroo pouch of the overlarge sweatshirt she wore. "Don't worry your pretty little head, my sweet. No one will be looking for us there. They're all chasing their shadows hundreds of miles away, thanks to your old friend Phil Auclair."

Phil? Phil was the one who'd betrayed her? She'd trusted him. Bared her soul to him. Who better, then, to know what would hurt most.

With one gloved hand Rafe squashed her cheeks and forced her glance to meet his. "It's only fitting, after all, that you should die where both your parents did. You were such a close little family."

Chapter Sixteen

Gray found Pamela's car parked not far from what was left of the Serendipity Gallery, nose out, ready for a quick departure.

Plain brown on the outside, it nevertheless packed a lot of horses under the hood and housed enough electronics on the dash to give a pilot cockpit envy.

As he sat in the driver's seat, the empty holster at his side seemed to mock him. If his own bullet killed Abbie, Gray could never forgive himself. A helpless, savage anger roared through him. Abbie would not die. Not on his watch. He redoubled his effort to learn all he could from what Pamela had left behind.

The painfully neat car gave up nothing other than the bank of electronics. He stared at the various screens. Most were dark, but a few showed LED readings. He punched Kingsley's number into his phone. "I found Pamela's car. It was still parked near the gallery."

"I'll give Mercer your location. He's on his way to Brattleboro Memorial in Vermont. It's nineteen miles from Shelburne Falls. You were right—she's listed as Lara Bancroft. Broken hip and leg, bruised ribs."

Gray hoped her every breath was a trip to hell. "Make them take away her painkillers."

"I'll pass on your request." The snap of Kingsley's suspenders popped over the line. "We got a tip on Vanderveer's location."

"Yeah?"

"According to an inside source, he's still in Boston in an abandoned warehouse."

"The same inside source who's been whispering sweet information into Vanderveer's ear?"

"Auclair," Kingsley said. "Falconer's watching him like a hawk."

Suspicions needed the backup of proof.

"I need to know what these things do." Gray described the gadgets that seemed to operate on a battery backup, since the key wasn't in the ignition to feed them juice.

"That last one's a tracking device," Kingsley said.

"The dot just started moving." Abbie? Who else? It had to be Abbie. Getting Abbie had been Pamela's focus from the start. His heart jumped with hope. If the dot was moving, Abbie was alive. He wouldn't entertain any other possibility until he'd found her again. "I made Abbie get rid of everything she had. How could—" Gray swore and hit the steering wheel with the heels of both hands.

"What?"

"Steeltex," Gray said, spitting out the word. "How does it work?"

"It transmits visual information about color, light and patterns through the fiber to make whoever wears it nearly invisible against any background."

"Could it also give information about location?"

"Microdots are woven in to locate a downed soldier.

The latest model contains conductive fibers in the chest area that can monitor the vital functions of an injured soldier. This information can be relayed by wireless signal to a remote location like a field hospital."

He should have figured it out sooner. The only thing that had followed them the whole trip was the piece of Steeltex that had ripped from Pamela's suit as she'd run from him. He'd picked it up because it was classified material and he didn't want the locals to question its presence on the island.

"Abbie," Gray said, searching for keys under the floor mat, in the glove box, under the seat. "I know where she is."

"Read me the coordinates."

Gray started reading the numbers and the phone cut off. "Kingsley?"

No answer, just dead air.

He'd run out of minutes.

No keys. No time for finesse. He shoved the car in neutral and pulled up the parking brake. In the toolbox in the trunk he located a flat-blade screwdriver. Under the hood he ran a wire from the positive side of the battery to the positive side of the coil. He crossed the two wires on the starter using the screwdriver. The engine cranked over. Using the screwdriver he unlocked the steering wheel and pushed the locking pin away from the wheel. He nosed the car onto the road and floored the accelerator.

The blip on the radar kept to side roads and meandered as if it had no particular destination. Gray followed, driving as fast as he dared on the winding roads. As long as the blip kept moving, he had a chance to catch up, a chance to get Abbie back. He'd messed up last night by not telling her she still owned his heart, that the address of his real estate didn't mean anything to him as long as she shared it with him. He could make her happy, and she sure as hell made him feel good.

The prickling feeling at the back of his neck was fire-ant biting and burning. He had to get to Abbie. He had to find his golden girl in time.

Then the blip veered onto a too-familiar path.

Echo Falls.

He mashed the accelerator to the floor, giving all three hundred horses their heads.

But he was still too far away.

THE CAR CRESTED THE HILL, AND below him sprawled the town Rafe had once seen as the answer to his dreams.

"It makes such a picture, doesn't it?" he said. "Why don't you ever do landscapes?"

Abrielle simply stared out the window, ignoring him. Her wrists and ankles were bound. She couldn't escape him. And he pointed the pistol—Reed's pistol; the irony was so delicious he could barely stand it—at her, insuring her cooperation. For a second he let go of the steering wheel and yanked her face in his direction. "You will look at me when I'm speaking to you."

Her eyes were topaz-hard, but she obeyed.

All Rafe had worked for had come down to this. This chapter of his life would end where it had started. Echo Falls.

The slice of small-town America had come to him as a blessing. The picture-postcard perfection of it even had the stone bridge he'd seen in his vision. It had a close-knit community where Labor Day parades, win-ter carnivals, spring maple sugarings and summer strawberry festivals brought everyone outdoors. A perfect little town, with its own first family—the powerful Holbrooks of Holbrook Mills.

"I could have made it great," Rafe said, admiring the scallop of houses against the horizon and the mountains almost black in the background.

"By what?" Abrielle jeered. "Raping it? Just like you raped me."

He pried the tip of the pistol between two ribs and pressed. She winced. Instant respect. Why had his father made the notion seem so complicated?

Rafe had seen himself as part of it all, taking in the populace's adulation at all these functions. Abrielle would have made the perfect wife. She would have borne him perfect sons. And he would have grown this town, shown them what they could become under his guidance.

He would have had all his father had—fortune, family, fealty—and made it better.

His dream had grown on track. Until the preparations to bid for the Steeltex contract had started.

Holbrook had questioned Rafe's intentions. The fool had insisted on digging himself further into the red, putting peons ahead of profits, and almost lost the mill to his creditors. If Rafe hadn't been there to make sure things changed, they would never have won the Steeltex contract, never have gotten back management of the mill. They wouldn't have built up the company back into the black.

"Rape? I raped nothing. Our night of passion was consensual."

"Except for the part where you drugged me."

"Simply an unmasking of inhibitions. You were so

shy and there was no reason for it. As for your little town, I saved it. I got the mill operating again. Where would all these people be now if I hadn't found a way to make a profit?"

And if he hadn't found a way to make terrorists pay for the expensive production start-up costs that went into making Steeltex, the taxpayers would have had to foot a much larger bill.

But did anyone acknowledge his brilliance? No. Holbrook had turned his back on him, demanding his resignation. Abrielle had ignored him, preferring to spend time in her studio. He'd had to do something to get both their attention. He deserved it after all he'd done for them.

Her gaze latched on to his eyes as if she wanted to scratch them out. He rewarded her insolence with renewed pressure from the pistol's muzzle. Doubling over, she still managed to say, "They'd still be here with their families instead of having to look elsewhere to replace the jobs you cut from underneath them."

He jabbed the pistol's muzzle deeper into her flesh and twisted, his finger itching to press the trigger. She gave a satisfying grunt of pain. "It's a business we're running, Abrielle, not a charity. Without profit there's no growth."

"There are more important things than profit. My father understood that."

"Your father was a weak man." And weakness, Rafe had learned from his own father, was always exploited.

"My father was a good man, an honest man."

Rafe turned onto Mill Road. "I admire your loyalty. It's a good trait in a daughter. In a wife."

"I never planned to marry you. Not even after the baby."

He'd tried to do the right thing. Once he'd found out

she was pregnant with his child, he'd asked her father for his daughter's hand. Holbrook's answer: "Not as long as I'm alive." Well, what choice had Rafe had?

His child had been at stake. He couldn't let anyone take his son away from him.

Then once he'd been jailed under false pretenses, she'd cheated him out of what was his. She'd gone and aborted their child. *His* son.

For the anguish he'd suffered, for the time he'd lost, for the perfection of the vision she'd destroyed, he had to punish her.

And once she'd fixed her mistakes with the photographs, gave him back his insurance, he would close this chapter and start new elsewhere.

The detour sign led him away from the bridge and the upper side of town. Soon the stone bridge faded in his side mirror, and he wound down to the lower part of town.

They could take the town, the mill and the girl away from him, but they couldn't erase all the knowledge he'd collected over the past few years. Technology, intellect and good business-management skills were always in demand. Like his namesake, he would paint himself a new vision.

GRAY SWORE AND EASED HIS FOOT off the accelerator. Too late. Vanderveer had made him and was now taking evasive action. Gray had let impatience and fear drive him, and his lack of control had put Abbie in greater danger.

Narrow roads and kids out playing on the streets forced Gray to slow down even more. He needed to get Vanderveer away from the populated part of town to where he couldn't hurt any innocent bystanders. His brain mapped out the spider web of the streets he'd raced through all of his youth. He knew them inside and out. Shortcuts and the long way around. Vanderveer was still a newcomer.

Gray cut Vanderveer off at Summer Street, forcing him around Library Road. Anticipating ahead, Gray sped to Mechanic Lane and intersected Library Road in time to convince Vanderveer he wanted to take High Street and go up to the upper village. Watching the horizon, he took in movement in his peripheral vision. A mother trying to juggle two kids, a stroller and a diaper bag, stepped into the crosswalk in front of the library. She froze at the sight of Vanderveer rocketing toward her.

Too late to brake. *Look at where you want to go, not what you want to avoid.* Gray stared past the woman at the opposite sidewalk, willing Vanderveer to do the same.

Vanderveer twisted the steering wheel left and narrowly avoided the woman and her kids. Gray followed suit. A quick peek in his rearview mirror showed the woman huddled safe on the sidewalk, comforting her two crying kids.

Plotting his course, Gray left Library Road at Prospect Street and went around the Pine Grove Cemetery. He popped in front of Vanderveer, compelling him to charge toward Mill Road. There Vanderveer could turn either right or left. Right would take him to the mill, where armed guards stood. Left to the bridge still awaiting repairs. Either way he was toast.

Vanderveer turned left, accelerating now that the road was clear. Nothing but grass fields on either side of the road. Gray followed close behind and prayed Vanderveer didn't make a mistake. Not with Abbie in the car.

Gray had to get him to stop before the bridge. He accelerated, edging his right front bumper along the left rear flank of Vanderveer's car in hopes of sending it spinning onto the grass.

Vanderveer's car spun around, but he got control and plowed through the orange detour-warning sign and the construction barricade. He picked up more speed, intending to hurtle through the gate on the other side.

Gray braked, cursing Vanderveer. He was going to drive right into the granite blocks piled and waiting for repairs to begin. The bastard was going to kill himself and Abbie rather than face the consequences of his actions.

Vanderveer's car screeched to a halt, burning rubber. Trapped with nowhere to go but through Gray or into the water.

Gray steered Pamela's car sideways, blocking Vanderveer's car on the bridge.

To his relief, too-blond hair on the passenger's side bobbed through the smoky glass of the windshield. Abbie was alive. But his relief was short lived. Vanderveer could still kill her—especially if he felt he had nothing to lose.

Engine idling, he waited, hands tight around the steering wheel. System in overdrive, everything in him urged for action.

Vanderveer was armed. Even if Pamela hadn't cached him any weapons, he'd stolen Gray's. A trapped rat tended to panic, and the last thing Gray wanted was for Vanderveer to use Abbie as a shield.

Vanderveer executed a one-hundred-and-eighty-degree turn and revved the engine as if he was about to ram into Gray's car. Instead the car crept forward—just out of pistol range. In case Gray had acquired another weapon? Maybe Vanderveer wasn't as stupid as he looked.

Keeping his focus on Vanderveer's every move, Gray spared Abbie a glance, and a fist squeezed at his heart. Her dyed hair made a beacon against the smoked glass. He couldn't see her expression, but her posture was warrior-princess ready. *Don't do anything foolish, Abbie.*

Bright sun reflected off rushing water below, making him squint. The day was warm, a stark contrast to the cold icing his gut. Cornering Vanderveer without backup was stupid, but he couldn't let Abbie out of his sight. He had to get Abbie back. He had to keep her safe.

Using the door as armor—not that it would provide much cover—Gray stood, dangling the flash drive he'd found on his run to Shelburne Falls between two fingers. "I have what you want. I'll trade you your freedom for Abbie."

Vanderveer's side window opened. "Do you take me for a fool? For all I know, that stick simply holds your collection of X-rated calendar girls."

The bully had aged, but his tactics hadn't. Once, Gray had feared retaliation, so had turned to carefree posturing and shades. He was never in his own skin. Not at school, not in the Navy, not in the Marshals Service. And most of the time not even at Seekers. Only with Abbie had he been able to risk being himself.

How could he have missed how empty his life was because of his fear of letting anyone see his real feelings? If he'd had the courage to do so earlier, how much richer would his life be now? Why did he have to wait so damn long to figure things out?

This time he had to fight the bully naked—no shades and no posturing. He didn't care about image, about looking weak, about avoiding being the target. All that mattered was Abbie and keeping her sunshine beaming.

Vanderveer wanted to play games; Gray had been playing this one all of his life. "I take you for a highly intelligent man with a strong survival instinct. You want to live. I want you to live. And this—" Gray waved the flash drive "—holds what you need to get your freedom."

"Consider the source."

"Yeah, consider him. He wants the girl. Do you think he'd do anything to jeopardize that? And you want the photographs. We trade. We both win."

"Why would you want someone who rejected you thirteen years ago?" Vanderveer scoffed.

Because she brightens every life she touches. "Some of us get stuck in the past. For me, life hasn't been good since I left Abbie behind."

"What can you possibly offer someone poised and polished like Abrielle?"

Love. Something Vanderveer couldn't because he couldn't feel—not love, not anything. If love was a fault, then Gray was a willing victim. "Nothing. I can give her nothing except myself."

"A loser and a coward. You live with dregs. What kind of a life is that?"

A good one. *One that takes scum like you off the streets and puts them behind bars where they belong.* "That's right, Vanderveer. I'm a loser and a coward. But either way I have what you want. And you can have it if I get Abbie back."

"I don't need what's on that flash drive. I always get what I want. With or without the photographs I will go on with my life."

"Without the photographs, you can avoid jail. With them, you won't ever get out again. Al-Khafar is ready to sing."

"Al-Khafar isn't in custody. He never showed."

"Because he was stopped before you arrived."

Even through the smoky glass Gray could see Vanderveer's derisive shake of the head. "And here I thought that perhaps you did have a modicum of intelligence. I had snipers waiting. How else do you think I got away? Al-Khafar never showed."

"Can you take the risk?" Gray asked.

"Can you?"

Gray held up Pamela's BlackBerry. "Dates and times. I've got 'em." He'd hoped he wouldn't have to play this card. The government needed this data to close the case against Vandervecr—not just for murder but for treason—and to figure out the extent of the damage Vanderveer's treason had done. Falconer's voice wavered through his conscience. *It's not just Abrielle, Reed. There's WITSEC's reputation and the lives of soldiers at stake.* Gray shut off the voice and focused on the situation on the bridge. "It's all here in Pamela's appointment book. Every time you met with al-Khafar, what he purchased from you and when."

"You're making a big deal out of nothing." Boredom listed through Vanderveer's voice.

Gray started reading the information in the data window. "June 13, Pamela notes that you've ordered her to shoot anyone guarding her. The date matches the shooting death of a Maine cop. June 12, Pamela notes you ordered her to retrieve a Steeltex uniform from behind the false backing in your bedroom closet. June 10, Pamela notes that you've ordered her to shoot the deputy marshal who was guarding Abrielle but to take care not to hit the subject or Phil Auclair—"

"Pamela is simply an overeager assistant. I can't help

her delusions. You have nothing there that can incriminate me in any way. I was in custody at the time. I conducted no business, as per the rules."

"Oh, okay. Let's scroll back further then. Let's see…here we go. March 17 of last year. You met al-Khafar in a Boston pub and for a mere million sold him a sample Steeltex uniform. April 10, you met him at the Public Gardens on the Common and arranged for delivery of half a dozen uniforms. Ah, looks like you got more this time. What, no bulk discount?" Gray tsked as he pressed the button to scroll down. "Need more? Doesn't look good, Vanderveer. Especially with Pamela in custody. She's going to want immunity. What do you think she'll trade for that? It's such a bitch trying to run with a broken hip and leg. No chance for her to get away. She'll have to sing."

Vanderveer remained sitting still, pistol—Gray's own Glock—pointed at Abbie's head. A surge of terror blasted through him, drenching him in sweat, but Gray suppressed it. No matter what, Vanderveer was going to shoot them both. He had to stay open for an opportunity to give Abbie a chance to flee.

"Open all the car doors," Vanderveer said.

He probably wanted to make sure no one was hiding in the back seat, that Gray was indeed alone. Armed, Vanderveer had the advantage and knew it. Gray did as he was asked.

"Walk toward me."

Below him water hurtled over rocks and crashed over pilings. Defenseless, hands up at his sides, flash drive and handheld computer cupped in his palm, he took easy steps forward.

"Stop."

Gray obeyed. The fight-or-flight response had kicked in big-time, washing adrenaline into his system, making his nerves jittery. He wished for shades to dim the sun's glare and hide his eyes. But even without the prop he was good at making himself look relaxed.

"Now hand over the computer."

Gray shook his head as if he was truly sorry he couldn't cooperate. "Not until I see Abbie."

"Look through the window."

"Make her get out of the car. When she's halfway to me, I'll put down the flash drive and the BlackBerry and back away."

Vanderveer opened his car door and, as Gray had done, used the door as a shield. Pointing the pistol at Abbie, he ordered her to get out. "Come to me."

Abbie got out of the car. Her gaze jumped from Vanderveer to him and back. She was going to take a chance. She was going to bolt. *Don't do it, Abbie.*

"I'll shoot him," Vanderveer said. "Do you understand?"

Abbie nodded and shuffled around the car, her ankles bound with duct tape. Ugly bruises purpled her legs beneath her shorts. Vanderveer was going to pay for each and every bruise he'd put on her.

"You're looking for a fight that doesn't have to happen," Vanderveer said as he hooked an arm around Abbie's chest and butted the pistol against her temple. "Whatever happens here is your fault. If she's hurt, if she dies, it's on your conscience."

The only way to beat a bully, Gray learned long ago, was to pretend you were smaller and weaker—make them look big by letting them make you look small.

Don't let them see your pain.

Helpless to help Abbie, Gray could only watch as Vanderveer shoved her forward and melded into one grotesque silhouette against the glaring sun.

"Put the computer down," Vanderveer ordered.

"Let Abbie go."

"I'm in control here, Reed. Put the damn computer down."

Just as Gray was about to put down the stick and computer, Abbie jerked her bound hands out of the kangaroo pouch of the sweatshirt she wore. Her fist, curled around something he couldn't quite make out, thrust upward.

A flash went off.

Then a gun.

Chapter Seventeen

Abbie was afraid. More afraid than she'd ever been. Everything around her took on a surreal quality—the stabbing sun, the roiling water, the pitted granite. But she couldn't let Rafe win because if she did, then all of those who'd died protecting her had done so in vain. For a year she'd cowered in fear. She'd become someone else. She'd given up all she cared for—family, friends, career. For a year she'd beaten back her grief with only one goal in mind—make Rafe pay for murdering her father in cold blood. She wasn't going to give up this close to the goal.

As Rafe prodded her toward Gray, a chill swan-dived down her spine. Gray had on his brave face, but his eyes gave away his worry. Rafe would see that. He would use it. He wouldn't let them walk away. He was going to shoot them both. First Gray, then her. She didn't want to lose him. Couldn't lose him. Not to Rafe.

A serene calm came over her, filling her with strength. She reached into the pocket of her sweltering sweatshirt, flicked on the camera's flash button and almost sagged with relief at the batteries' hum beneath her fingers. Loosing a warrior's cry, she thrust up her tied arms and pressed the test button for the flash.

Temporarily blinded, Rafe reflexively let her go. As she rammed forward, she shoved his weapon hand down. His gun went off. The striking bullet chewed off bits of granite and spit them out.

Instinct kicked in and she sprang away before he had a chance to recover. "Run, Gray!"

Just as if it were July at the quarry and Gray sat on the beach, eyeing her behind his mirrored sunglasses, pretending he wasn't, she took a breath, raised her arms and jumped.

GRAY CHARGED TOWARD VANDERVEER. He'd thought he'd known fear, but when Abbie arched over the side of the bridge, he realized he hadn't. Never like this. Never with every fiber of his body. Never as if his soul were being ripped right out of his body.

She was a strong swimmer. A survivor. This was just another dive.

Vanderveer raised his weapon.

Striking fast and hard, Gray head-butted Vanderveer in the gut. Both tumbled to the ground.

Weapon in hand, Vanderveer rounded a punch toward Gray's face. Gray clenched his jaw and pushed himself forward, trying to avoid the blow. It landed hard just below his ear, making his head ring and snaking pain throughout his jaw. Gray answered with an uppercut that broke Vanderveer's nose. Blood flowed.

An evasive maneuver on Vanderveer's part found them both on their feet. Before Vanderveer could raise his weapon, Gray locked Vanderveer's wrist in his left hand, grabbed the barrel with his right hand and twisted, breaking Vanderveer's trigger finger. Vanderveer screamed his outrage. One last shove downward and Vanderveer released the weapon.

Breathing hard, Gray pointed his own Glock at Vanderveer's chest. "It's over."

As Vanderveer swiped at the blood still running from his nose, a flat smile stretched his lips. He lurched forward. Gray squeezed the trigger. Vanderveer flung himself over the bridge railing and fell into the fast-moving water twenty feet below. His body disappeared under the white froth.

Gray swore. Vanderveer had gone after Abbie again. Gray hated bridges. Hated the way the rushing water made him feel as if someone had a hand to his back and wanted to push him over. Fighting vertigo, he scanned the banks of the river. Where was she?

Nothing. No Abbie on the shore. No Vanderveer. Did he have her?

Gray hiked his legs over the granite railing and jumped feetfirst, aiming for the channel in the middle of the river. After he hit the water, he spread his arms and legs to slow down his descent. He kicked for the surface. Fighting the force of the current dragging at his body, he sputtered and started looking for Abbie. The roar of the water as it broke against the rocky shore and the bridge pilings filled his ears. His arms and legs were fast tiring as he treaded water.

Then something flashed in his peripheral vision. Too-blond hair bobbing against the dark gray of wet granite. Alive? "Abbie!"

Abbie, still clinging to the bridge piling, turned her head. And when she saw him, the bright beam of those golden eyes and that golden smile tugged at his heart like a lifeline.

He'd almost lost her. He'd almost let Vanderveer take her away from him. He wasn't going to let anything else keep her from him.

THE CURRENT SMASHED GRAY right into her, knocking her grip from the piling. His arms wrapped around her so tightly, she had trouble breathing. She stretched her duct-taped wrist up and over his head and hung on for dear life, relief shaking through her that he was still in one piece. What had happened to Vanderveer? Had Gray thrown him off the bridge?

"Since when do you know how to dive?" she asked, desperately trying to keep tears back.

A grin sloped across his tanned face. "From watching a beautiful swan dive off a ledge at the quarry. I had to find you, Abbie."

Her throat too thick with tears to speak, she nodded. Together they swam for the rocks where Mercer now waited. He gave them a helping hand out and they sprawled on the grassy knoll above the rocky shore. "You two okay?"

Gray nodded. "Still standing. Vanderveer?"

"He washed up downriver, but he's not moving."

Gray ripped the duct tape from her wrists and ankles and patted her body down as if he expected to find every bone in her body broken. "She needs medical care."

"On its way," Mercer said, rising from his crouch. An odd smile quirked his lips. "I'll fish Vanderveer out."

"I'm perfectly fine," Abbie said, pushing Gray's hands away, then holding on to them, reluctant to let go of him for even an instant.

But he didn't let go. He took her deeper into the haven of his arms, all soaking wet and wonderfully alive. The wide open silver of his eyes connected straight to her soul, reflecting the truth of his heart. He loved her. She tried to speak, but the words choked in her throat.

"I'm never letting you go again, Abbie. I can't give you the world. All I have is me. But nobody will ever love you as much as I do."

And that was more than she'd ever hoped for. "Yes."

He looked confused. "Yes, what?"

"Wherever you go I'll follow. I won't make the same mistake twice." She could never live in the mansion again, not after her father had been killed there. She didn't know what she would do about the mill, about Echo Falls, about anything, but she was sure of one thing. She could do anything, anywhere, as long as she had Gray in her life. "All I want is you, Gray. I have forever and I will forever. And that's more than enough."

THE TRIAL WAS POSTPONED UNTIL Rafe's condition improved. What did they expect? That his spine would miraculously heal? That he'd rise from this prison hospital bed and walk into the courtroom? His blasted spine was crushed. He'd never walk again. He'd never stand again.

"Nurse!" His voice barely projected past his own face. He'd been calling for five minutes and nobody answered. It wasn't as if he could scratch his own itches anymore—as if he could feed himself or dress himself or even breathe for himself. A machine at his back took that function over for him, making speech a halting indignity. He had to get out of here. Soon.

"Nurse!" The force of trying to speak turned his throat raw.

The door to his left swooshed open. A big, broad, bald man entered, wearing white scrubs. "You rang."

"I've been ringing…for the past ten…minutes. I need to make…a call." The effort sapped his energy more quickly than he'd expected.

"Sorry. You get one call a day and you used it up with your lawyer."

"I need…to talk to him…again."

"Sorry." The man went about his business as if Rafe was a piece of meat on a slab.

"I demand—"

The nurse glared at him, his dark eyes cold and empty. "You're not in a position to make no demands."

"I can…pay you—"

A rocky laugh echoed in the room. "With what?"

"I have…money."

The nurse sneered. "Not from what I hear."

"Just let me…call. You'll see."

"Sorry, man. Gotta go with the sure thing."

The nurse put down his chart, then reached behind Rafe's neck. Rafe floundered, choking, looking desperately for breath. He couldn't fight. He couldn't do anything except lie there helplessly. The nurse bent down toward him and whispered, "Mr. al-Khafar sends his regards."

Chapter Eighteen

"Hey, Hollywood, I heard you took up diving." Kingsley grinned at Gray from the computer console where he was setting up today's daily briefing in the basement bunker of the Aerie.

"It's a real rush." As he walked by, Gray jabbed Kingsley in the ribs with an elbow. "Thanks for everything."

Dimples practically cutting his face in two, Kingsley dropped the octopus of wires he was holding and copped his best *GQ* imitation of Gray. "No sweat."

"What happened to your suit?" Skyralov, who was filling a mug with hot water for his usual dose of green tea, looked him up and down. "And your shades?"

Gray glanced down at his jeans and light blue polo shirt. "I'm going for the Saturday-afternoon-college-football-watching look." Grinning, he pumped a fist in the air. "Go Aggies."

Skyralov's laughter filled the room. "Even in jeans you still look too much like a magazine cover."

"He sweats." The disembodied voice came from the wall where Mercer stood with an unusual sparkle to his green eyes.

"Like a horse," Gray agreed, no longer caring if his

admission marred the image he'd carefully constructed for the rest of the team.

Skyralov smirked. "Who'd have guessed?"

"I always knew he had it in him," Kingsley said, plugging in the final wire.

Gray dropped into a leather chair around the cherry-wood conference table. Farthest from the door—his usual post. He reached for one of Liv's famous orange-date muffins.

Harper looked up from the notes he was busily scribbling onto a lined pad of paper. "Watch out. He just got his butt chewed by three different agencies trying to cover your behind."

The "he" in question strode in and took his place at the head of the table. The room became so silent that the burp of the coffee machine in the corner sounded like an insult.

"Okay, bring me up to date," Falconer said, opening the top file in the pile before him.

Grasping his red suspenders, Kingsley gave the daily security briefing.

Mercer followed with an update on the Vanderveer case. "We recovered all the evidence left behind by Vanderveer and Pamela Hatcher. She's off to jail to await trial. Al-Khafar's still on the loose, but Hatcher kept meticulous notes and there's a record of all the information Vanderveer sold al-Khafar. Damage control is possible."

"Vanderveer's death saved the taxpayers the cost of a trial," Gray said, wondering who'd gotten to Vanderveer in prison.

Mercer nodded. "With this being the second death in that facility in less than six months, prison authorities have no choice but to launch a full investigation."

Nodding, Falconer turned to his cousin. "Harper."

Harper scowled at his notes. "The inside man at WITSEC turned out to be Phil Auclair's wife, Claudia. Her dissatisfaction with the state of her marriage showed up on Vanderveer's radar. She wanted her husband to retire, and he wasn't ready. She and Vanderveer struck a deal. She'd tell him what her husband was working on, and he'd ensure an early retirement, not to mention facilitate that early retirement with a financial bonus. When she didn't want to play anymore, he threatened her husband's life. Wasn't until Vanderveer's death was announced that she relented and filled in all the details. She was a tough interview."

"You got her to talk." Falconer went over the rest of his agenda, then glanced around the table. "Anything else?"

"Laynie McDaniels died last night," Skyralov said, his expression somber. "She's the latest victim of the marriage con I'm hunting. She never came out of her coma. Her funeral's on Thursday. Simply stranding his wives with debts up the wazoo doesn't seem to satisfy our serial marrier anymore. If this guy figures it's easier to kill them than to just leave them, his next victim could be in grave danger."

Falconer's frown deepened. "Any leads?"

"I followed his tracks from Louisiana to Alabama. Just got a hit in Florida. I'm heading down there as soon as I get out of here. He seems to be following the coastline. Has a thing for boats."

"Keep me posted." Falconer closed his folder. "That's all, gentlemen. Check your PDAs for updates. Reed, stay behind."

Harper squeezed Gray's shoulder as he left. Everyone knew a reaming was next on the agenda, so they all filed out without a glance.

Falconer contemplated him with his hard eyes and sharp face.

The weight of silence pressed at Gray. "You would've done anything for Liv."

Falconer nodded, leaning back in his chair.

"I did the same for Abbie."

"You didn't have to go it alone."

Gray popped a careless shrug. "I thought there was a mole inside."

"And you don't think I could've handled that?"

Gray met Falconer's gaze straight on. "He's your cousin."

"He's not here because he's family. He's here because he's good at what he does and got a raw deal from the agency that was supposed to be watching his back." Falconer rose and gathered his files. "Just like the rest of us."

"I know that now."

"Good." Falconer's mouth skewed sideways. He handed the files to Gray. "Welcome home."

ECHO FALLS WOULD NEVER LOOK the same to Gray. Not after seeing it through Abbie's eyes. The little town sparkled under the summer sun. The people he passed as he wound his way through the lower village took on individual faces with stories of their own.

At Peanut Row he slowed. The engine of his rescued Corvette idling, he stared at the home where he'd grown up. He'd had some good times here. Why had he blocked them out of his memory? He massaged the stiffness cranking the tendons tight in the back of his neck. Now that he was here, he wasn't quite sure what to do.

He twisted off the ignition and strode across the street to the red door. Kingsley had brought Brynna—at her insistence—home today. Gray wanted to make sure she was all right. Taking in a breath, he knocked.

A volley of small yips answered him. "Quiet, Queenie!"

"Bryn, it's Gray. Can I come in?"

The silence on the other side of the door became black-hole deep. "Please, Bryn. I'm not walking away this time. There's been enough silence between us."

Footsteps padded against the linoleum of the hallway. The lock turned. Then the door creaked open and Bryn appeared, holding her little Yorkie in her arms—a shield between them. Her face bore a series of black-and-blue bruises. A small patch was shaved from her head and now sported a bandage where she'd had stitches. "I'm so sorry, Bryn. I never meant for you to get hurt."

"I know." She moved aside and opened the door all the way. "Come in."

Queenie sniffed at him and a low growl rumbled through her small body. Bryn smiled and the smile looked good on her. "Better watch out, she bites."

Gray gave the dog a wide berth and walked into Bryn's office. The damage there looked like a war zone, everything broken as if someone had taken out their anger against each object in the room. "You don't have to stay here. I can help you sell the house and get started elsewhere."

Silver eyes watching him as if she expected him to vanish at any second, she stroked her little dog's ears. "This is my home. I want to stay."

Gray righted a toppled chair. "I missed you, you know."

Bryn blinked at him, then turned away.

Great. He was making all sorts of progress today. He

picked up a broken frame that held a five-by-seven of the same photo of him and Bryn he carried in his wallet.

A scraping, shuffling sound came from the hallway. He glanced over his shoulder. Still holding the dog in one arm, Bryn was dragging a garbage can from the kitchen. She stopped and stared at him.

"I still have that picture, too," Gray said, brushing away the shards of glass. Sixteen-year-old Bryn, playfully jostled with eighteen-year-old Gray to hog the camera. Her head leaned against his shoulder and his hand rested around hers. Both their smiles had enough electricity to fire up a dozen birthday cakes. A few months later their worlds would change. "Abbie caught us true, didn't she? You and me, we were always fighting for space. But if you look closely, you can also see that we care about each other. If I'd known how things were going to turn out for you, I would've dragged you away with me."

Bryn walked over to him and slowly leaned her head against his shoulder. "I missed you, too."

Throat working overtime, he risked dismemberment by dog and reached his arm across her shoulder. "Talk to me, Bryn."

And between a river of tears, she did.

GRAY LIVED ALONE AND LIKED it that way. The tiny piece of real estate was his kingdom. Here he made the rules and there was no one to tell him they were wrong. Here he was who he was and it didn't matter if he wasn't good enough or strong enough or anything enough.

But when he walked through the front door of his condo and saw Abbie in the kitchen, her golden smile beaming just for him, he couldn't imagine why he'd thought living alone was so great. And when she came to him, fit herself into his arms and kissed him, the burden he'd carried all the way home lifted.

"How's Brynna?" Abbie asked, worry pinching the corners of her eyes.

Forgiveness would take time, but they were working on it. "I'm going to help her rebuild her office."

"I'm so glad." Abbie feathered her fingers through his hair so gently, it set off a wave of tenderness. That was happening a lot lately, and getting used to all these feelings inside him would also take time. "How was your meeting at Seekers?"

"I survived." He pressed his nose to the golden hair she'd had repaired to its original color and inhaled the sweet honey-and-almond scent that was so much her.

"I'm sorry for not trusting you about your own people," she said, leaning her head against his heart. He sighed with pleasure.

"You weren't in a state to trust anyone. Not even me."

"I'm still sorry I put you through all that."

He kissed her slowly, savoring because there was time, plenty of time.

"I heard from the lawyers today," she said, breaking away. "The mill will be going back into production. The creditors appointed a new CEO, and we're working something out. I won't lose total control of the company, but I won't be running it either. He's a good man. He'll take care of the mill the way Dad would have."

"You don't have any qualms about giving up the business or putting up the mansion for sale?"

"None." She laughed and its song warmed his heart. "It's such a relief, actually. No more pressure."

"What about Echo Falls? We could move there if you want." An hour's commute from Nashua or an hour's commute from Echo Falls didn't really make a difference.

"No. I can work anywhere, and you need to be closer to your office. I'll go back. I still have connections there. I'll stay active in the women's club. And Brynna's there, so we'll visit often." Abbie frowned at him. "You do still have a job, don't you?"

"Falconer didn't fire me."

"That's good, isn't it?"

"That's good." Being a Seeker was what he was. He was good at it. He couldn't imagine doing anything else. Still, there was Abbie. Could she really want this pared-down version of her life? "I'll be stuck doing scut work for a while, but eventually I'll get to lead another case."

"I knew he wouldn't fire you." Triumph lit her eyes as if she'd just won the lottery.

She didn't realize what her prize entailed. He wouldn't lie to her. He wanted her to know what she was signing on for. "You know what that means, don't you?"

"Of course—you'll be doing the job you love."

He shook his head. "It means I could be gone for days, maybe weeks at a time."

She cocked her head in question.

"You deserve someone who's home every night."

She chuckled again, as if he was the silliest fool she'd ever met. "I deserve a husband who's happy. I deserve a husband who loves his work. I deserve a husband who wants to come home because that's where he wants to be. You'll be coming home to me, Gray. That's what I deserve."

"Husband?"

She flicked his shoulder playfully. "You didn't think I'd make it easy for you to disappear on me again. I plan on shackling you as soon as possible. I won't let you go again."

"Oh, yeah?" Now that conjured up a whole album full of possibilities he was dying to try. He slid his hands down her arms and took hold of her wrists. "I do have a set of handcuffs. Want to try them out?"

Laughing, she dragged him to the kitchen. "I have something to show you." Spread on the table were real-estate listings. She picked one out of the pile and handed it to him. Her front teeth skimmed over her bottom lip, and she waited expectantly. "What do you think?"

The picture showed a Victorian-style home complete with a front porch, flowerpots on the steps and a Welcome flag flying. A colorful play set peeked from one end of the house. He grinned at the goofy dog sprawled on the drive-way. He'd bet the photographer had done his best to remove the shaggy beast from the picture and had to finally give up. This little house looked like Gray's idea of heaven. Abbie didn't need a mansion. She never had. She deserved a home filled with love and color and life. "Where is it?"

"It's right in Wintergreen," she said, breathless. "You could jog to work, if you wanted."

"And let the guys see me sweat?"

"They wouldn't care."

No, they wouldn't. And knowing that gave him a sense of acceptance. "Does it come with the dog?"

She peered at the picture and her mouth curved up at the corners, giving her that angelic look he carried with him in his heart. "We could ask."

He caught her hips in his hands and moved in close. "Is this what you want, Abbie?"

Her arms looped around his neck, and she pulled his head close to hers. "Look into my eyes, Gray. What do you see?"

His future with Abbie spread before him, and the picture it formed was a dream come true.

"It's a deal. I'll take it all, Abbie—you, the house, the dog. Everything."

* * * * *

LIV'S ORANGE DATE MUFFINS

3/4 cup of pitted dates
1/2 cup flour
1 orange, unpeeled, cut into eight sections
1/2 cup orange juice
2 eggs
1/2 cup cold butter
1-cup whole-wheat flour
3/4 cup flour
3/4 cup sugar
2 tsps baking powder
1 tsp baking soda
1 tsp salt

Put dates and 1/2 cup flour into the bowl of a food processor with a cutting blade. Pulse until the dates are chopped uniformly. Add the pieces of orange and pulse again. Add the orange juice, eggs and butter and pulse until a homogeneous mixture forms.

Mix together the dry ingredients and add to the food processor. Pulse until all the ingredients are wet (don't overmix).

Drop mixture into prepared muffin tins. Fill to just below the edge. Bake in a 400° F oven for 15-20 minutes. Makes 12 big muffins.

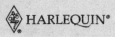
HARLEQUIN®

INTRIGUE®

and

JOANNA WAYNE

present

SECURITY
MEASURES

September 2005

Falsely imprisoned, Vincent Magilenti had
broken out of jail to find Candy Owens,
the mother of his child and the woman
whose testimony had sent him away.
But when their daughter disappeared,
Vincent would do whatever it took to
protect them…even if it meant going
back to prison.

*Available at your
favorite retail outlet.*

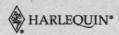

HARLEQUIN®

INTRIGUE®

As the summer comes to a close, things really begin to heat up as Harlequin Intrigue presents...

Big Sky Bounty Hunters: No man's a match for these Montana tough guys...but a woman's another story.

Don't miss this brand-new series from some of your favorite authors!

GOING TO EXTREMES
BY AMANDA STEVENS
August 2005

BULLSEYE
BY JESSICA ANDERSEN
September 2005

WARRIOR SPIRIT
BY CASSIE MILES
October 2005

FORBIDDEN CAPTOR
BY JULIE MILLER
November 2005

RILEY'S RETRIBUTION
BY RUTH GLICK,
writing as Rebecca York
December 2005

Available at your favorite retail outlet.

www.eHarlequin.com